HosKaren Publishing

This work has been self-published to expedite its availability while the author searches for a mainstream agent/publisher. It was deemed essential to get the book in the marketplace, where it might begin helping others.

For more information, comments and contacts, please visit:

www.GeoffCoatesBooks.com

In June the River

A NOVEL

Geoff Coates

In June the River

By Geoff Coates

A HosKaren Publication

ISBN: 978-0-615-25508-8

This is a novel inspired by personal experience.
Similarities to names used or people depicted are coincidental.

To Karen, of course

1

Gramma

To this day, the memory of my grandmother and Aunt Migget remains as much a part of the cottage as its ancient, sagging timbers. They have been dead many years, but I easily picture them lazing in their wicker rockers on the wide screened porch, Gramma with her tea and knitting, Mig with her beer and crosswords.

I spend more time in those old rockers myself these days. And as I find myself regarding each spring not only as the birth of another season but as one less season to go, I realize that during my long separation from this summertime wonderland I loved as a boy, it was they I missed as much as I did the cottage, and the grand blue river. Gramma was my one true friend. In the few years that I knew her she brought peace and comfort to my disordered young life. She was everything a grandmother was supposed to be, and everything I thought a mother should be.

When she died the cottage days of my youth died with her. I could no longer spend my summers there, and I often wonder now whether things might have gone differently if I'd been able to keep returning each year, to rejuvenate my spirit and hopefulness, to live part-time that glorious lighthearted life, to hide for a spell from the unrest at home, and from the real world that would get the best of me.

Migget was Gramma's niece, our father's cousin. From my childhood until I saw her in her last years she never seemed to change. She claimed to be on her deathbed for thirty years. She lived almost into her eighties, despite suffering numerous ailments, some genuine, including emphysema and asthma, which she nursed every day with three packs of Camel straights and a case of Carling's Black Label. She smoked the Camels down until they burned her fingers. She poured the beer three fingers at a time into a small juice glass, so that every swallow that wasn't either en route to her gullet or on immediate standby stayed cold in the bottle longer, not that her beers hung around long enough to suffer much.

She appeared on the porch every morning in a faded housedress and settled into her rocker to oversee the river. As soon as Hubert, a great blue heron, glided past low over the water on his way to work, she checked her watch to see if it was too early for her first beer, and it never was. Beyond that she couldn't care less what time it was. It was summertime.

By noon on hot days that housedress had hiked up to her hips, the better to expose her ample foundation to the cross breeze through the screens. She didn't always wear underpants, I discovered one day. She snorted and jiggled when she laughed and she told wonderful stories. Migget loved to fish and was good at it, and knew as much about the river as anyone. She'd been quite a looker and an accomplished singer in her day, but she and her husband Tom had been in a horrific car crash in which she'd been disfigured, though not terribly so. Family legend had it that she nevertheless decided to kick back with a cold one and spend the rest of her days watching the river crawl by. She read thousands of books in her lifetime, worked the New York *Times* crossword almost like dashing off a letter, and rarely lost a card game of any kind.

For years she mail-ordered a powdered preparation containing belladonna and God knows what else from California. She used it to revitalize herself when her breathing became labored, sprinkling it on crumpled tissue, setting it ablaze, then tenting a towel over her head and sucking in the smoke with heaving gasps. She'd be brand new in no time and firing up another Camel.

Mig was the proverbial lovable slob, and my siblings and I adored her. Her husband was on the road a lot when I was a kid. Uncle Tom had thick wavy hair, a toothy smile under a sporty mustache, a booming laugh, and he drove a slate gray Cadillac with a suicide knob on the steering wheel. They had no children, and I suspect that spending several summers with this kid went a long way toward soothing any regrets they may have had.

I've heard people say I was the nicest little boy, but I know I was a pest. When Tom was around he sent me on missions. When I was ten I asked why we didn't have a boat. He told me that you've got to have a dock to have a boat, and on a powerful river like the mighty St. Lawrence you need a hell of a pier to build the dock on. Now if a strapping young boy spent a summer or two in the river stacking boulders the size of medicine balls, bare-handedly erecting a head-high sixty-foot jetty that would be a formidable undertaking for the Army Corps of Engineers, why Tom would scare up some lumber and slap a dock on it and we'd go get us a damn fine boat. I put about three hours into the project, bruised my toes, pinched my fingers, got slapped against the seawall a few times by waves I didn't see coming, and decided we didn't need a boat.

I spent every summer at the cottage from the time I was old enough to doggie-paddle until I was twelve, playing in and on and by the river. Gramma and her sister Inez, Mig's mother, had inherited the Thousands Islands property from their father, who had bought it in 1908 from the family that had built it around 1880. They had married brothers but had been widowed many years. My summers were spent with Migget and Gramma, and with Inez, who smelled like a wet dog.

Gramma put me in her lap and read me *The Little Trapper* about a thousand times. She never raised her voice or thrashed me with the buckle end of a belt, or locked me in a closet, or hid my favorite toys or my coonskin cap, or made up stories about misdeeds I'd committed, or got mad at me for no reason. She asked only that I let her know what cottage I was playing at, and that I stay off this or that deep-water pier unless I was with a grownup. When I did something good she told me so. When I did something bad she told me why it was bad. She said she loved me to pieces and stuffed my face with warm apple pie and molasses cookies. She believed me when I lied. She believed that kids were to be loved no matter what, and that play in the sun and water was all a small boy was supposed to do.

All of Houghton's Point was my back yard and I knew every corner of it. The cottage owners all knew everyone else's children, and looked after them. I had some seasonal friends, kids who came and went over the summer, and a few who stayed the whole season as I did. And my sister Rudy and brother Jim were usually there as well, though they were older and had their own friends and pursuits. But for the most part I thoroughly enjoyed being by myself, as I would all my life, producing my own adventures, making my own discoveries, satisfying my own curiosities, and dreaming.

I loved exploring the rickety old boathouses that had been sagging and lopsided for so long that they may as well have been built that way—riverbank shanties that smelled of gas and oil and where countless fish stories had been hatched and honed. Warped plank countertops were hollowed and chipped by generations of knife strokes that had gutted who knows how many bass and pike and maybe a few muskies. Makeshift shelves drooped from the weight of cans of hardened varnish and paint, and rusted tins of fishing reel parts and pulleys and bolts, unused for decades but saved just the same, as if to honor the long gone grandfathers who had put them there. Peculiar old gadgets and crusted crude tools hung from corroded nails in rough-hewn support posts smoothed by the ages. The singular sounds of boat lines groaning and squeaking and of waves slurping lazily at rocking hulls echoed eerily under the low flat roofs. Big northerns and jack perch wandered in from the busy river, and on sunny days the boathouse water extracted the outside brilliance and took on an iridescence as if illuminated by a mysterious radiance from below, showcasing the fish in an enormous glowing aquarium. They looked so easy to catch, and too content to bother.

The focus of the small cottage community was the general store and its upstairs pavilion, perched on the Point's highest ground, overlooking the river. A heavy wooden bench in front bears the initials I carved in it then, and those of dozens of others whose childhood faces I remember still. I helped behind the counter in the store selling penny candy, employing a policy of one for you and one for me that I would later in life apply liberally as a bartender. And in the morning it was my job to raise the flag on the pole out front, and in the evening lower it and fold it in proper military fashion as the storekeeper had taught me. He lived in the dock house on the long main pier along the shore in front of the store, where passenger steamers had once stopped regularly. I thought he had the neatest job a man could have, living so close to the river that he could fish out his window, running the store, hoisting the flag, selling pop and candy.

Life on the river with Gramma was smooth. No hidden shoals. She spanked me only once. I took my fishing rod and a dried-up third of a worm out on one of those forbidden docks alone one day when I was six. I caught a northern pike almost as long as I was. I managed to haul it onto the dock but I couldn't get the hook out because the fish kept snapping at me like a dog. So I left it on the line and dragged it home by its lip to show Gramma.

She came out in the yard when I called to her, and needed only a glance at my trophy to know where I'd probably caught it. She asked if I'd landed it all by myself, and I proudly said yes. Then she asked if there was anyone else there to see me catch it, and when I said no, there was no one else around, she slapped my young fanny until her hand must have stung, then laid me down in the yard alongside the pike and went back in the cottage. As I stared into that pike's puss, all I could think about was how she knew I'd been on that dock, and why she never said a word about the size of that fish.

That was the same summer I saved a kid's life, off the pier next to the sand-bottomed boat slip we were allowed to swim in. Some of us kids from around the Point were under the supervision of a young mother who'd settled under a tree with a paperback book and an infant. I saw a large toy yacht bobbing in the river where the water was eight feet deep off the pier. Bubbles broke the surface around it and two tiny hands were wrapped over it. I got on my stomach and pulled the boat out and that baby was hanging from it, motionless. His face was the color of fish belly. The kid didn't know he was headed for the Promised Land, but he wasn't going without that boat, and it saved him. The mother stomped over and smacked his backside so hard for crawling off that he blew a quart of water in her face. Then he screamed with all the gusto befitting the occasion, but he never loosened his grip on that little yacht. He probably has a real yacht now. Maybe I've waved to him.

I remember hearing guides on the tour boats announcing on loud speakers to their passengers that presently they were passing poor man's paradise, Houghton's Point. A few of the Point residents didn't appreciate the description, but for the most part that's what it was. The Point certainly couldn't compete with Millionaire's Row, where ornate mansions towered over felt-like lawns and preened gardens on private islands near Alexandria Bay, each one boasting more rooms and balconies and servants than the next, where cabin cruisers and skiffs and gleaming mahogany launches were sheltered in boathouses more elaborate than our cottages. Ours were simple utilitarian structures, some prettified by gingerbread trim, but otherwise as unpretentious as the folk who rocked on their porches and fished and swam from their docks, and to whom they were paradise enough.

For a young boy in the care of his grandmother it was a wonderland of peace and exploration. I splashed and yelped and lobbed gobs of sea moss with my summertime friends in the shallows of the bay shores. We outgrew our life jackets and leaped from piers and boathouse roofs into the cold clear deep, stretched out on our backs to warm ourselves on wave-polished slabs of sun-baked bedrock, watched the seagulls flap and dart among lofty swaying pines centuries old, marveled at the grace and power of the herons gliding low across the river, lay on boathouse roofs at night and counted shooting stars, and for timeless weeks in the heart of summer were inclined to do little else.

2

Natalie

I awoke as if from a coma. My crusty eyes opened slowly on a strange and blurry room. For a drunk, waking up is when the nightmare begins. He isn't sure how or when he got to wherever in hell he is, or if what he's waking up to is a morning, afternoon or night. He doesn't know if he's in his bed, a stranger's bed, a hospital bed or a flowerbed; or if a sergeant, a surgeon or St. Peter is standing over him, or some woman's husband with a five-iron.

And, if he hasn't yet graduated from being fairly functional to living in self-imposed seclusion, the hours ahead will entail an almost theatrical production of schemes and lies as he struggles to balance his ability to cope with his incessant need to be sufficiently soused—hopefully without anyone noticing. This day would be different.

I peered sideways from under some covers. In the faint light of a table lamp a suitcase against the wall looked familiar. Clothes draped over the back of a chair looked like mine. I was curled in a ball, shivering and sweating in tangled pajamas and bulky robe, a yellow terrycloth cocoon. The sparse and ordinary furnishings might adorn any motel room. I waited for something to register. My mouth tasted like kipper.

The awareness arrived with that hollow thud in the gut that signals impending doom—that dreadful moment when the deal goes down; when the variety store manager catches you red-handed stuffing a stolen toy gun in your dungarees; when the boys' dean waves before your eyes the pass you forged with his name; when a traffic cop pulls you over and you suddenly remember the baggie full of amphetamines under your seat and the three pounds of pot in the trunk; when your woman asks how you managed to get lipstick on your underpants working late at the office. I remembered now exactly where I was. Detox ward. Drunk farm. Up the creek and down the road, tucked away in the rolling green hills of Pennsyltucky. It might as well have been Pluto.

I had arrived that afternoon in a state of calm but total intoxication, thoroughly unaffected by my new surroundings and ready for my nap. As usual, I'd worry about where I was when I came to. I hazily recalled walking a long quiet hallway, supported by someone at my left arm. I didn't remember undressing or being undressed or getting into bed. Nothing new there. I felt as if my blood had been drained.

I still hadn't moved and was afraid to. I wiggled my toes to see if they worked. I was not unfamiliar with feeling like road pizza upon waking, but this was a state of numbness and delirium beyond any I'd ever known. I recalled having undergone an exceptionally earnest onslaught of self-abuse the previous day or two, but nothing I considered extraordinary for a body that had grown so accustomed to that kind of punishment. Maybe the machinery had finally shit the bed. I had no desire to budge. I wasn't sure I could.

Now, as the gravity of my condition became more apparent, it occurred to me that regardless of any other plans I might have had, wherever else in the world I would have certainly preferred to be, this room, this very bed, was probably as far as my stick-thin legs could have carried me anyway. And I'd have been content to lie dormant there indefinitely if not for another thunderbolt of awareness. I had to piss like a yak. I scanned the room but saw no door that could be a toilet. I rose to a sitting position, slowly and in jerky stages like an old cartoon. I swooned from the change in altitude, dribbling urine down my thigh. I didn't trust my legs but I had to get somewhere. I slid from the bed and managed four rickety steps before my knees gave out and I clattered to the floor like Jenga blocks. A fragment of self-worth was all that kept me from just letting loose, surrendering to the cold hard tile and emptying like a punctured wading pool. Just mop it up and throw me a blanket and leave me the hell alone. Forty years old and feeble. I reached the door on hands and knees and hoisted myself by the knob. I cracked the door and called to a nurse at a kiosk in the hall. A rest room was down the corridor, she said. Maybe fifty feet, she guessed. Too damn far. I told her my legs didn't work and I asked for something to leak in.

I'd just shuffled unsteadily back to bed when the door breezed open. The lady flicked a glaring overhead light on and tossed me a crook-necked plastic bottle, and left. I sat in bed with legs splayed. One trembling hand tried to steady the jug. The other, using thumb and forefinger as if holding a roach, clumsily tried to maneuver what in my decrepit state had shriveled up like a half-dead mushroom that was now launching anticipatory spurts three feet high in all directions, while the bottle danced hopelessly out of reach like a scene from a demented puppet show.

This would never work. Satellites couple in space easier. Standing apprehensively and leaning against the bed, I straddled the jug like a sickly old milk cow and made the connection at last, opening the floodgates and issuing a groan they could have heard in Topeka, just as the door blew open again.

I didn't remember what the first nurse looked like, but standing there now was Natalie Wood. She wasn't much more than twenty, her mischievous mouth and I dare you dark eyes unmistakable; and in a petite white nurse's outfit, custom tailored by her own exquisite form, she never looked sexier or softer, sweeter or warmer, more inviting or willing, more like the most trouble you'd ever want to be in. I froze at the sight of her. The mushroom shut down as if I'd snapped a rubber band on it. We stared at one another for two seconds that seemed like two minutes, and it felt like a kick in the nuts that Natalie should see me like this.

She smiled a smile that asked how much I wanted her, and it was precisely then that I understood what I was, what this stunning young woman saw when she looked at me, what I had done to my mind and body and whatever fair appearance I might have once had, what I had done to my life, what my beautiful and compassionate wife Kay had so long endured, what my friends and family must have thought of me, what a disgraceful waste and piece of crap nobody I had become. There was a time when I would have supposed smugly that a beauty like Natalie would be attracted to me. But all she saw was an aging stooped-over has-been with a pasty face and glazy eyes, his hair matted and greasy, his toothpick legs quivering, his lifeless dick drooped in a jug. She asked how I was doing. Her voice was like honey. I asked her how it looked like I was doing.

"Let me know if you need any help," she said. Finally she turned and left, magnificently, tossing her silky black hair as I knew she would. When the door closed I woke up Topeka again, and cried.

***

Having filled the bottle, I resumed my fetal position and was about to drift into another well-earned coma when the door swung open again. This time it was a whole parade: Natalie with a clipboard, a smiling young Marcus Welby with a stethoscope and other gear, and a broad-beamed girl with a tray of food that smelled like my high school gym locker. She set it down next to me and I nearly bathed her in bile, the yellow toxic waste that accumulated in my stomach while I slept because my overworked liver couldn't process it. It tasted like rancid orange juice when it gushed from my gut whenever I awoke. I had started my days that way for so long that throwing it up was as much a part of my morning ritual as getting the newspaper off the stoop. Any sane person would freak out if they spewed that disgusting fluid even once. I'd been doing it every day for months. It was a precursor to severe liver damage and evidence enough that I had begun the slow and ghastly progression of drinking myself to death. I had been in a state of late-stage alcoholism for some time, maybe years. I previously had been critically ill with alcoholic hepatitis, but had resumed my regimen of insane drinking as soon as its symptoms began to abate, despite my doctor's admonishment that my next bout of drinking could kill me. And I'd been drinking uncontrollably for ten years since. It's astonishing what the body can endure; but end-stage alcoholism, with its irreversible brain damage and eventual multiple organ failure, at one time an indiscernible danger on the distant horizon, was now just down the road a piece.

I sat up to be polite and asked the girl to move the food. Dr. Welby said I'd had quite a nap, which I didn't find unusual. I'd come mid-afternoon and it was now nine o'clock. Evidently I'd misplaced a day. I'd arrived the previous afternoon, he told me, and hadn't stirred in thirty-two hours. No wonder I'd had to piss.

My emaciated body took turns feverishly seeping sweat and shaking violently from the chills. I needed to puke. I twitched all over. Dizziness rolled in and out like waves at the shore. My lips trembled. I told the doctor something was definitely wrong, I was really sick. He said I was suffering withdrawal symptoms, which apparently was medical jargon for a hangover fit to cripple a Clydesdale. I wasn't accustomed to hangovers, and certainly not lasting ones of this magnitude. I had never believed in that paying the piper nonsense, feeling like crap all day and waiting minute by minute for the appointed hour at which it was deemed socially acceptable to jump back in and start hammering myself into a stupor again. It was like slicing a hand open in the morning and waiting until cocktail hour to bandage it. A friend of mine used to bust my chops about drinking all day because he always waited until five o'clock to have his first one. Then he drank a quart of scotch in a sitting and within an hour he'd be talking like he had a mouthful of Tampax. So what was the difference? I merely spread my consumption out more sensibly. As some lovable lush once said, you don't get hangovers from drinking; you get them from stopping.

But this was obviously no ordinary hangover. I had been dangerously sick from drinking and drugging for so long that a major collapse had been inevitable and imminent. I was finally experiencing physical meltdown. The morning after the decade before. I tried to grasp the veracity of it. It felt like overwhelming defeat, but at the same time like captivity. I remembered now that I had consented to come here. No one had forced me, and no one could make me stay. And for a few seconds I actually entertained the notion that I should just say fuck this, I'm outta here. Get dressed, grab my bag, call a cab or stick out my thumb, get to a bar or liquor store—this from a man who was physically incapable of walking fifty feet to take a leak.

The doctor said he'd been informed of the condition I'd arrived in, and asked what I'd consumed before coming. He had no intention of judging me, he said, but for medical purposes he needed to know what and how much I'd poisoned myself with. I had to think about it. The day before leaving Rochester I'd drunk three or four random beers, snorted at least a gram of coke, popped half a dozen Xanax, smoked four or five joints and my usual fifty Winstons, knocked back a couple of shooters of Grand Marnier and a couple more of Cuervo, gulped a tumbler of cheap chablis, and, over the course of the day, devoured a quart and a half of vodka. All told, about the same as I'd consumed on a daily basis for as long as I could remember, except for the cocaine. I usually couldn't afford coke and bought it as a treat for a special occasion, like an unexpected Tuesday, or like the day before being carted off like a pathetic bum to a drunk camp. The Xanax pills were designer downers my doctor at home had prescribed for me some months previously to "take the edge off so I wouldn't drink so much." They worked just fine. I washed them down with booze.

The morning of my departure I blew off what coke I had left, took several long swallows from half a quart of white whiskey I'd hidden behind some books, downed four Xanax, and smoked a joint. I returned to the book shelves twice and finished the bottle, and hit up Kay's gallon of white wine, cradling it in the crook of my arm and guzzling from it like a hillbilly moonshiner. I hadn't any idea what this rehab business would entail, but it seemed likely it wouldn't get underway with a cocktail hour, and I had no intention of starting the adventure on an empty stomach. I drained three martinis at the airport before boarding the plane and had two while in the air—all that the stingy bastards would allow me during the brief flight.

In cases of advanced alcoholism, one's level of tolerance comes full circle. Although years of heavy drinking may have enabled him to consume and tolerate escalating amounts of booze, the drinker's system now can't detoxify as quickly and proficiently as it once could, so that even small amounts of alcohol can get him drunk again. But I had never been a sloppy drunk, and I was still capable of putting away humungous quantities of alcohol without appearing to be intoxicated, which enabled me to be served in public several more beverages than those to which a body might ordinarily be entitled. And so, though already fried to a crisp by lunchtime, I scored four more martinis in fifteen minutes during a half-hour layover in Pittsburgh.

The server had clearly spent years climbing the ladder of his noble profession to attain a station of such esteem—daytime service bartender in an airport lounge—and would, like a hundred before him, retain that exalted position only until he figured out how to beat the metered pourers on the whiskey bottles. He told me to take a table and a waitress would be right with me.

"I really don't have time for a waitress, thanks," I said. "I'm not going to be here that long. Just make me a fast vodka martini on the rocks, easy on the ice, hold the fruit, hold the vermouth, if you would." He said it was a service bar and I could only be served at a table. I put a twenty on the bar. I told him I'd suck that drink down before the waitress could find her pencil. Then I begged. He looked around surreptitiously, then poured the typical airport bar's ludicrous version of a martini. I knocked it back, asked for another, then another.

He asked if I was afraid of flying. "Not any more," I said. "One and done." He hesitated, looked around, pursed his lips. I said, "Look, if it's any consolation, I was shit-faced when I walked in here." He relented.

I planned on hitting the bar at my destination airport as well, after the last short leg of my journey on one of those shaking and rattling flying shuttle buses that barely clear the treetops and have no business being airborne. Unfortunately, the driver that Hell Hole Hospital had dispatched to fetch me intercepted me at the arrival gate instead. How he knew me I couldn't imagine. Maybe he'd been tipped to look for a pale, gaunt-faced six-foot-two string bean who looked like he'd gone toe to toe with the devil and got his ass kicked. Or maybe he knew from experience to recognize the most apprehensive and disorientated passenger to step from the plane.

When we got in his car he said, "You've been drinking."

I said, "No shit. What'd you expect?"

"I never know what to expect. But a lot of incoming patients make an effort not to drink for a few days before they get here. Makes the adjustment a lot easier, you know?"

"No, I'm afraid I don't know," I said. "If I was capable of going a few days without drinking I wouldn't fucking be here, would I?" Then I passed out.

***

Dr. Welby nodded at the food tray. "You should be hungry."

"I don't think so."

"It'll make you feel better."

"I don't think so."

"You look like you need a good meal."

"I think we both know what I need," I said, "and it sure as hell isn't hospital meatloaf."

"You won't get a drink here. Can't do it." His smile was sad.

"You're going to make me suffer."

"Don't worry," he grinned. "We won't let you die."

"Swell."

***

Kay and I had been together for eleven years but had only been married a few months. She'd known for some time that the booze was getting the best of me. My parents both knew I had a problem, of course. My father liked his cocktails too, but, as he would readily point out, never had it affected his work. His health had been failing. He had previously overcome open-heart surgery and he'd had a cancerous third of a lung removed. Both surgeries had damn near killed him, but they had enabled him to add to his life span a number of years in which he'd managed to get back to his previous form, playing golf as miserably as ever, working and drinking just as much. But the cancer had returned and his life had been reduced to a daily battle with increasing pain that he'd tried to fight with a regimen of bourbon and Vicodin, Percodan or Dilaudid, concealing his agony from us all the while. He had cared a great deal for Kay and had hinted more than once that he'd love to see us marry. He got his wish and died four weeks later.

It was a lovely wedding, and friends talked about the open-bar reception for weeks. Before the wedding I waited in the vestry off the altar with my brother. We lived in different worlds, but I'd felt obligated to have him as my best man. It was early June on a sweltering day. It must have been ninety degrees in the chapel and even hotter in the stuffy room. I had a vial of coke in my pocket that I desperately wanted to get to without my brother noticing. At one point he busied himself at a bookshelf and I moseyed over to a window, opened the vial, and tried to pour a smidgen into the cap. A chunk the size of a pea tumbled out. I quickly inhaled it with an almighty swoosh that slammed it to the back of my nasal passage just as the door opened and we were beckoned to the altar. Throughout the ceremony tears poured from my eyes, snot ran over my lips, my face twitched and contorted like a mime being electrocuted, I snorted like a pig, the minister gave me some curious looks, and the buzz was simply awesome.

***

Kay had found me that way again, curled up in bed like a child, shaking, gagging to keep down the bile. I'd usually wobble to the bathroom and puke it up when Kay wasn't looking. I couldn't let her know I had to do that every day. She might think I was sick or something. It didn't matter. I couldn't veil the eyes, marble-veined and yellow, afterwards bulging grotesquely from the heaving. I couldn't conceal the sweat dripping from my sallow face, or my flammable breath, or the telltale discoloration of my cheekbones. I couldn't hide the stench of alcohol waste seeping from my pores, or that I was twenty pounds underweight and looked a dozen years older than I was. Most mornings I couldn't get downstairs without a bracer, my legs trembled so.

I'd wait for Kay to go down for coffee. I'd sneak to the bathroom and vomit, then to the spare bedroom I used as an office-studio-library-den-nest-cave-hideout. Behind some books I'd locate among a collection of bottles the one that wasn't yet empty. I never finished all the booze at night; I knew how desperately I'd need it in the morning. I'd slug down some vodka, hurry to the bathroom and throw it up, slug down some more, throw it up, and keep doing it until it stayed put, until the glow finally spread through my body like hot creamy soup, until I thought I could face another interminable day.

She sat on the bed and pleaded with me. Rarely had I seen her cry. We had a friend who'd gone away. Johnny Gimlet had been about the worst drunk either of us knew, but not any more. I called him and got the number for the local substance abuse agency he'd gone through. Nice people, all business. Drinking problem? They'd be happy to see me that very day, two o'clock. Barely enough time to get properly medicated, but I managed, and then some.

The interview began with a somber man telling me he could see I'd already been pretty well into the sauce that day. Not only had they been able to fit me in that afternoon, but I'd been assigned the staff genius to boot. After he verified that I was a prime candidate for "the program," he made a couple of phone calls. "We have a bed for you in Pennsyltucky," he told me. "You'll check into a detox."

"Detox? What the hell for?"

"Standard precaution for someone in your condition."

"What condition is that?"

He almost chuckled, but restrained himself. "Let's just say that it would be dangerous for you to abruptly stop drinking without medical supervision."

"I wasn't aware I was going to abruptly stop drinking."

"Well, you are."

"Just like that?"

"Isn't that why you're here? You leave tomorrow."

"Tomorrow? I can't leave tomorrow."

"Why not?"

"I can't just leave. I got stuff to take care of."

"What stuff?" There was no stuff, and he knew it. He'd already concluded from our interview that I had no job, no responsibilities, no schedule, no commitments, no plans, no purpose, no stuff. I told him he didn't leave a guy much time for a last hurrah. He said, "You've had your last hurrah." He was mistaken.

***

There was a fruit cup on the tray and I managed to eat that. The doctor and his entourage had left. I'd been given a physical and pronounced alive. I curled back into my ripe pajamas, the first I'd worn since childhood, and my yellow cocoon. Kay and I had argued about packing the robe because it was so bulky. Now I was living in it, soaking it with my foul sweat one minute and trembling in its chilly dampness the next, my tattered thoughts ricocheting around a vacant, bewildered head, bouncing from fear and hopelessness to defeat and disgrace, nausea humming constantly in the wings. The very concept of tomorrow, or anything beyond this agonizing minute, was a total void.

How the hell did it get to this? How could I end up here, in a hospital for hopeless juiceheads, like a Mad Dog 20/20 gutter bum, a garden-variety drunk, a common souse, in a goddam detox, an institution, a sanitarium, a clinic for the chronically pickled? The only thought I could muster, while sliding into another deep sleep, was that I had managed to find at last what I must have been searching for all along. The end of the road. Not quite.

***

It was another nine hours before my eyelids unglued themselves again. Yet another nurse stood over me, this one announcing that it was time to get up and join the others. I didn't want to join any others, or meet any others, or play with any others, or look at any others, and told her so. She said I'd slept almost the entire time since my arrival, something like forty hours, and that this wasn't to be my regular room. This was an admitting room, for patients newly arrived who were not yet up to a community experience. She said that thereafter I would share a room with another brain-fried space cadet, partake of society in the dayroom, and eat my meals in a dining hall. I told her I wasn't ready for anything nearly as demanding as that and ducked under the covers like a two-year-old until she left. Shortly afterward the chick from the kitchen bounced in with another tray of disgusting food, which remained untouched. About mid-afternoon I awoke to find the nurse standing over me again. She said simply, and without much warmth, "Time to get up." I grudgingly raised myself to a sitting position and was suddenly overcome by all the inspiration I needed to do anything at all—a putrid stench something like decomposing flesh escaping from the parted lapels of my robe.

The ordeal of my showering would have been almost comical if it weren't so pathetic. A shower was in a room down the hall, fifty feet. Too damn far. I needed to lean on the nurse to walk it. I had a death grip on the plumbing with one hand while I awkwardly washed with the other. I didn't dare let go. I shivered in the near-scalding water. I gawked at my unstable legs. My thighs weren't much bigger around than my calves. The basketball legs were long gone. The nurse stood outside, asking if I was all right every few minutes, as if I were an old man who might suddenly fall and break something. As if I couldn't be left unattended. Like an invalid.

But I was slowly becoming coherent enough to begin exploring my circumstances, my thoughts alternating from defiance and anger to submission and surrender, from being mad as hell for being subjected to this degradation to feeling grateful for being in good hands. I was experiencing the typical seesaw of emotions that comes with the neighborhood—from dejection to acceptance, the overwhelming fear, and the awful truth. My entire adult life had been spent in a bottle. All the events that should have highlighted my existence, which measured together make a man what he is through his experiences and achievements, had been hazed over and rendered forgettable and regrettable by a lifelong miasma of chronic drunkenness and indifference. Everything in my life worth having had been drowned in booze: a former marriage to a spectacular woman that produced two children so removed from my life that I had no idea what they looked like; a newspaper career that had taken me from cub reporter to editor and award-winning columnist and photographer; a rare opportunity as a songwriter in the country music capital of the world; an escalating career as a public relations consultant; a cushy job as correspondent for the nation's leading publisher of retail trade magazines; God knows how many valuable professional associations; lifelong friendships compromised by dishonestly, thievery, and exploitation; and any number of relationships with decent, attractive women whom I'd treated like expendable whores.

But I hadn't just lost these opportunities and people. They hadn't merely been the unavoidable casualties of my sordid lifestyle. I had discarded them, disposed of them, tossed them aside like empty bottles and crumpled cigarette packs. And I had been breaking my beloved Kay's heart as she endured having to witness my wasting away. I gripped the showerhead like a microphone and wanted to scream into it like a rock-and-roll front man *I'm sorry I'm sorry I'm sorry.* The steaming water pummeled my face and the nurse asked again if I was okay.

***

As I sat in my new room late in the afternoon, properly scrubbed and clothed, I felt the sensation of hunger. I couldn't think of a thing that appealed to me, but I at least sensed for the first time the need to eat. My new roommate was Arthur, who seemed pretty cognizant. He had arrived the same day I had, but evidently in much better shape. He escorted me to the dayroom and introduced me to the other drunks and addicts. There were about twenty in all, in various stages of detoxification, some a little more chipper than others, most no more lucid than I was. A couple greeted me warmly. Others offered feeble waves and weak grunts. Some were twitching, others sleeping, others pacing. One girl yakked non-stop and annoyingly loud, perhaps fearing that if she shut up for two minutes she'd realize how awful she felt. All awaited the announcement to head to the cafeteria. Arthur said the food wasn't half bad.

I feared that I still wasn't capable of going too far. The shower and the effort of dressing had pretty much sapped me. I shared this with Arthur, who said he understood and assured me of his help. I made it to the cafeteria but told Arthur I didn't think I could stand in line for food. He said he'd get a tray for me. I sat at a large round table and meekly said hello as others joined me with their food. When my tray arrived it held only a bowl of soup and some crackers. Arthur said he figured I wasn't ready for anything heavy yet. Arthur was right.

After failing my first attempt at a mouthful of soup, I assumed I was the butt of a traditional practical joke. Who the hell gives a man who's shaking like a jackhammer a bowl of soup? The first spoonful was empty before it cleared the rim of the bowl, but I jerked it over my shoulder anyway. The second went all over the table. The third bounced off my chin and splashed down my front. The fourth spoonful made it to my lips but the spoon didn't. I must have looked like a spastic conducting the philharmonic. I tried drinking the soup from the bowl itself and made even more of a mess. I looked around, certain that everyone in the cafeteria was rolling with laughter at the new boy.

So this was the procedure. One flew over the drunk farm. Bring the poor sick bastard to his knees. Like I didn't feel enough like garbage. Smother me in humiliation. Wait until I'm just conscious enough to realize what a total waste of skin I am, stripped of any semblance of self-respect, shuddering like an old fart on his last legs, trying to piss in a bottle with my stinking jammies around my ankles, and send in the most delicious broad I'd ever laid eyes on to ask if she can help. Haul my bewildered butt to this kiddie cafeteria shaking so bad I'm on the verge of D.T.s and can't hold my own dick still let alone an eating utensil. Throw me in a roomful of lobotomized losers from the village of the damned and serve me a bowl of scalding fucking soup so I can burn the skin off my chin and splash it all over myself for today's entertainment. This is how they detox your sorry ass. This is how they treat a helpless scared-to-death drunk on his first day in the souse house. How do you like it so far, party boy?

But no one was watching. There were about a hundred other

patients from various sections of the rehab center. My announcement to the other detoxers at our table that the soup was evidently an initiation ritual of some sort raised a couple smiles. They'd probably painted their own fronts with soup. And when I asked after lunch if we'd be gathering in the dayroom to thread needles and practice our calligraphy, the rise from a few was evidence that in spite of my former protestations I had indeed joined the others; and that no matter what happened to me here, I might just retain the one behavioral trait that throughout my life had condemned me to chastisement and saved me from insanity. Stripped of my wiseass humor, I'd curl up and die like a maggot in the sun.

We laughed apprehensively and put up brave fronts, strangers all and painfully uncomfortable and frightened, instant comrades tossed in a stew of uncertainty and shame, tolerating the misery because we had no choice. Kicking and screaming or waving white flags, we wiped soup from our chins and braced ourselves for whatever ordeal awaited us—and all without chemical help. I had arrived at this crossroads, this way station to wherever, two days before. I had not gone that long without a drink or a drug for as long as I could remember. This alone was something like a miracle.

***

Over the next several days, however, as my withdrawal symptoms began to abate and my inborn rebellion came to life again, I found it necessary on several occasions to point out to doctors, nurses, and counselors that they obviously didn't realize with whom they were dealing and that their usual tactics would prove useless on me. Those other mind-addled meth-heads, booze hounds, snow-snorters, crack-smokers, pill-poppers and skin-jabbers might be desperate and damaged enough to fall for their brainwashing bulldip, but not this kid.

At one point a doctor happened to mention during a routine exam that the twenty-eight-day rehab I had reluctantly signed on for did not include the luxury holiday in the detox ward.

"What the hell are you talking about?"

"The four-week rehabilitation program doesn't start until you get out of detox. You must have known that."

"How would I know that? I was told I was going away for four weeks of rehab. For some crazy reason I took that to mean I was going away for four weeks. How the hell long is detox?"

"Depends. You're still pretty shaky. In your case at least a week, maybe more."

"And it doesn't even count as part of the four weeks of rehab?"

"Actually, the rehab might take longer than four weeks."

"Wait a damn minute. You can't commit someone to a four-week program and then tell him after he gets here that it's going to be five weeks or six weeks. Where do you get off doing that? Jesus Christ. That's like sentencing a guy to four years in prison and when you get him behind bars you tell him six might be better. What the fuck."

"We can do without the language."

"The language? Golly gee, Doc, I'm sorry all to hell. I've been grossly misinformed and I ain't happy about it. I've been railroaded. Blindsided. You're screwing around with my life here and you're offended by my language?"

"We're trying to *save* your life here. Look, the objective is to help you overcome your addiction by putting you on the proper path to recovery. For most people that takes four weeks. For a few it takes a little longer, just as some people need more days in detox than others.

It depends on your condition and how you respond to treatment. If it's determined that you're not stable enough to stay clean and resume your life, you may need more help. It wouldn't make any sense to make this treatment available to you and then release you before the treatment is complete, would it?"

"I don't believe this. I got a career, you know. I happen to be a professional, and I'm thinking this so-called hospital is anything *but* professional. I was expected to be on leave for four weeks, not four months. You gonna pay me what I'm losing by being away from my career all that extra time? Who the hell do you people think you are?"

The doctor smiled. They all had that denigrating grin down pat. *Having successfully completed the required course of studies, Dr. Ernest Pudpuller has been awarded a degree in advanced clinical smirkage by the University of South Dingleberry College of Condescension.* He was either trying to smooth the feathers of a typically ticked-off novice, or he realized full well that in my present state of affairs I had the professional prospects of a three-legged pack mule. I found it incredible that these clowns seemed to know what made me tick as soon as I walked in. They weren't easy to bullshit, and I was a bullshitter extraordinaire.

"I suggest," said the doctor, "that you go down to the dayroom and read over the serenity prayer."

"What the hell's the serenity prayer?"

"It has to do with accepting things we cannot change. It's posted on the wall in the dayroom, along with excerpts from the book of Alcoholics Anonymous, what we call the Big Book, some quotations, adages and the like. The displays are all over. I'm sure you've seen them."

"Yeah, well, I didn't come down here to read Mother Goose posters, you know?"

"Suppose we just take this a day at a time, shall we? You're still exhibiting a lot of withdrawal symptoms and you're still unsettled and confused. You've been here a few days and you're still pretty agitated."

"Gee, I can't understand why. Yeah, that's me, Doc. Agitated, confused, dopey, grumpy, shaky, and if you'll excuse my saying so, highly pissed."

On day five I got to sit down with a counselor for a chat. She asked about the world I came from.

3

S.O.B.

It sure would be easy to blame it all on my mother. I was destined to be an alcoholic, but I wish she hadn't encouraged me quite so much. She asked me once, when my siblings and I were older and on our own, why none of us could come over without getting drunk first. I said, "Good question. Maybe you should think about it."

Ida Jean Thompson was the youngest of three sisters. She abhorred the name Ida and forbade anyone to utter it even jokingly. She insisted on Jean. As a young woman she'd had the most radiant smile, the longest and most statuesque legs, the most endearing personality, and the biggest tits in Auburn, NY. A knockout her entire life, she carried that grille with a good deal of authority and had a remarkable way of arriving everywhere twice.

To say that our mother was enigmatic is to pay her the ultimate compliment. As Oscar Wilde said of himself, she lived in terror of not being misunderstood. Contrary by both nature and design, she was predictably unpredictable always, which made her as maddening as she was marvelous, as vexing as she was vivacious. Her devoted admirers accepted the fact that her exasperating behavior was as much a part of the dynamic package as her exuberance, humor, and glamour; and the few friends to whom she remained close for many years, who did not make the mistake of trying to correct or challenge her, tolerated her infuriating tendencies simply because they adored her. Her children certainly fit into that category as well, though we had to maintain a higher degree of forbearance because of a vindictiveness and temper of which few people outside the house would have thought her capable. It was like living with Lucy Ricardo on crack.

I can't expertly diagnose her emotional problems, but my siblings and I saw behind her compensatory facade many symptoms prevalent in bipolar disorder, borderline and histrionic personality disorders, panic disorder, paranoia, schizophrenia, and chronic and progressive great big pain in the ass disorder. I believe she nevertheless had the looks and guts to do or be whatever she wanted. So many people we've known over the years have said she should have been an actress, which is like saying that Wilt Chamberlain should have been tall.

I also believe she was capable of killing. I'd like to think she couldn't bring herself to murder anyone intentionally—if you don't count the times she added toxic cleaning solutions to the old man's liquor bottles—but her episodes of anger often reached a frightening intensity, and there were several occasions in our childhood when it appeared that she might indeed be homicidal. I think that these incidents scared her as much as they did us, and that after one of her real rip-snorters she took refuge in her room and got down on her knees.

My younger sister Maris, who may have gotten closer to her than any of us, believes that Mother never enjoyed a thoroughly happy day her entire life. Even as she appeared to be in high spirits, we knew that anguish simmered within, real or imagined, waiting to erupt at the slightest provocation. And on the occasions when an aura of happiness seemed to prevail, she apparently couldn't bring herself to trust it, and would invariably find a way to sabotage it. Even as adults, we never spent an hour under her roof when we weren't walking on eggshells.

Thanksgiving dinners were traditionally disastrous. I don't recall one that didn't turn ugly over the turkey. The old man had never learned to carve one correctly, and none of us, save Mother, could care less. We each got a generous slab of it on our plates and gave thanks for it. Since these feasts were always painfully drawn out in their preparation, the old man was inclined to sedate himself with additional manhattans, thereby weakening further his fragile tolerance for criticism. He'd take up fork and carving knife and set to work, and without fail Mother would make a derogatory comment about his procedure, igniting the inevitable fireworks, which culminated on one occasion, much to our delight, in his sailing a drumstick across the table and caroming it off her forehead. She returned fire with a side-armed sweet potato and dinner was served. As I look back on those festive gatherings, I still imagine her arriving at the table and being fully cognizant that all she had to do to have a peaceful holiday dinner for once in our lives was to keep her mouth shut about that turkey; but not once did she contain herself.

At the same time, it was hard to imagine any other mother being as much fun as ours was whenever the sun broke through the thunderclouds that darkened most of her days. She could be so loving and caring when at times the appearance of a bona fide compassion upstaged her inexorable drive to manipulate those around her. Those good times and affectionate deeds, when she could be such a marvelous mother and friend, are as memorable now as the bad ones. But when I find myself recalling them, I realize they were not exceptional. She was only doing then what mothers normally did. They were only remarkable in their contrast to the draconian behavior we'd grown so accustomed to.

One summer day, when we were still quite young, she planned a picnic for us while the old man was working, and on the way to the park in the family convertible there occurred one of those thunderstorms that materialize without warning. It was just the sort of curveball that would send her into a screaming rage, and for which she would somehow concoct a way to blame and punish one of us. But she calmly pulled the car to the side of the road and pushed the button to raise and close the convertible top. With the rain thumping the canvas over our heads, she opened the picnic basket and passed out sandwiches and lemonade, turned on the radio, and we had the best picnic ever right there in the car. Just when we expected her to turn into a raging storm herself, she turned instead into Mary Poppins. She could go either way like flicking a switch.

She was such a joy to be with when she felt good, and on the rare instances that she bared her soul to us as we grew older, she claimed that she wanted more than anything to be a good mother, and even confessed to lacking some of the psychological tools essential to the job. But time and again her venomousness would confirm that her interludes of tenderness were not to be trusted, and that she could not be trusted with ours. When we warmed to her enough to confide and share our secrets, or ask her advice on a personal dilemma, she stowed the intimacy away as a squirrel stores nuts, digging it up months or years later to use against us, dropping it like a bomb when it would be the most devastating, usually in the company of others. In the psychological warfare she waged perpetually against her loved ones, she maintained an arsenal of such weapons to which she could resort if a confrontation wasn't going her way. She always had a dagger concealed and at the ready.

She told me once that she didn't think she knew how to love or how to show love. I don't think she knew how to *be* loved either. A carton in my attic contains bundles of letters she wrote to her sister Teddy in her slow, deliberate hand. I have them because they were never sent. It was a way of venting for her, writing at length about her longings and failures, her exasperation over the old man's seeming indifference toward her feelings, her inability to cope with the burdens of motherhood, her children's ingratitude and selfishness, her mother-in-law's interference in the management of the household, her chronic depression and unhappiness. One handwritten letter covers both sides of twenty-seven pages of narrow-lined legal paper, devoted exclusively to her frustration over not having any time to do anything. But the theme that prevailed in all those letters was her steadfast belief that she was unwanted.

Our grandmother moved into our house before I started kindergarten. My parents fought a lot anyway, but Gramma's involvement in the household matters added another dimension to the constant friction. Mother was infuriated by the old man's reliance on his mother's judgment and approval, especially since they were usually in contrast to hers. We found ourselves turning to Gramma for nearly everything, particularly affection and sympathy. In her eyes we were always the innocents, and she knew we had to turn somewhere. When Mother was having "one of her spells," as our grandmother called them, we took refuge with Gramma, our only safe harbor, while our father wrestled with his ever-conflicting devotions to the two women who controlled his life.

I crapped my corduroys in kindergarten one day. It came on so fast I didn't even have a chance to get permission to use the rest room. I pretended it hadn't happened, even as my classmates zeroed in on me as the source of the horrendous odor. When I awoke after naptime I had the whole floor to myself. The other kids were jammed against the walls as if they'd been thrown by a tidal wave. By the time I got home my trousers were cemented to my ass. Mother accused me of deliberately filling my pants to get attention. Gramma came to my defense, and it was she who pried my clothes off, cleaned me up, and dried my tears.

Ida was born in 1911. It says so on her birth certificate, which I've seen. She claimed it was wrong, of course. She was really born a year later. I don't think her assertion had anything to do with pretending to be younger than what was established by the most indisputable documentation on God's green earth, but rather that her birth certificate couldn't possibly be as mundanely accurate as yours or mine.

She was every inch a woman and knew everything there was to know about being one. That sounds sexist, but our mother was herself sexist in the sense that she overcame every obstacle and sidestepped every comeuppance by drawing from an inexhaustible supply of feminine charms, emotions, privileges, courtesies, and theatrics as instinctively and adeptly as a craftsman selects the precise tool for the job at hand. What the rest of us refer to as a woman's prerogative, Ida considered law. She didn't merely appreciate being treated like a lady; she demanded it. She deemed it not only acceptable but compulsory to arrive fashionably late for anything from major surgery to an audience with the pope, not that she'd ever grant him one.

We often attended church as a family and never were we seated in her preferred front pew when the service started. We waited in the car until she dramatically emerged from the house like the belle of the ball at about the same time the service was beginning a few blocks away. We arrived just in time to make the second seating, when she proudly led her brood down the center aisle the length of the chapel, flashing her dazzling smile, lofting those gifts from God left and right by way of greeting the congregation, and signifying that the service could now get underway.

When we were young we didn't really care that our mother was such a control freak. We'd adapted to it. But rarely could we justify the ferocious tantrums that erupted when she couldn't have her way, often over the most trifling of occurrences, and we were helpless to predict their severity. Sometimes she'd work herself into such a lather that she'd forget what she was pissed off about in the first place. One of her outlets was to storm out of the house, doors slamming in her wake, get in her car and smoke backwards out the two-hundred-foot driveway with the accelerator to the floor. It wasn't an easy maneuver. One shoulder of the narrow driveway dropped off suddenly to a deep gully that had swallowed more than a few delivery vans, cars, and subsequent tow trucks. The other side was bordered by a rock garden that had claimed its share of fenders. At the end of the drive was a huge boulder painted white to mark the apron so that drivers pulling in at night wouldn't misjudge the entrance and take out the picket fence, our father among them.

One evening when she caught one of us stirring Kool-Aid in the wrong direction, she slipped into maniac mode, screamed uncontrollably for half an hour, and stomped out the back door keys in hand. We heard the car door slam in the garage and watched from the kitchen window as she squealed backwards down the driveway, burning rubber and disappearing past the side porch beyond our view. After something like this happened there was silence in the house. We kids didn't dare say anything. We never knew what the old man's stand was going to be. He usually defended her, mostly because he was so devoted to her, but also to keep his own ass out of a sling. She had obviously found herself lost and disoriented in another emotional blizzard, leaving us again mystified about what was really bothering her. If we'd asked what was wrong and how we could help, however, she'd question our motives and sincerity. As we learned to understand over the years, she usually didn't know what was wrong herself. She was just plain angry inside.

The front doorbell sounded. It was our minister who had happened along. He frantically shouted to the old man, "Jean's in a terrible predicament. She's driven up on that big rock at the end of the driveway and can't get the car off. She's teetering back and forth and gunning the engine and screaming bloody murder." The old man said, "Good. Leave her there."

***

My father was Mr. Campus at Hamilton College. He wanted me to attend Hamilton. With my high school grades, I wouldn't be allowed on that campus to mow the lawn. He was Phi Beta Kappa and Phi Beta everything else, tops in his class academically and socially, handsome, talented, ambitious and funny.

I learned from my mother that at college social gatherings Huey could sit at a piano and play and sing the popular songs and show tunes with professional pizzazz, cut a rug with the best of them, knock back cocktails better than most, and be the life of the party wherever he went. He chaired any number of school organizations, sang in the glee club and played in the band, participated in sports if by no means a jock, was elected class president, edited the yearbook and campus newspaper, headed the most prestigious fraternity, probably never missed a party, and still managed to ace nearly every course. Yeah, he was one of those.

He was a tenacious student and insatiable reader who was fascinated by history and had an astonishing capacity for remembering names and dates. His weaknesses included golf, convertibles, booze, Camel cigarettes, and Ida Jean Thompson. He was decent to a fault and the most honorable man I have ever known.

Among my many disappointments is that I was such a disappointment to him. He expected great things from me. It must have deeply pained him to see my dreadful report cards. Spelling, proper grammar, and passable writing skills had come fairly easily to me, yet I earned D's in English on a regular basis. In my junior year in high school I got drunk before my final English exam and slept through it. I flunked the course altogether, despite earning straight A's in an honors course in advanced composition writing. That just blew his mind. He learned early that I'd never match him scholastically, due to a severe lack of giving a damn on my part, and while he hoped that I would achieve some measure of success as a writer, later in his life he may have been content to hope that I'd achieve a measure of success in anything at all.

My father had barely begun college when his own father died. The loss might have inspired in him a greater determination to succeed, but

I suspect the determination was already there. He staunchly believed that if you want something you have to work for it, an ethic I apparently hadn't inherited. He agreed with Thomas Jefferson's observation, often falsely attributed to renowned football coach Vince Lombardi, that the harder you work, the luckier you get. But, contrary to Lombardi, he believed wholeheartedly that winning is neither everything nor the only thing. That much I did inherit, and gratefully. It does matter how you play the game.

Huey earned his master's degree in English literary history and taught English composition at Hamilton before working in public relations for what was to become Rochester Institute of Technology. He then joined newspapers in Auburn and Syracuse and eventually our local afternoon daily, the Rochester Times-Union. He distinguished himself as a consummate reporter and editor whose commitment to accuracy became legendary in the newsroom, and whose knowledge of local history was second to none.

The sheer magnitude of his vocabulary and his gift for precise phrasing made him an exceptional writer to begin with. His photographic memory, a keen sense of what made a good story, a wealth of integrity, and the speed with which he could put an article together made him a journalist's journalist. But it was his genius for nailing the heart of a story by getting to the heart of the reader that afforded him a way with words that moves me still.

While city editor and then assistant managing editor, he produced a daily column that showcased his gift for reaching everyman, dispensing with compassion and humor a wisdom characterized by a camaraderie with fellow parents, wage-earners, sports fans, neighbors, and citizens of every stripe who shared the same pleasures and challenges of life regardless of station. He maintained a high regard for all who did their best with the tools they had, and thus treated the trash man, mechanic, factory worker and doctor and lawyer with the same degree of courtesy. In 1955 he published a book of some of his favorite columns. I've probably read it a hundred times, pulling it out when I get to thinking about him, and finding in its pages a lesson in good writing, and a reminder of what a fine man he was.

This is the side of my father that my siblings and I have clung to all our lives, the side we will always cherish. His other side was the one with which he coped with the ever-maddening love of his life, a side that was not always pretty or commendable. In one of her letters to her sister, my mother described an incident at the kitchen table one night when he kept making grotesque faces at her like a kindergartner. She had probably pushed one of his several sensitive buttons, and he had no doubt been to the trough a few times and had resorted to childishly antagonizing her in response. I can picture him doing it. Mother explained to her sister, "I think he hates me because he loves me."

She may have been right, although I think it was more a matter of his hating himself for loving her so much, for being so much at her mercy. She knew she was impossible to live with and delighted in it. She knew that his willingness to suffer it came not from fortitude but from allegiance, and she abused his devotion relentlessly.

As a father he had his shortcomings as all fathers do. He did the best he could, or at least the best he knew how. He was not one to throw the baseball around in the back yard when I was young, but he had season tickets for box seats at home games of our International League Rochester Red Wings, for whom Stan Musial and George Sisler had played, and whose player and managerial rosters would include Frank Robinson, Johnny Mize, Jim Palmer, Earl Weaver, Harry Walker, Bob Gibson, Don Baylor, Eddie Murray, and Cal Ripken, Sr. and Jr. For years I thought our team must be the best in the league because the Wings were the only team that wore white uniforms. He often took me to the locker room after games to meet the players and get autographed baseballs.

He took me to see welterweight and middleweight boxing champion Carmen Basilio train in his gym in Alexandria Bay; and I sat with him in front row seats to watch Bob Davies, Bobby Wanzer, Arnie Risen, Maurice Stokes, and Jack Twyman of the Rochester Royals, who in 1951 beat the New York Knickerbockers for the NBA championship.

As a newsman he scored tickets to many events, the Shrine circus, concerts, theater productions, boxing matches, auto shows. Once he took me to a show starring Dean Martin and Jerry Lewis. The warm-up act was a skinny colored kid wailing on a harmonica, Little Stevie Wonder. He couldn't have been more than thirteen. The old man always had books of free passes to the downtown movie theaters—the RKO Palace, Loew's, the Paramount, all long gone now—and I treated my friends.

I made a Little League team one year but was not a good player. I had always thought it odd that he would drop me at the field and pick me up afterwards, but would never join the other fathers in the bleachers. He watched me play in one game, from his car, parked at the side of the road by the playing field. I understand it now. He didn't join the other fathers out of some belief that he was above them in any way. He just didn't feel like one of them. He could write to them, or about them, or be friendly at a party with them. But he couldn't sit in the bleachers with them like a regular dad because he felt out of place, out of his element, not one of the boys, diffident and uncomfortable. How well I know the feeling. On the other hand, he might have been embarrassed that I was such a crummy player.

We were thought of as having money because of the appearance my parents projected. My father was well known in the community and highly regarded. When he switched to broadcast journalism and became evening news anchor for a local TV station, he became Rochester's version of Walter Kronkite, at what I suspect was about a tenth of the salary. He was as skilled with the spoken word as with the written, an accomplished lecturer and popular emcee at community affairs, as well as a radio news announcer; but he was extremely uncomfortable in front of the camera and never quite mastered an appearance of poise. He nevertheless delivered the evening news with an air of fatherly trust that endeared him to viewers, who had no idea that he had never done a broadcast sober.

He dressed in Hickey-Freeman suits almost exclusively, not that he could afford them, but because he had once written a column about Frank Sinatra's visiting Rochester to be fitted at the prestigious and world-renowned local clothier for a movie. His superiors had deemed the column an obvious plug for the company, but my father viewed it more as a plug for Rochester and a newsworthy item of public interest. In any event, he was thereafter rewarded with suits at generously discounted prices. He belonged to a country club only because his membership was paid in part by his employer. He drove flashy convertibles that he bought several years used, among my favorites a '53 baby blue Buick Roadmaster. We lived in a superior neighborhood in a large house with a big yard that he could barely meet the second mortgage on.

We were rich in many ways, certainly, and lacked very little. Yet I can picture my father stepping suavely out of his shiny convertible for a gala party at the country club, dressed impeccably in an elegant suit, my glamorous, radiant mother on his arm, and with all of about five dollars in his wallet.

My parents shared so many enjoyments that at times they seemed proverbially made for one another, and yet clashed with such ferocity that it often seemed implausible that they could stomach each other's company. There were times when their fighting became so fierce that I cowered in my bedroom and prayed for the screaming and crashing to stop, only to be terrified all the more when it did stop, fearing that one of them was mortally wounded. Yet in spite of it all my father simply worshipped her, and defended her often when he knew she was dead wrong. He told me more than once that he'd have divorced her in a second if it weren't for us kids. I didn't believe it then or now. He could never live without her.

In the course of his work my father met many famous and important people, including presidents, the pope, generals, sports stars, and entertainers. More than once he telephoned the White House to wish Richard Nixon a merry Christmas, and got through to him. He thought the world of Nixon. We argued when I refused to vote in the 1968 presidential election because I objected to having to vote for a lesser of evils. He told me that ignoring my right to vote was blasphemous. But I would not vote for Nixon for reasons clear to any upstanding hippie, and I would not vote for Humphrey solely because he wasn't Nixon. And I certainly wouldn't vote for Wallace. I asked my father what was worse, someone who doesn't vote at all, or someone who'd vote for Captain Kangaroo as long as he was Republican. He didn't speak to me for a week.

On a Thursday evening, August 8, 1974, I was at the house watching TV with my parents as Nixon delivered his resignation speech. My father was granite-faced. He had given Nixon the benefit of the doubt throughout the Watergate fiasco, and what he was hearing now seemed incredulous. He was devastated, and he took Nixon's demise personally. When Nixon concluded his address, my father stared at the TV and muttered, "You goddam two-faced bastard." He looked at me apologetically, revealing a rarely displayed acknowledgement of having been mistaken.

In another such acknowledgement, he had never hidden his distain for the flower generation's protests against the Vietnam War and had objected to my participation in them, especially my joining the March on Washington in November of 1969. But as the blunder of America's involvement in Vietnam became clearer, along with the feebleness and deceitfulness with which the government attempted to justify it, my father came to believe that we'd been right to protest all along, and in fact had been downright American about it.

Above the fireplace mantel in our living room was a large mirror five feet across, and every Christmas season it wore a different hand-scribed holiday greeting in poster paints. My parents' friends and neighbors traditionally dropped by each year to share the spirit and spirits, and to see how we'd decorated the mirror. We kids and Mother would offer suggestions, but applying the message and artwork was always the old man's job, like carving the turkey, and none of us would dare interfere.

One year as Christmas approached I took it upon myself to paint on the mirror a gigantic peace sign, which was not yet widely recognized by my parents' generation. When my father saw it he said, as I thoroughly expected him to, "What the hell is that?" I told him it was the peace sign. It had no meaning for him whatsoever. He probably thought it was some sort of swastika. He said it was hideous and demanded I clean it off. I refused. I told him that I was sorry if he didn't know the internationally recognized symbol for peace on earth, but that if it bothered him so much he could remove it himself. But it stayed. And when his friends dropped in over the holidays and a few asked what it was, he explained, "It's the peace sign, of course. What did you think it was?"

4

Trouble

We didn't realize until we were teenagers that our mother had real psychiatric problems. Even then, in the early sixties, we didn't know any appropriate medical terms for her behavior. We just figured her for an exceptionally gifted lunatic. But when I was a child and she used my Tinker Toys for kindling because I didn't hang up my coat—or because I did—it just didn't occur to me to make allowances for her rampant chemical imbalance.

We may have thought all mothers were like that. And by the time we were old enough to realize that maybe her batty behavior wasn't her fault, we'd taken so much crap from her it was hard to muster any compassion. Besides, I wasn't all that sure she didn't enjoy being nuts. We could never understand the sudden changes. One minute we might be sharing a pleasant project with her at the kitchen table, like sorting through her beloved collections of odd cigarette lighter parts and broken shoelaces, and the next thing we knew it was raining cast iron skillets.

I never knew what to expect when I walked in the house after school. I'd see her through the kitchen window wearing her constipated librarian face, one of her favorites, and I'd amuse myself by throwing snowballs at passing cars until someone else came home.

I didn't stand a chance with her one on one.

Once when I was seven, playing with toy cars with my friend Dave in my room after school, Mother called up the stairs and asked me to take out the trash. In the first place, what mother bothers a contented, quiet, occupied kid with a frivolous chore like that? I said something like "Do I have to?" and thought that was the end of it. Ten minutes later the old man stomped in the room, told Dave to hit the bricks, and thumped me a couple of good ones. It wasn't the first time I'd been bonked for no apparent reason, but curiosity made me wander downstairs to find out why my bell was ringing this time. The trash was strewn across the kitchen floor, slimy garbage, coffee grounds and all. According to my brother, when the old man walked into the slop after coming home from work, Mother explained that she'd pleasantly asked me to take out the trash and I'd told her to go to hell; and that she'd made the mess to make me clean it up as punishment. When I told my father I hadn't said any such thing, I got walloped again for lying.

Another time I asked her for some money so that my friend Hammy and I could go to the corner store for Popsicles. She gave me a half dollar and a pat on the head. Hammy and I washed down the Popsicles with Cokes and added some gum and other junk, and without trying too hard we spent it all. When I got home she asked for the change. When I told her there wasn't any, she shot me that twisted-face scowl of hers, the one that could start up small appliances from across the room, and when the old man came home she told him I'd stolen five dollars from her purse. What's a kid supposed to do with a mother like that? It's a wonder I'm not a serial killer.

Dear teacher: So that you'll know what you're getting into, I feel obligated to warn you up front that what you have here is one troubled little boy, cute as I am, who is going to make you wish you'd gone into nursing instead. I need attention and plenty of it. My older brother beats the snot out of me on a daily basis. I have a dad who's too busy and a mother who has more moods than teeth. If I had an ink well I wouldn't dip Susie's pigtail in it; I'd pour it down her neck. Nobody wants me around. I don't even feel like I belong when I'm talking to myself. I have severe younger brother syndrome. My daddy plays golf instead of taking me fishing and camping. His mother lives with us. My parents sleep in separate bedrooms and argue all the time. I need a hug, and maybe some candy. I have a new best friend every week. I'm a middle child, for God's sake. My mother is loony. Any day now I'll be disemboweling neighborhood cats and biting the heads off sewer rats. I'm small for my age. I'm going to be an alcoholic and a drug addict, you can bet on it. I am class president of the class clowns your professors warned you about. My brother gets a new Rawlings baseball glove and I get a dried up webless piece of crap handed down from Shoeless Joe Jackson. My brother gets a brand new snow shovel and I get the old one with the loose floppy blade and the corners all bent up so that it catches on everything and runs the handle through my spleen. My mother makes pabulum you could use for adobe. My brother got a new bow and arrow and they gave me a target. I always have the top bunk and my brother gets the lower. Every night he launches me six feet out of bed with his feet. Crashing to the floor disrupts my sleep pattern. My dad finally makes me my own bedroom by nailing up beaverboard in an unheated attic that a polar bear wouldn't last a night in. My parents have turned family dysfunction into an art form. I have to wear my brother's old clothes. I hate going to school, I hate going home, and I ain't all that crazy about you.

My kindergarten teacher, Miss Morose, was older than dirt. She had always loved children. She had a special place in the classroom for the kids she loved best, a chair in the corner. She must have loved me most of all. My first grade teacher, Miss Barnwhistle, was only twenty-two and in her first year of teaching. She resigned after a month to get a hysterectomy. In second grade Mrs. Skidmarks had me transferred to another class mid-semester, where my new teacher learned in no time why that had happened. In third grade I got a new teacher in October when Mrs. Manatee came down with a mysterious illness and moved to South Dakota. In fourth grade Mrs. Wagonstern determined that I needed to be needed, so I was given the much-envied job of delivering milk to all the classrooms on a cart that apparently wasn't meant to do stairs. You wouldn't have thought there was that much milk in those little bottles, or that much glass. In fifth grade I disrupted the class so many times one day that Mr. Brutalia put me in a wardrobe closet so I couldn't watch a breathtaking filmstrip on the export products of Paraguay. His coat was in the closet, along with his Lucky Strikes and matches. In sixth grade Mrs. VanWrinkle gave me failing grades in everything. She retained the entire class for seventh grade as well, except for me. I was transferred to Mrs. Stratford's class. Mrs. Stratford gave me good grades and plenty of attention and we got along fine.

I wanted Mr. Bliss' job. Mr. Bliss was the custodian. He pushed wood shavings up and down the hall with an extra-wide dusting broom that made the floors shine. I thought that was a swell job. Mr. Bliss spent a lot of time in his custodial office being keeper of the paste, the sweet-tasting white glue that was so delicious. He kept it in a big ceramic crock and we needed a note from a teacher to get any. I wanted to be master of the paste.

In that final year of grade school, on a snowy day in March, my friend Artie rushed in after the lunch recess and excitedly told Mrs. Stratford about seeing some old lady cross the street and get squashed by a beer truck. That old lady was my Gramma, and my life was about to change.

***

Our grandmother had lived with us about seven years when Mother apparently convinced the old man that other arrangements had to be made. How he'd coerced her into letting Gramma live with us in the first place I can't imagine. Mother couldn't abide having her authority compromised, and her frequently disparaging treatment of the old man lost a good deal of its sting when he had his mother to turn to for absolution. He found Gramma an apartment just a block away, where I often went for lunch recess and after school. The old man stopped on his way home from work almost daily. It was an acceptable alternative for all concerned, and a far better arrangement for Mother.

Gramma was crossing the road by her apartment on her way to a drug store when the beer delivery truck turned the corner and ran her over. She survived briefly in the hospital but there was no hope. It was the gloomiest day I'd ever seen in our home, made worse by the gruesome way in which she had met her end. None of us had ever seen our father sob. Never had we seen him so overcome. Mother even shelved her usual theatrics and seemed genuinely grief-stricken.

As we struggled to absorb the horrible shock there was an uncharacteristic calm in the house. Mother remained somber, only losing her grip momentarily the day of Gramma's memorial. When we arrived at the funeral home and took our seats in the chapel for the service, Mother was horrified to discover that, despite her specific directions, Gramma's casket was open. Mother was claustrophobic and hated the sight of open coffins. She could deal with a closed casket, but it was the visualization of the dearly departed openly reposed in a box upon which the lid would ultimately be lowered that bothered her.

We'd barely been seated when she stood and blared loud enough to make Gramma jump, "We'll just see about this! I left *explicit* directions that this coffin was *not* to be left open!" She stomped out as stunned heads turned, and could be clearly heard in another room berating the stammering funeral director, calling him negligent and a disgrace to his profession, demanding to know how on earth he could possibly have made such an inexcusable blunder, and threatening to never pay one dime for his services.

That done, she marched triumphantly back into the chapel and took her seat. Shortly thereafter, in an attempt to make things right, the undertaker walked quietly to the casket and closed the lid right in front of her, whereupon she fainted. Or at least pretended to.

When our grandmother's will was read some weeks later it contained a specification that was far more significant than we kids then realized. Gramma had bequeathed her half share of the cottage property indirectly to the four of us grandchildren, bypassing our father, her only child. The details meant little to us at the time. We were told that the cottage would one day be ours, and that's all I needed to hear. Migget, her niece, who already held title to the other half of the property that had belonged to her late mother Inez, would also have use of our intended half for her lifetime, after which it would go to us. And, since Mig and her husband Tom had no heirs, we would logically inherit the property in its entirety upon their deaths.

The specifics were the focus of several window-rattling arguments between my parents, as my mother questioned why the old girl had deprived her son, and therefore Mother in turn, of the cottage inheritance.

We kids, meanwhile, grudgingly accepted the fact that our summers at the cottage had come to an end. As much as I'm sure Migget loved us, with our grandmother gone she felt no responsibility to accommodate her cousin's kids beyond perhaps an occasional brief visit, though no definite invitations would be forthcoming.

I don't think my older brother and sister were nearly as distressed as I was about forfeiting our summers along the river. They were in their mid-teens and had numerous other avenues to follow. And though I understood that it might be a long time before my dream of returning to the cottage came to fruition, I nevertheless held it fast to my heart long into adulthood. Especially when I felt lost and alone, I saw the cottage as the one ray of light on an otherwise gloomy horizon. I always believed that, deep down, the cottage by the river was all I ever wanted. It was the only place I knew that held only pleasant memories, where I had always felt safe, and had always felt loved.

5

Roy Pratt

R oy Pratt had a bad back. That was his explanation for needing the smoother ride of a heavy car, especially on the rutted gravel road through the woods to his cabin. The heaviest car you could get in those days was a Cadillac convertible, and Roy Pratt bought a smooth new ride every year. The first one he docked in our driveway was cherry red with cream upholstery, in '59 when Cadillac became king of the tailfins once and for all. That Caddie would be the first car I ever drove.

Roy hurt his back moving a boulder the size of a beer keg in the creek next to his cabin on Long Indian Lake. When the rainbow were running he piled logs and large stones against one bank to form a pool along the side, like a park and rest area, where he snatched parked and resting trout with his bare hands if he had a new audience. Otherwise he just speared them. Either way it was illegal, but Roy figured the trout were cutting through his yard, and he was only doing what natives had done hundreds of years before, no doubt in that very creek, maybe at that very spot, probably with spears.

I was between grade school and high school when he wheeled his fire engine into our driveway that summer, parking it in the front where I hoped my buddies might ride by and see it. The whole family walked around the car like it was roped off at an auto show, almost afraid to touch it. Roy let me get behind the wheel. The luxurious seat was big as a sofa, and I could smell the fine soft leather baking in the sun. The dashboard was a shrine of knobs and dials.

My dad looked lustfully at that car, but he'd never own one, even later in life when he had the means. He liked his sporty convertibles, but a sled like that was a little too showy for him. It suited Roy Pratt just fine, though. He drove it like the captain of an exquisite yacht, cruising the city streets and sailing the highways with the top down, his snowy hair fluttering in the wind.

A life-long bachelor, Roy was in his mid-sixties and financially comfortable. He was semi-retired from the investment company he had founded and spent his free time at his cabin. He came into our lives as easily as an uncle we hadn't seen for many years, as though we'd known him all along. And he would be my deliverance from the anguish of knowing that my summers with my grandmother were gone. This was my first summer without her, and without the river.

In no time at all he miraculously replaced her in my life in every way and then some, as if it had been ordained that I was ready for a new mentor, a new wing to nestle under when things got crazy at home. My brother Jim had met Roy through a friend who had been to Roy's cabin. Roy was invited to the house for dinner to meet our folks. I didn't know it at the time, but the arrival of that Cadillac was my ship coming in.

He was tall and solid-looking, neatly dressed, tanned to a bronze, and he had a sly yet comforting smile with well-kept teeth not altogether straight. He wasn't a handsome man, but the ladies would call him dashing. He seemed remarkably sturdy for his age, though he stooped a little, and I would soon discover upon seeing him in his preferred summer outfit of faded khaki shorts and tee shirt that for an older man he had an exceptional physique.

My father served Roy one of his legendary mahogany bullets, which wasn't anything more exotic than an oversize rock glass with two ice cubes adrift in a droplet of sweet vermouth and enough four-dollars-a-quart Three Feathers whiskey to fell a rhino. Mother asked about his single life and he gave his stock and perfect answer of never having met a woman like her. He had a number of lady friends, he said, and Mother commented that she was sure he had. She said she thought he'd be quite a catch, and he said with a wink that yes, he'd been caught a few times.

Within an hour Roy Pratt seemed to have passed my parents' scrutiny, revealing himself as a kind and affable man who lived the good life and enjoyed sharing the fruits of his prosperity, particularly with kids, since he had none of his own. An unassuming businessman, country gentleman and outdoorsman, prone to off-color remarks befitting his seasoned singleness, he was an easy talker who enjoyed my old man's humor and Mother's sarcasm. A former Scout leader and recipient of the Silver Beaver Award, the highest honor for service in a local Scouting council, Roy said he adored children and took great pleasure in enabling young boys in particular to discover some of the joys of the outdoors to which they might not ordinarily have access. This in particular came as good news to my father. I think the old man felt a little guilty that he wasn't inclined to offer his boys more opportunities with outdoorsy pursuits. His idea of roughing it was playing golf in a drizzle. He'd enrolled us in Boy Scouts and summer camps, but he wasn't about to venture into the wilderness himself.

It was with my parents' blessing, then, that a couple of weeks later I eagerly accepted an invitation for a weekend at Roy's cabin. They saw me off as I sat beaming in the passenger seat of his elegant car, my skinny arm draped over the doorsill like a big shot. It was like sending me off to camp. They knew I'd be in good hands and would benefit from some new experiences. It apparently hadn't occurred to them that Roy could be a pedophile.

The drive to the lake was about an hour and a half, through farming country east and south of the city. We stopped in a small village to get supplies. We left the main road and drove through meadow and forest for a mile or so on a narrow unpaved lane, down the bank of a deep ravine, and into a picture postcard. What Roy had modestly called his cabin in the woods was a thoroughly enchanting lodge, a one-story ranch-style log house nestled in the lap of a glacier-carved canyon that opened on Long Indian Lake. The modern kitchen and bathroom were spotless. The focus of an expansive living room was the biggest fireplace I'd ever seen, capable of accommodating fat logs five feet in length, flanked by a pair of enormous red leather armchairs.

Several gleaming tables had been handmade from huge slabs of walnut. Superb paintings of landscapes and wildlife hung on walls of real wood. A brilliant oriental adorned a lustrous yellow pine floor. Surrounding the cabin Roy claimed some fifty acres of woods and fields, and owned a thousand feet of shoreline. Through a gigantic picture window I saw a stunning panorama of the glistening lake rippling ashore just twenty yards away. I saw a speedboat with sizeable outboard at the end of a long dock, and on the shore were a canoe, rowboat, and a small sailboat. Beside a rushing stream an outbuilding housed his lawn tools and other equipment and a large sleeping loft with several beds. Across the yard a three-sided shed protected a double bed just a few feet from shore for the more adventurous overnight guests.

For a kid who had just lost his treasured haven on the river and the grandmother that had made his life there so splendid, the entire setting appeared most capable of sufficing. I felt as if I'd stumbled into a brand new version of paradise. Roy was like a grandfather. The only real grandfather I knew lived in Auburn with my aunt, but I'd only seen him a couple of times, and he was old and didn't say much.

Roy told me to make myself at home and look around, and to stop calling him Sir. I opened a coffee table drawer that was packed with girlie books, as Roy called them. In those days porno magazines weren't easy to come by, but there were issues of nudist colony magazines that showed real pussy hair, a paperback book of dirty cartoons, and, most incredible of all, half a dozen old photos the likes of which I didn't know existed. I stared at them for an hour. The guy had a dick as big as my arm. I'd never seen a picture of a man's hard dick. In some of the pictures he had it buried in the woman's crotch. In others it was in her mouth. Roy called it Frenching.

In another drawer I saw a carton of cigarettes, and Roy said I could help myself if I wanted. I'd been smoking for a couple of years when I could steal one here and there. Now I was carrying my own pack of Marlboros, and a cooler twelve-year-old you never saw. All Roy said about it was that I was not to smoke in the woods. And the first time he cracked open a can of beer he asked if I wanted some, and of course I did. I drank half of his. After that he always gave me one of my own. Goodbye apple pie and molasses cookies.

In subsequent trips to the cabin he allowed me to sit next to him and help steer the car, and sometimes, on back roads through the countryside, he let me get behind the wheel on my own and drive the big Caddie for real while he operated the pedals. He allowed me to take his speedboat on my own, and we went water-skiing and canoeing and sailing. We took long hikes in the woods, deep into the vast canyon along the stream, which he called *his* stream. It seemed to go on forever, but one day we hiked all the way to a lofty waterfall that Roy said was where the stream began. We shed our clothes and stood under its pounding shower, and then behind it under an overhang, peering through the downpour at dancing, floating rainbows.

But the most exciting treasure revealed to me at the cabin was a secret panel inside the back door that housed an assortment of rifles and shotguns, mine to use for the asking. Roy thought that the powerful kick of the shotguns might be too strong for my slender shoulder, but he allowed me to take a .22 rifle into the woods by myself, where I experienced my first invigorating conquests in the wild, blowing chipmunks and sparrows to smithereens, and forcing imaginary hombres to freeze in their tracks, while I blasted chunks of bark from their torsos shooting from the hip.

But my newly discovered hunting career came forever to an end the day I came face to face with a deer. We stood there only about forty feet apart, staring at one another, and the deer didn't flinch or move at all when I raised the rifle to my shoulder and squeezed off a single round. I thought I'd missed him entirely, but after a few seconds he just keeled over. I had no idea where I'd hit him. It isn't easy to kill a deer with a single .22 bullet. I was so excited I ran half a mile through the woods to get Roy Pratt at the cabin. It seemed like five miles getting back to the deer with him in tow. He looked at the deer and his face turned to stone. He told me I'd shot a doe, which was absolutely forbidden. Roy was pissed. He said that game wardens had a way of appearing out of nowhere, but he was just as concerned about other hunters who might report it if they came across that doe, such was the gravity of the offense. He said we'd need a neighbor's help, and we trudged off to Wally Higgins' cabin about twenty minutes away. The three of us hiked back, Wally with an assortment of knives, a shovel, rags and some rope. When we got back to the deer, Wally went to work and Roy Pratt told me to watch and learn.

Wally slit that animal open and the smell and sight of its guts made me gag. Roy began pulling out its innards, yanking sometimes to free them while Wally hacked away inside the cavity. Wally made some quick whacks with the blade and Roy's hands emerged from the bloody cavern cradling the deer's heart. He made me hold it. It jiggled like Jello in my trembling hands while Roy and Wally finished disemboweling the carcass and digging a hole to bury the entrails, minus the liver that Wally slid into a coat pocket. Tears poured down my face. The heart was still warm, sticky and gooey and dripping blood. Finally Roy took it from me and handed it to Wally, who added it to his pocket. They replaced the dirt in the gut-filled hole and covered it with a big rock. Roy handed me a rag to wipe my hands with. Wally rigged the deer with ropes tied to its feet and Roy helped him hoist it to his shoulders so that he could carry it to his cabin. Wally lumbered off, saying something about venison stew that I knew would never pass my lips.

Roy and I walked wordlessly home. He told me to wash my bloodied hands and arms in the lake. He said that maybe I should give the guns a rest for a while, until I could be more responsible. He left me alone on the shore and I stayed there for an hour, afraid to go in the cabin. I washed my hands twice more. I thought about the big shiny eyes on that doe. I was reminded of the eyes on a monstrous northern pike I'd once been punished for catching.

The day after that dreadful experience I was stretched out on one of the day beds in the living room under the big picture window, looking through one of Roy's nudie books. When he started playing with my cock I wasn't startled in the least and experienced no negative feelings whatsoever. All I knew was that it felt good.

6

Cherryl

My abominable high school career began in a dreary formerly abandoned downtown elementary school building where no two clocks wore the same time and only half the toilets operated. I can't take credit for the wayward clocks, but I might have been responsible for passing out those M-80 firecrackers (depth charges, we called them) with wicks that burned underwater. They packed a lot more punch than cherry bombs, and when you flushed down a live one you'd best not be sitting on the throne when that sucker blew.

The old building served as a halfway house for the eastside eighth graders who had finished elementary school but had to wait a year before construction was completed on the much-ballyhooed new East High, the most innovatively designed high school complex in all the land. Today it looks like a sprawling compound of warehouses, but back then it was considered downright futuristic. I fell in love on opening day with the first girl I saw who had bumps in her blouse. When I got home that afternoon I carved her name in my wrist with a razor blade and an awl—so deep that I could still read the scar when I graduated—and spelled it wrong.

My mother spotted the ragged artwork at the dinner table and slapped me so hard I heard an opera. Then the old man reached over and landed two of his patented blows, one for the carving and one for the spelling. He wasn't one to slap or punch, but he'd perfected a glancing thump off the forehead with the heel of his hand that made your frontal lobe hum pretty good.

That girl, pimples and all, was this thirteen-year-old tinkle-snapper's first chance at the real deal, and I didn't let an opportunity go by to grope for parts. I was doing just that in our basement after school one day when my mother walked in on us. For a woman who could produce enough noise to trip air raid sirens, she was quiet as dust when on patrol.

I later heard her telling the old man that it was time to give me the talk. It must have been a double delight for her, putting me through the embarrassment and him through the agony. He cornered me in my room that night and began by informing me in his usual erudite fashion that one of the phenomena of becoming a man was that my peeenis was going to become erect on occasion. I didn't have the guts to tell him that I was already well aware of this marvel. At that age it seemed like most of the time I had a raging woody you could hang a golf bag on. I'd have considered it phenomenal if my peeenis *wasn't* erect on occasion. We were poles apart as father and son in those days, and for another ten thousand days for that matter. But on the degree of discomfort we shared in that session we were as close as blood brothers. He detested talking about sex or body functions.

About all I thought about in those days was getting a hand on that girl's knockers. She was pretty stingy with them for a girl who obviously enjoyed having them so much. One Saturday I biked over to her house ostensibly to do homework with her. She was waiting on her front steps, so I did some trick riding. I cruised by no hands and with my eyes closed and smacked into a parked car. When I'd dragged my mangled bike and body to her steps and sat down, trying to act as if that wasn't the first Oldsmobile I'd spanked, I realized my prick hurt. I looked down and saw blood dripping out of the crotch of my jeans. She told me I didn't look so good. She helped me into the house and her mother called her son from his room. I'd always been intimidated by him because I knew that he knew that my life's work was to get into his little sister's panty girdle.

He led me to the bathroom and told me to drop my jeans. My underpants were sopping red. He told me to slide them off. I couldn't do it. He knelt on the floor and did it for me, gently, his hands trembling. He whispered "holy shit." Tears splashed off my cheekbones. I suddenly got cold all over. I thought I was going to puke on his head. It was a long time before I dared look.

In being hurled from the bike I had caught myself on something, and it looked like I'd ripped the head of my cock about a third of the way off. My whole lower body throbbed and my legs started to give out, but he held me against the wall with his hand on my heaving belly. He cleaned the blood off with a wet washcloth while I stared transfixed at a gleam in his long, lacquered pompadour, wondering when I'd be old enough that my parents would let me have hair like that, Elvis style, combed back and swept up without any part. Right now I was a scared sobbing kid who had all of six or eight struggling pubic hairs and who'd permanently mangled his pecker before he even got a chance to put it *in* anything.

The wound still leaked blood, but he had cleaned it enough for us to see that more accurately I had a nasty inch-long laceration—not as damaging as first thought, but evidence enough that I nearly did rip the head off. He said, "You're a lucky little fucker, you know that?"

He made a thick pad of toilet paper and put it lightly on the wound. This hood with the hot Chevy and leather jacket and sideburns and shiny ducktail hair would roar about this over beers with his buddies later. Now he carefully slid my briefs and pants back up and carried me to a bedroom and laid me on a bed. My girl wasn't allowed to visit and I wasn't keen on seeing her.

I heard her mother on the phone to my mother, saying the word peeenis a dozen times. Evidently parents so rarely got to use the word out loud that whenever the occasion warranted it they liked to get their money's worth. I heard her report her son's opinion that I'd no doubt need stitches, like I wasn't terrified enough. Our family doctor eventually arrived and said that stitches would not be necessary and that the gash would not heal before the entire school heard about it, but fairly soon thereafter. It was a good week before I could whack off again.

***

If my grade school teachers had thought that the rigors of high school would cure my inattentive and disruptive classroom manners, they had a lot to learn. It only took me a few weeks to make the sort of dean's list you don't tell mom and pop about, and by the time I graduated I'd been suspended about twenty times and expelled forever six times. One year I got thrown out on the first day.

My teachers kept waiting for me to buckle down. A good many of them have died waiting. Wherever they are these days, I hope they appreciate that I now know everything I was supposed to learn in their boring classrooms, and they needn't have branded me with grades from the depths of the alphabet just because I didn't learn the stuff at their convenience. Now that I'm at the age where I cover my mouth when I cough not so much to be polite, but to keep from blowing my teeth across the room, I think I know an obsolete triangle when I see one.

In my freshman year I made the basketball team. Several decades later I still hold an East High record that is likely to stand until the school falls down. I was on the varsity team for four years and never set foot in a game. My deplorable grades rendered me ineligible, and the fact that I was not particularly crestfallen I recognize now as typical of the attitude I maintained toward most of my endeavors for much of my life. It was the best of both worlds for me. I had the status of being on the varsity squad but didn't have to bother learning any plays. One year I tore the ligaments in both my ankles and had to wear casts during the one season that I was, in fact, eligible to play. Perfect. I'd probably have been a star, of course, but alas, they wouldn't let me off the bench. I always had an excuse for failure.

For some reason I lost interest in my first high school love, or the other way around, I don't recall. I never did get a hand inside her blouse. The name on my wrist is long gone but I still have the scar on my peeenis. It reminds me of a girl named Cherryl, and of what a lucky little fucker I was.

7

Riddance

Roy Pratt was an ephebophile. He had sexual partners more his own age, but took a special liking to adolescent boys. Typically, he sought out troubled kids who were discontented at home and overwhelmed them with paradise. I could not have been a riper candidate for his affection, and his timing was perfect.

Like the grandmother he so smoothly replaced as my wing to nestle under, he lifted me from my despair and laid at my feet all the bliss and adventure a boy could ask for. I don't think that the prospect of his sexual advances being wrong either morally or legally even occurred to me. His paradise was an escape, his affection a diversion. I maintained a three-year friendship with him, yet never felt any homosexual tendencies of my own. I remained preoccupied with invading the upper and lower attire of any girl I could get my paws on. Still, I hungered for any entertainments and pleasures that would make my life more tolerable, and they were mine for the taking at both Roy's cabin and at his apartment in the city. Already I was adhering to a simple doctrine that would guide me for much of my life: if it feels good, do it; if you want it, have it.

His apartment, where I sometimes spent the night, was a one-bedroom bachelor pad. I'd hitchhike or take a bus to his downtown office on weekdays during the summer, and we'd walk to his apartment several blocks away. I'd call my parents and tell them I was there and might as well stay the night, and they never seemed to object. There, as at the cabin, I was free to smoke his cigarettes and drink his liquor and leaf through his nudie books. I could watch late TV and stay up as long as I wanted, and take lengthy, leisurely showers that seemed to stay hot forever.

Roy had a number of young friends, all from good homes where things were not so good. I occasionally shared weekends at the cabin with some of them. We swam nude in the frigid lake and water-skied, speared carp by lantern at night, explored the expanse of Roy's woods and fields, held target shooting matches with his array of firearms, fished and boated and ate wonderful meals, drove his convertible to the local town and cruised around though none of us had a license, studied his nudie books as if cramming for an exam, smoked and drank and cursed and jerked off, and in general gorged ourselves on taboo pleasures like members of an elite and clandestine cult.

I had introduced a couple of my own friends to Roy, though certainly without the objective of luring them to his brand of affection. I just wanted to share the utopia I had stumbled into. I didn't even know whether Roy was fooling around with them. It wasn't something we discussed. We didn't ask, we didn't tell. Roy kept his encounters one-on-one; and, characteristically, he had finely tuned antennae that enabled him to single out which boys to leave alone.

One night at his apartment Roy Pratt blew his brains out. That was the official story. One of Roy's young friends, a buddy of mine, had run away from home. His parents thought Roy was harboring him at his cabin. They were friends of a police detective whose help they enlisted. The detective arranged for state troopers to raid Roy's property at the lake, but no one was there. The detective and the boy's father then went to Roy's apartment, and when they banged on the door Roy answered in his underwear. The boy was not there either, but another boy was.

As the detective questioned Roy, that young man appeared from the bedroom, naked, his prick at attention. The detective told Roy he was under arrest and directed him to get dressed. Roy went to his bedroom and took a handgun from his dresser. There is no one alive today who knows what happened next in that bedroom. The detective and the missing boy's father are long dead. The boy at the apartment had returned to bed, and would later report that when he saw Roy take the gun out he hid under the covers. He heard two shots and felt the weight of Roy's body fall on him. He squirmed out from under to find the sheets soaked with red and the walls spattered with bloody tissue, but apparently hadn't seen what happened. The runaway boy had been hiding somewhere else entirely and wandered home the next day.

The official story never rested right with me. Roy's gun was a .45. You just can't shoot yourself in the head with a .45 twice. I imagined more plausible scenarios. The detective followed Roy to the bedroom, saw him take out the gun, and, anticipating that Roy might turn it on him, shot in self-defense. Or the detective saw Roy put the gun to his head and did nothing to stop him, and put a second round into him for good measure. Or, once the detective saw that gun, school was out. Just seeing it gave him license to do what he likely ached to do anyway—just blow Roy Pratt away.

There was no one to share my doubts with, because no one cared. To parents and the authorities the important thing was that the world was rid of that perverted cocksucker and he wouldn't be bothering any more kids. But for me the criminal and depraved facets of Roy's lifestyle were eclipsed by the loss of a gentle and generous benefactor I felt I had once loved like a grandfather, and by a measure of guilt as well; for it was I who had introduced him to the boy who'd run away, and subsequently felt at least partially responsible for his ghastly death.

Many years later, with a belly full of vodka, I ran into the father who had accompanied the detective that night. I was always writing stories or starting some spellbinding novel, and I was consumed then with the prospect that the tale of Roy Pratt would make a great book. I asked him to verify some details from that ill-fated evening. It was obvious that he didn't appreciate my bringing the matter up, but he humored me. I outlined my scenarios and asked him point blank if any of them might be closer to the truth of what had happened. He claimed he didn't know. He hadn't gone in the bedroom that night so he couldn't say what had transpired. But when I asked if, hypothetically, it had been he who followed Roy to his room, would he have shot him? "Absolutely," he said. "Twice in the head."

I can't condone what Roy Pratt was or what he did, but he never harmed any of us or forced us to do anything against our will. There was never even a suggestion of penetration, at least not to me. I have to think that the other boys accepted his advances as I did. We were young and crazy and rebellious, looking for a good time anywhere we could find it. Roy Pratt used us for his pleasures, and we used him for ours.

One can hardly pick up a newspaper these days without learning about people in all walks of life being accused of exactly the same behavior; and despite the fact that charges of pedophilia have become almost commonplace, the crimes remain scandalous and inexcusable. In Roy Pratt's day, they were utterly unspeakable.

There was no funeral service. His existence was erased. I don't know how or why my parents learned the terms of Roy's will, but they told me he had bequeathed his Caddie convertible to a brother, his cabin and other possessions to a sister, and $650,000—no trifling sum in those days—to the local chapter of the Boy Scouts. His name was never again mentioned in our house.

As long ago as that was, I am still puzzled by how my parents could have been so blind. Their adolescent son spent overnights with a never-married man in his sixties on a regular basis and went away for entire weekends with him, usually just the two of us. There were many episodes in my youth that serve now to corroborate how acquiescent my parents could be as long as I was out of their hair and not in a jail cell or hospital; but their apparent indifference toward my relationship with Roy Pratt remains inconceivable.

When they learned of his death and the accompanying details, they asked if Roy had ever "done anything to me." I said that he hadn't. End of conversation. They heard what they needed so desperately to hear, accepting it as gospel while undoubtedly suspecting I was lying. They pursued it no further, perhaps in fear that they might have to concern themselves with whether I had suffered any lasting repercussions. They just wanted it all to go away, as if it never happened, to be buried along with Roy Pratt.

It's so much easier now to understand that their successes and failures as parents were largely proportionate to mine as a son. I must have let them down as often and as much as they allowed me to stray and wander. It is just that kind of blindness and apathy in which dysfunctional families are rooted. Their love was always there. I never doubted that. They had set up their easel and equipped themselves with the requisite canvas and brushes, their palette adorned with the finest oils in all the popular and time-proven hues; and like all parents they had a vision, a finished image in mind, and plenty of inspiration.

They just didn't always know how to paint very well.

8

No Pity

In my early teens it was only natural for my buddies and me to rebel against the caste into which we'd been so unjustly born. We had been reared in stately old homes on the oak- and elm-lined streets of one of Rochester's most enviable neighborhoods. We'd been force-fed an education in the district's highest-ranking elementary school and had frolicked on its grassy playgrounds with other equally beleaguered middle-class Caucasians. At home we'd been inundated by a wealth of playthings in paneled basement recreation rooms and spacious yards. We'd been periodically turned over to heartless Little League and Pop Warner coaches, and exposed to the brutalities of Scouting and the YMCA. Some of us had even been tortured with music lessons.

We'd been dressed in cleaned and ironed clothes and crammed with nourishing meals by stay-at-home mothers. Mere begging had rewarded us with just about any material thing we wanted, and in return we'd been asked to perform an occasional chore. And in spite of this atrocious upbringing it was nevertheless hoped that we might exhibit a semblance of gratitude for the multitude of advantages with which we'd been so pitilessly encumbered. It's a miracle we didn't all turn psychopathic.

It was our destiny then to become a gang so dreaded by the community that authorities and citizens cowered under our reign of terror and intimidation. By the time we were fifteen we had orchestrated a coldblooded auto theft ring, stealing our own parents' cars with abandon, and transporting them across neighborhood lines and back without remorse. Many a homeowner lived in fear that he was next to learn that his children's missing swing set had been located in a four-way intersection downtown, to find that his swimming pool had been filled to the brim with lawn furniture donated by thirty of his neighbors, or to discover that the horrendous ripping and crashing he heard behind him as he left for work in the morning was half his gutter system being dragged down the driveway by rope tied to his bumper.

One of our more thoughtful enterprises was that of tying up a house with clothesline conveniently left for that purpose in the homeowner's yard. We'd double the line for extra strength and tie it securely to the front and back door knobs, stretching it so tautly around the exterior of the house that neither door could be opened from the inside. We threw the bird at one guy we'd done this to while he bellowed out his window that we were in big trouble because he knew every one of us. He finally managed to open a door enough to cut the line with a knife, rushed out and jumped in his car, and chased us down the street with his picnic table bouncing down the road behind him. Anyone else would have called the cops or at least our parents, but we figured he'd spare himself the embarrassment, his being the chief of police and all.

I didn't know how it was at home for most of the guys. I did know that a couple of them got whacked around pretty good, not that it slowed them down any. But our mischief was for each of us an escape.

We'd do absolutely anything for a laugh, and we laughed until our jaws ached. They were wondrous, silly times, and we laugh about them still, aware, of course, now that we are property owners ourselves, that we'd kill any little bastards who pulled that crap on us, if we could catch them. No one ever caught us. We knew every back yard, hedge, fence, gate, dead end, and dog in the neighborhood.

On the home front in those days, while my sibs and I were busy being the ungrateful, indolent slobs Mother repeatedly accused us of being, family warfare continued to break out on a regular basis. And yet, when the doors weren't slamming, when we weren't screaming at one another or ducking kitchen implements, when my mother wasn't locking herself in her bedroom or locking us out of the house, we laughed uproariously and carried on like a close-knit family of circus clowns. When all of us were still living at home, rare was the occasion that everyone was in good spirits and no one was in the dog house, but during those times I would not have traded our family for any other.

We never knew when our father might appear at the dinner table wearing some ridiculous hat he'd found in the attic, or bring out a book and eloquently recite a chapter backwards, or when my parents might break into song and dance and act out a scene from a Broadway musical in the middle of the kitchen, or when brother Jim might suddenly embark on his Dance of a Thousand Mirrors. He'd thunder through the house like a deranged buffalo, posing in the mirror of every room that had one, checking his hair, grinning debonairly, clambering to the next room, up and down the stairs, out the door to look in the side-view mirror on the car, around the outside of the house to find his reflection in every window, back inside running full tilt mirror to mirror again, golf club in hand, never uttering a word, sometimes for up to an hour. Jimmy was never what you'd call right.

Our family definitely wasn't out of *Father Knows Best*—more like *Father Doesn't Want To Know Shit*. Since his principal objective was to stay the peace and keep the apple cart upright, the old man generally maintained a complacent manner toward us, asking only that we help make our mother's workload a little easier wherever we could, and for God's sake stay out of scrapes that would jeopardize the family's precious if spurious reputation or interfere with his weekend golf. For our mother's part there was no pleasing her under any circumstances, and we came to accept that there wasn't much point in trying. If I told her I climbed Mt. McKinley backwards on a unicycle while balancing a flowerpot on my head, she'd ask why I hadn't scaled Everest. I once miraculously got a final A in algebra in summer school—possibly the first time in the history of either side of the family that someone had aced a mathematics course—and all she talked about was how inexcusable it was that I'd only gotten a C in American history. A kid can get a complex from crap like that.

Mother's antics and fits of anger, and subsequent battles with the old man, seemed to reach a new plateau in our teenage years. We kids gathered at the top of the stairs and listened to the screaming and cursing. We always knew when the tempers were nearing crescendo by the quality of the old man's swearing. He rarely used dirty words, even on the golf course, so whenever the choice expletives began echoing through the house we knew the main event was about to get underway.

One day after they'd had a particularly fiery altercation the night before, Mother was nowhere to be found. We had one car in those days and it too was gone. Mother and car were away for two weeks, though a phone call to her sister confirmed she was visiting her in Amsterdam, NY, where she sometimes went for extended visits when the pressures of being a mother, a wife, and a human became too unbearable for her. We kids enjoyed these absences, despite having to live on peanut butter sandwiches and scrambled eggs, but the old man took them a little harder. Taking a bus to work was an inconvenience, and bumming a ride to the golf course was embarrassing.

When she returned, she denied having left at all. When the old man asked where she got off disappearing for two weeks, she calmly announced that she had no idea what he was talking about and hadn't gone anywhere. As usual, we were at the top of the stairs waiting for the curtain to go up.

"You snuck into my bedroom while I was asleep, you took the registration to my car out of my wallet, you took my keys and stole the goddam car," bellowed Huey.

"I don't know *what* you're talking about," said Mother. "I never touched your precious car keys."

"Then you must have stuck your *tit* in the ignition," he screamed. The symphony of crashing and yelling that followed was one of their fiercest, but at least there wasn't any bloodshed. In a couple of days the incident blew over, as they always did. Mother began acting as if nothing at all had happened, and the old man, as usual, let the matter drop in exchange for a smidgen of fragile peace in the house.

One day she intentionally got herself arrested for shoplifting at the supermarket after a blowout with the old man the night before. He was news director at a local TV station then. Mother was aware that throughout the day he and his staff reviewed police reports that arrived continuously via Teletype, and it was her objective to mortify him by having the report of her arrest appear in the newsroom for all to see. It did. She hadn't anticipated that the episode would blossom into anything more than that, but it turned out to be even more fulfilling than she could have hoped. Apparently she had been quite deliberate about the theft, brazenly stuffing items into a large purse while looking the store manager straight in the eye as if daring him to do anything about it. He had called the police and had every intention of pressing the issue, despite knowing who she was. The old man's humiliation was subsequently raised to a higher level because now they were going before a judge.

The old man told us later that she performed one of her finest Lucy Ricardo routines for the judge, and he wasn't amused. And when he rejected her portrayal of a mischievous scatterbrain whose playful antics had got out of hand, she suddenly switched strategies to her superior woman above reproach approach and threatened to have the judge disbarred. When that tactic failed, she launched herself into a full-blown hysterical tizzy that pissed the judge off so much he ruled that her behavior justified psychiatric evaluation. Any woman who would go to such extremes to get back at her husband over an argument, who would set out to blemish his exemplary reputation in the community by deliberately getting arrested, and who would even insult and threaten a judge to his face was in need of professional help.

It was probably the first time in her life that she'd been unable to bullshit or flirt or tizzy her way out of a jam. The judge declared that the charges would be dismissed only if she completed a series of sessions with a psychiatrist. He might just as well have sentenced her to a Caribbean cruise. The sessions lasted for a year and cost the old man a fortune. He'd owned some residential property in Auburn that he'd inherited, and he had to sell it to pay the cost of her treatments, which came to an end when the psychiatrist announced that he had been unable to accomplish a thing in terms of therapy, that she had turned every session into a circus by refusing to give him a straight answer to anything, and that he couldn't possibly help her.

As for her punishment, it was ruled that despite the ineffectiveness of the treatments she had satisfied her obligation to the court, even if succeeding in sticking it in everyone's rear in the process. The psychiatrist committed suicide. There was no evidence to suggest that there was a connection between his apparent personal problems and my mother's stint as a patient, but we couldn't rule out the possibility.

The only true vacation my parents took together was a cruise to San Francisco on a luxury liner out of Miami. They were to fly from Rochester in the early seventies, when the dangerous new menace of airline hijackings by terrorists had necessitated the first security checkpoints at airports. Mother had never encountered such security measures, and I'm sure the old man led her to the boarding gate with a great deal of apprehension. And, as if on cue, he told us later, when a security officer began going through her carry-ons, Mother said loudly, "Oh by all means search my things. I never go anywhere without a bomb in my purse."

It was three hours before they were finally allowed to board the plane, which had been quarantined on the tarmac all that time and the other passengers evacuated. FBI agents had grilled her and the old man while their identifications were verified. Security personnel had turned the jet's cargo hold upside down to locate and examine their luggage. Agents had tried in vain to impress upon her the havoc her remark had created throughout the airport. Since many of the other passengers on that flight were booked on the same cruise ship, the liner had also been delayed for hours with a thousand on board. And throughout it all she had no idea what the fuss was about, and at no time then or afterwards did she express a morsel of apology. To her, the whole adventure was a great big hoot. It was classic Ida Jean.

***

As my older siblings were leaving their teen years behind and I was nearing eighteen, it was hoped that our mother might have learned to take things in stride and chill out a bit. After all, there wasn't much we kids could do that would surprise her any more. But while she now had her hands full with Maris, who was embarking on her own teen years and quickly developing into an attractive, long-legged, well-endowed hellfire just like her mom, we older kids had pretty much exhausted our tolerance for her relentless intimidation, and frequently found ourselves standing firm against her assaults and giving them right back at her.

On occasion, these confrontations flirted with being of a more physical nature, when Mother elected to play her hole card if a verbal melee wasn't going her way. Many times she took a swipe at one of us with the hope, we came to realize, that we'd make the mistake of swiping back. She bruised easily, and the tendency served her well.

She enticed every one of us to cross that defining line that would transform a verbal clash into a corporeal one—taunting us so unmercifully that it was all we could do to keep from letting her have it once and for all—because once we raised a hand, victory would instantly and unmistakably be hers. We were not inherently violent, with the exception perhaps of my brother, but she drove us nearly crazy, especially when she took to humming. She'd be mad about something, and when we'd try to find out why she'd ignore us and hum. We'd raise our voices and she'd just hum louder. We'd even offer politely to break her neck for her, and she'd just keep humming. My God it was maddening. None of us ever hit her, but we came very close to it. There were times when I seriously considered killing her, and I often lay awake at night plotting how to do it. In my imagined schemes I couldn't just bump her off, like shooting her from a distance. We had to be face to face so that she'd know she was meeting her end at my hands. We would both be laughing hideously, she because I'd spend the rest of my life in prison, and I because it would be worth every last day of it.

I still have the saber Mother tried to behead my brother with. She claimed it had belonged to an ancestor in the War Between the States. It's a legitimate Civil War sword, produced by Ames Manufacturing Co., Chicopee, Mass., in 1864, but whether it had hung from the belt of a forefather of ours remains questionable. She also claimed we'd had kin on the Mayflower, in the Battle of Lexington, at the Alamo, Wounded Knee, and Valley Forge, and that we were descendants of a famous frontiersman who swam the length of the Mississippi and invented corn on the cob and clothes poles, so who the hell knows.

I don't know what started the fight, but when I ran upstairs to see what all the ruckus was about in Jim's bedroom, I saw her going at him wild-eyed with that sword, both hands on the handle, round-housing it left and right like a crazed buccaneer, screeching hysterically, while Jim deftly back-peddled and ducked and side-stepped her slashes and swoops like a veteran swashbuckler, and enraged her further by growling "Har Matey" with every swipe. When he saw his chance, he lunged and tore the saber from her hands, raised it over his head like an executioner, and brought it down with a crashing blow that missed her by inches and pulverized the footboard of his bed into so much kindling, thereby bringing the argument to an abrupt conclusion. When the old man got home and wanted to know what the goddam hell happened to the furniture, she and Jimmy embarked on another big screaming match over who tried to julienne whom first.

One night when Jim was twenty, Mother tried to brain him with his own sand wedge during a confrontation and in the tussle caught her bare toe on a castor of a bed. It bled so much you'd have thought she'd sliced it clean off. She dragged that leaking toe from one end of the house to the other before taking to her bedroom and locking the door. Jimmy split. The old man returned from a speaking engagement and it looked as though there'd been a massacre. Blood was everywhere. When Mother finally allowed him to enter her room, she looked as if she'd been worked over with a two-by-four. She told him Jimmy had beaten her up. When Jim came in later, the old man, fortified by several cocktails, attacked him, and Jim had no idea why.

My brother maintained a primitive psychology toward dealings of an aggressive nature, be it with friend, foe, or family: If you hit me, I'll hit you back. In the fight that ensued my father did not fare well. Jim picked him up and threw him bodily through a glass-topped coffee table and was commencing to punch him in the face when I jumped in. With a surge of strength that came from I know not where, I threw my older brother across the room, slamming him against a wall. He gave me a startled but murderous look and bolted out the door. My father lay half unconscious amidst the shattered glass and splintered wood, bleeding heavily from a gash in his forehead. His glasses lay smashed on the floor. I cradled his head in my lap and dabbed at his wound with my shirttails, not sure what to do, until he finally regained his senses. He was badly hurt. He later took some sutures in his noggin and learned that several ribs were broken. Jim never slept in that house again.

One night three years later I found myself in a similar predicament when my mother got mad and came at me swinging a sponge mop, slashing the metal edge toward my head hard enough to embed it in my ear like a cookie cutter. Instinctively I blocked the mop-head and shoved her only hard enough to make her step back, whereupon she fell down on her own accord, wailed like a banshee, and retired to her bedroom with the door locked. When my father was later allowed in her sanctum, he found her covered with abrasions and the yellowing of skin where spectacular bruises were beginning to blossom, the result, she told him, of my having beat the tar out of her. He made me go in and look at her, to see what I'd done. She was a mess. She looked straight at me, through me. Her lip was cut open. Her front was bloodied. One eye had swelled shut. Red marks were everywhere. Her neck looked as though she'd been strangled. I was banished from the house.

I never found the right time later in life to tell him what had happened that night. I should have, but he suffered enough because of her. The incident was just another scrap of regrettable history, one of so many incidents equally pathetic that had washed over the falls. At the time of the encounter he had been powerless to challenge her accusations, but I suspect he'd known all along, as I certainly had, that every mark on her had been self-inflicted—as they had been in the incident involving my brother, and as they had been on another occasion when she appeared at the home of our minister equally bruised, battered and bloodied, claiming that the old man had beaten her and thrown her down the cellar stairs when in fact he had not laid a hand on her.

He was not always as innocent, however. He never actually hit her that I know of, but there were incidents when he grabbed her or pushed her forcefully into her room, resulting on one occasion in her suffering a broken collarbone. It is nearly impossible to explain such manhandling of a woman in a way that anyone could accept or condone, but it is just as difficult to relate the lengths to which my mother would go to instigate it. Unfeeling as it sounds, I don't recall an occurrence in which my mother was mistreated that she didn't have it coming; and if the old man had ever actually taken to really whacking her, I don't think any of their friends would have blamed him a bit.

When we were young there were many times when my mother might herself have been arrested for physical abuse. There were times later on when her mental instability might have gotten her institutionalized. There were definitely occasions when she should have been pitied, but we had no pity left. How sadly ironic it seems now. At the core of her troubles was her adamant denial that she had a problem—not unlike that of an alcoholic. Submitting to a regimen of earnest psychotherapy meant admitting that she was seriously unbalanced, which she would never do. We have little doubt now that she was in fact bi-polar, or what was referred to then as manic-depressive. She may never have been officially diagnosed as such, however, and in any event she wasn't taking whatever medications were available then specifically to treat the malady. Instead she switched between tranquilizers and uppers as her divergent moods dictated, thereby exacerbating the consequences of mixed bipolar symptoms, when experiencing the simultaneous effect of both mania and depression that is characteristic of the disorder.

Throw into the mix her own multi-faceted and erratic personality, and what you have is a package of cross-wired circuitry that a psychiatrist could spend a lifetime trying to unravel. We were therefore constantly at a loss to determine how much of her behavior at any given time was due to her mental instability and how much to the fact that she thoroughly enjoyed play acting. Keeping those around her on pins and needles was a hobby to her, and few things seemed to fulfill her more than a thunder and lightning tantrum. She actually seemed to prefer being furious, which would explain why she invented scenarios that provided her reasons to detonate. What a waste of such an incredible lady. She was petrified of being mentally disturbed, yet remained so for life because of her inability to accept that she was.

My sister Maris related a story to me about an incident many years ago at the dinner table. The old man mentioned that while tidying up the cellar he had removed a large bucket of fill stones and thrown it out. Mother had apparently intended to use them in the garden at some point, but my father had said that the bucket had been there for years and he was tired of walking around it.

Mother went into a full-blown rage, yelling hysterically about how he had no right to touch her stuff, about her never being allowed to keep one damn thing for herself, about his throwing out those stones deliberately to infuriate her, screaming uncontrollably and pounding her fists on the table until the old man fled the room. When he'd gone, Maris told me, Mother turned to her with a smile and calmly said, "I have no idea what stones he's talking about. I didn't even know they were down there."

9

Camelback

What was to become a spotty and largely unsuccessful career as a singer-songwriter took root in Arizona when I was nineteen, after I'd flunked out of a Rochester community college that I'd chosen because it accepted idiots. Apparently idiots in particular were expected to attend classes now and then. I went west to seek my fortune in a '51 Chevy woody with a friend who had earned a cross-country scholarship to Arizona State, picking up old Route 66 in St. Louis. I left home with fifty dollars in my pocket. It was gone by the time we got there.

I remembered my mother once telling me that if I ever found myself truly hungry I should buy a bag of popcorn. It only cost a dime in those days and it was nourishing and filling. My friend's brother knew a local who let us stay at his apartment for a couple of days, but when my buddy moved into his college dorm I was on my own, sleeping on a chaise lounge by the pool at the apartment complex and, sure enough, living on popcorn. I ran into a guy who told me I could probably get work at the Camelback Inn, which he said was always hiring dining room and kitchen staff. The hotel—now a renowned Marriott resort and spa but at that time privately owned—was a huge, sprawling complex at the base of Mummy Mountain with a broadside view of Camelback Mountain, Phoenix's most distinctive natural landmark. The personnel manager said I could start as a busboy. The job included a room, maid service once a week, laundry service for my work clothes, three meals a day, use of the hotel pool, tennis courts and other facilities at times designated for employees, and $100 a month plus tips. I figured I could live with that. The one ironclad rule was that I was not to mingle with the guests during off-duty hours. But I could mingle all I wanted with the other employees, a good many of whom were young waitresses, and I figured I could live with that too.

It turned out to be a hell of a gig. I worked and partied with others my age whose futures were equally open for anything, and got to wait on celebrities and people of wealth who were drawn to the resort by the enchantment of its southwestern decor and relative seclusion. J.C. Penney stayed there for a couple of months on the American plan, leaving at the end of his stay a seemingly enormous blanket tip for the wait staff of several hundred dollars, which, when calculated with the cost of all the meals he'd had, came to about three percent.

I waited on Ann-Margret, who was a year or two older than I, and by all accounts one of Mother Nature's most exquisite creations. My job as bus boy was to make sure she had plenty of butter pats, and she got enough to butter a battleship.

I soon became a waiter, raising my level of respectability enough to be accepted by the other waiters and waitresses who had previously found it demeaning to socialize with a lowly busboy. We lived in a separated sector of the hotel complex, where we were pretty much free to do as we pleased as long as we confined our activities to our own community.

Rare was the night that an after-work party wasn't going on in someone's quarters, but no matter how much booze was available at any given affair it wasn't nearly enough for me. I remember a night that someone had brought a quart of tequila, passing it around for everyone to take a slug. I'd already chugged a half dozen beers, but when the bottle came to me I turned it up and just kept drinking, gulp after gulp, until someone snatched the bottle away and passed it along. The selfishness of the act meant nothing to me. The rudeness sailed over my head. I saw an opportunity to consume straight alcohol, I wasn't sure if the opportunity would present itself again, and I made damn sure I got my fill. It made perfect sense to me, a simple matter of mathematics. For whatever reason, it was obvious to me that the other people simply didn't drink as heartily as I did, so therefore a greater share of the refreshments was earmarked for me.

That was the night I took old Snowball for a spin. Snowball was the hotel mascot, a white burro that was showcased in a small corral near the hotel entrance, and that purportedly had been the white donkey Jeffrey Hunter rode in his role as Jesus in *King of Kings*. Snowball was retired from the movie biz and probably well past his riding days, but he didn't seem to mind getting out for a road trip into the desert. When we sauntered back from our stroll I saw hotel staff frantically running around looking for their missing mascot, so I left him tied to a Joshua tree and moseyed home.

One day a posse of state police raided the employee complex and hauled away several waiters and waitresses on charges of heroin possession, which might explain why they hadn't seemed as enamored of alcohol as I was. That a number of the fellow employees I had been partying with were junkies was news to me. Thankfully, no one had approached me with the stuff. I knew next to nothing about drugs then, even those of the recreational variety. And while I would always maintain a reluctance to poke a needle in my skin, my insatiable thirst for any kind of buzz and an even greater appetite for feeling like I belonged could easily have swayed me. In that regard I could be grateful for a change for having been left out of the festivities. Besides, I'd make up for it later on with just about every other drug known to man.

***

I had been musically inclined since studying classical piano as a child with an eighty-year-old spinster who had gnarled, arthritic fingers and lived over a garage with her grand piano and a cat. She hoped I'd get through one of Beethoven's concertos without screwing it up at least once before she croaked, and I did. I played it as well as Beethoven ever did, I think, and not nearly as loud. My mother was forever dragging me to the piano to play for company, and if I made a mistake she'd claim I did it deliberately to embarrass her. I had a great ear and feel for the music, but by my teens the interest had faded, along with prospects of my pursuing any avenues as a classical pianist. I later studied with a more contemporary teacher who had me playing such things as Zez Confrey's *Kitten on the Keys*, boogie, and ragtime; but again my enthusiasm made way for new interests and I gave up the piano for good.

In high school I'd been part of a folk group that performed at various functions. By the time I got to Phoenix I was leaning toward country music and had become a devout Dylan freak. He sang with a voice that came from you and me, as Don McLean later put it in *American Pie*, and while his style may not have been totally original, it was certainly unique to me and to mainstream America. More significantly, he sang stories, and did so with a poignancy that overshadowed his outlandish sound and gripped me firmly by the heart.

I bought my first guitar, a forty-dollar cheapie whose nylon strings were so far off the fret board you had to stand on the suckers with both feet to hold them down, along with my first Dylan songbook. The first song I learned was the *Ballad of Hollis Brown*, Dylan's mournful tale of poverty eleven verses long, accompanied by a single guitar chord throughout, an open E minor requiring two fingers, the easiest chord of all. I was immediately wailing away at my first song and beating that chord to death. Soon I graduated to some common three- and four-chord combinations with which I could play any number of tunes, and before long I was writing my own songs.

As I began playing in front of other people, bolstered always by plenty of alcohol, my own material constituted the bulk of my repertoire and always would. Unless you are strikingly original and exceptionally talented, however, most people want to hear songs they're familiar with. I maintained the belief that when you sing songs no one has ever heard before there isn't a person on Earth who can say you aren't doing them right—a distinct advantage when you get so hammered you forget half the verses.

It had long been apparent to me that I drank more than most people my age, but as I entertained early thoughts now of a career in songwriting and singing, I was at the same time, if unconsciously, laying the foundation for the much more demanding vocation of full-time lush. I didn't recognize it as such, of course, but I had already graduated from the school of social drinking and was studiously pursuing my masters.

I was too young to drink legally in Arizona and couldn't frequent the bars. My roommate was of legal age and bought me a couple of six-packs of Coors before going out at night. Often I'd leave a party where the booze was scarce, and go to my room where my six-packs awaited. I stocked up on paperback books, particularly the Ian Fleming spy novels. I waited until the dining room lights shut down at closing to sneak into the hotel and steal crackers or anything else I could find. I'd stay up half the night reading, munching, slurping down Coors, strumming the guitar. The two six-packs quickly became three and then four, and it became an almost nightly ritual. Often I'd disregard a party altogether, stay in my room, and drink a case of beer by myself.

I climbed Camelback Mountain drunk one afternoon with a bunch of other waiters and nearly dropped to my death from one of its peaks. With an elevation of just over 2,400 feet, Camelback is a renowned hiking and bouldering attraction now, with designated trails and steps and railings and several mapped-out routes of varying difficulty, depending on one's level of expertise. Back then there weren't any such amenities. You climbed it at your own risk, finding a way to the top any way you could, and the only trail guides were reptilian. The first thing to do to prepare for mountain climbing in hundred-degree desert heat is chug two six-packs and take a pint of hard stuff for the journey up. You also want to wear shorts and tennis sneaks with no socks to give the rattlers and lizards something to gnaw on.

We decided to split up and take different routes to see who could reach the top fastest. I arrived first, and when I walked across the summit's plateau I saw that the cliff on the other side was nearly vertical, a sheer deadly drop but for a foot-wide ledge that protruded from the mountainside just five or six feet below the precipice. How clever I thought I'd be to lower myself to that ledge and then come crawling over the top when the others arrived to make it look as though I'd scaled the steep side.

That ledge wasn't nearly as level as it appeared from above—more like forty-five degrees—and it wasn't as much a ledge at all as an outcropping of loosely packed shale and sandstone that began crumbling and breaking away as soon as I lowered myself down to it. I was literally running in place like Wile E. Coyote on the face of that cliff, frantically grabbing at rocks to hold onto but pulling out handfuls of loose stone instead. There was no doubt in my mind that I was about to die. I clawed at that cliff and tore skin from my fingers and elbows and forearms and knees, screaming loud enough to wake up Cochise and the missus, until finally some other hikers arrived and formed a human ladder to drag me to safety. I sat on the ground with my knees around my ears and shook uncontrollably for half an hour. Only a brain deranged by alcohol could have devised a stunt so incredibly idiotic. Astounded and thankful to be alive, I vowed to God then and there never to succumb to that temptation again; and I can say with all honesty that I haven't climbed another mountain since.

I stayed at the Camelback Inn throughout the winter months until it closed for the hot summer season, then hitchhiked to southern California with another waiter named Brad who said he could put me up with a friend of a friend of a friend who had a place near Newport Beach. I had saved a couple hundred bucks, which to me was a small fortune.

I hung around for a few weeks and became friendly with a number of natives my age who struck me as being as carefree and reckless as I was but at the same time different somehow. At first I thought they were merely more laid back and went about their business at an easier pace, but there was more to it than that. After a while I pinpointed what it was. They simply didn't give a fuck. They answered to no one, did whatever the hell they wanted, didn't care whom they screwed over in the process, and would mug their own grandmothers for a pack of cigarettes. I considered myself admirably irreverent, irresponsible, disobedient and reckless; but compared to them I was a Boy Scout.

One day when I expressed an interest in learning to surf, Brad took me to a spot in Newport Beach at the end of the Balboa Peninsula known as The Wedge. Even experienced surfers rate it at a level of challenge somewhere between expert and psychotic, and only the most insane among them would attempt to surf it with a board. For upstate New Yorkers who have never surfed in their lives, it is most definitely not the place to learn. It is called the Wedge because of the dynamic and treacherous effect caused by a long stone jetty jutting into the sea. A humongous wave thunders off this wall, merging in a sideways motion with another incoming wave, where the convergence erupts into a two-story triangular crest of unimaginable energy that peaks and crashes in dangerously shallow waters. Depending on your timing, you have the choice of being sucked to Hawaii with its undertow or pile-driven into the ocean floor like a human tent pole.

And, because timing for rookies is dependant solely on sheer dumb luck, the beach was jam-packed with locals who, after mugging their grandmothers, enjoyed relaxing in the sun and watching victims wash ashore dismantled.

Brad instructed me in the proper procedure for bodysurfing this deathtrap. All I had to do was wade out a ways, and when a wave came crashing over me to dive for the bottom at the base of the wave at just the right instant so that the wave would roll over me instead of picking me up, and to keep doing that until I was out far enough to catch a really bitchin' ride. Then I had to time it just right so that I dived toward land in such a way that the crest of the really fine wave would push me along like a human surf board and carry me exhilaratingly back to shore. This sounded simple enough, especially after sharing a six-pack of Olympia and chugging a pint of Southern Comfort.

I tried the stunt exactly once, which apparently was par. I paddled out just far enough to meet a reasonably mammoth tsunami that picked me up like a frond of seaweed, tumbled me head over heels for an hour or so underwater, sucked me up into its jaws about twenty feet above sea level, launched me landward as if lashed to the front of a locomotive, and body-slammed me on the beach half drowned and totally naked. The really boss baggies Brad had lent me were now on a world cruise.

A week later my dear companion invited me to Bullhead City, AZ. It is a major vacation, tourism, and water sports hub now and sister city to the gambling community of Laughlin, NV, across the Colorado River at the northern tip of Arizona and southern tip of Nevada. But back then there wasn't much to it. It had been founded just twenty-five years before as headquarters for construction of Davis Dam, and the town proper didn't seem to have been modernized all that much since.

We were to be the guests of the family of a girlfriend of a friend of a friend who had a getaway retreat there, but the term "guest" had been used somewhat loosely in my case. Brad would be riding with the family on their private plane. I would be hitchhiking. I couldn't drag all my gear along, so a buddy of my buddy's buddy said I could stow most of it in the trunk of his car while I was gone. With some changes of clothes and incidentals in an overnight bag I headed out to thumb my way to Bullhead City. It was June. It was desert. The Mohave frequently boasts days with temperatures in excess of a hundred and ten degrees, and this was one of them. My sneakers were melting.

Upon arriving I was informed that no accommodations had been arranged for me at all. I could shower at the girlfriend's house, but I was to find sleeping quarters wherever I could, which turned out to be on the beach along the river.

I met a young lady at a party. She gave me the time of day. She invited me to her place later and told me to bring plenty of beer. One of Brad's buddies dropped me off. I naturally assumed that the invitation included overnight lodgings and conjugal privileges, but I was wrong. Her parents had turned their garage into an apartment for her so that she could come and go as she pleased. We sat around and guzzled beer, though I was already whacked when I got there, and when I made a move on her she backed off. I made another move and she told me to get the hell out. I guess she only wanted me for my beer. I hate broads like that.

Far from the noise of passing cars, the desert is eerily quiet in the daytime. Not so in the dead of night. I didn't really know how far from town I was, but I started on down the road under barely enough moonlight to make out the pavement. Off to my left I saw a faint glow on the horizon that I assumed must be the town, so my drunken brain reasoned that it would be faster to abandon the road and cut across the desert.

The reason one doesn't see or hear a lot of animals in the desert during the day is that most of them are nocturnal, especially the ones you could do without meeting face to face. That's when they do their hunting. Mountain lions and coyotes and such generally keep to the hills, but not exclusively. Gila monsters, diamondbacks, and sidewinders can be found anywhere thereabouts, as can scorpions of the lethal variety, black widow spiders, kangaroo rats and assorted desert rodents, skunks, foxes, and sundry other critters that tend to keep to themselves unless disturbed from their nightly activities by barelegged stupid people.

About a quarter mile into my trek over rocks and shrubs it started to sound like the San Diego Zoo at feeding time. I couldn't imagine what all was making the scampering, hopping, thumping, chattering, galloping and swishing noises around me, but the further I walked the more intense they became. I decided to sing. I picked up my pace considerably and sang all the Dylan tunes I knew, every song I'd written, the complete repertoire of the Beatles, the top fifty songs on the Billboard charts since 1958, and was working my way through Christmas carols and nursery rhymes when I realized that the glow on the horizon wasn't getting any closer and may have been Vegas for all I knew. I stopped and listened. Someone seemed to have cranked up the volume on the desert symphony. Then I heard, directly behind me, the unmistakable sound of panting. I hadn't realized that hair really could stand on end. Maybe I was imagining it. Nope, it was panting all right, and it wasn't coming from the ground, but directly behind my head. A six-foot prairie dog, maybe. Or maybe sounds carry across the desert like they do on water, I thought.

I slowly turned around, utterly terrified, and there atop a Saguaro cactus not two feet away at eye level stood the most gigantic owl I'd ever seen unstuffed, flapping a four-foot wingspan and glaring at me with eyes the size of eight-balls.

A two-foot bat couldn't have scared me any worse. I didn't stop running until my feet hit pavement again, and I miraculously found my way back to the girl's garage and pounded on her door. She reluctantly let me sleep on the floor. In the morning I walked back to town, sticking to the road. It took four hours.

Badly in need of a dip in the frigid Colorado, I parked my small bag by a tree. When I returned the bag was gone, and with it my glasses, wallet, and all the clothes I had with me but those I'd been wearing, which the thief had been courteous enough to leave behind. There was about forty bucks left in the pants, but the rest of what money I had was gone.

I'd had about enough of Bullhead City, AZ, and my so-called buddy and his buddies' buddies. I flirted with the idea of thumbing to Vegas and getting a restaurant gig of some kind, but I was nearly penniless and couldn't even clothe myself properly enough to apply for a job. Truth be told, I was feeling a little homesick, so I called my friend at Arizona State. He was about to head back east and he was nice enough to come fetch me. We even drove back to L.A. to find the buddy's buddy who had the remainder of my belongings in his trunk, but he was nowhere to be found.

We headed back to Rochacha in the same Chevy wagon that had turned 100,000 miles on the odometer when we'd crossed the Pennsylvania state line on our way westward the previous fall. It had since logged several trips to Mexico and California and was on its last legs. It sputtered its last breath somewhere in Ohio, and we made the rest of the trip on a Greyhound bus. I arrived home with empty pockets, the clothes I had on my back, and a sincere hope that Robert

Frost was right when he said that "home is the place where, when you have to go there, they have to take you in."

10

Interlude

In that interlude of nonchalance conceded to young men in search of themselves, my buddies and I exploited thoroughly what for many of us would be the last of our carefree days. We burned the rubber off our sneaks on the outdoor asphalt basketball courts, and off the tires of the first motorcycles and cars we owned on the neighborhood streets we had once terrorized on foot. We still lived at home, stayed out all hours, came and went as we pleased, and drank with both hands. We kissed the girls and made them cry.

We were inheriting an America in the throes of a social upheaval whose seeds may have sprouted the day JFK took a bullet, when we realized that not all was right in the cozy, comfortable country we had been brought up to believe was infallible. As children we had argued over the superiority of Jim Brown or Sam Huff, Chamberlain or Russell, the Yankees or the Dodgers. Now we took other stands, influenced by the myriad stimuli of the times, the God-awful Vietnam War paramount among them.

U.S. involvement in Vietnam's civil conflict had been intensifying throughout our high school years. We had been vaguely aware of some sort of trouble in a southeast Asian country few of us had ever heard of; but a handful of American military advisors dispatched in 1959 to aid South Vietnam had grown to some 23,000 by the end of '64, and U.S. air strikes were underway to stem North Vietnam's Communist aggression. When ground fighting began in the summer of '65, military draft calls increased dramatically, and the timing for us could not have been more significant.

Some of my friends enlisted in the military, with either a sense of patriotism or a hope that they might better secure non-combat assignments. Others played the waiting game with the draft, and lost. Still more dodged the bullet, literally, by joining the Reserves or National Guard.

At the same time many of us were awakening to the dawning of the Age of Aquarius, as the Fifth Dimension put it in song, when the moon is in the seventh house, and Jupiter aligns with Mars, then peace shall guide the planets, and love will steer the stars. However the planets may have been choreographed, all I knew was that this dawning of Aquarius business included drugs, and that the drugs were a perfect complement to the liquid narcotic I already revered. They welcomed me with open arms, and with a galaxy of promises.

Like a pied piper, Sgt. Pepper led me on a search for Lucy in the sky to a bridge by a fountain, where rocking horse people ate marshmallow pies, where Clapton and Cream wandered in a daze through a white room with black curtains at the station, where Dylan saddled up with a motorcycle black Madonna two-wheeled gypsy queen, saw darkness at the break of noon, and shadows even the silver spoon. I had no idea what they were talking about, but I could dig it, man.

I took any sort of job that came along, treating each as an

annoyance necessary only for putting drinking and drugging money in my pocket. I lost my job in the stock department of the telephone company because I was caught too many times sneaking out for lunch when we were forbidden to leave the building, and coming back sloshed. I lost my job as a mail carrier because I was spotted too often taking lunch breaks in saloons. I lost a variety of other jobs because I didn't feel like showing up, or came in late more often than not. If a party coincided with a work shift, I'd quit the job if need be. As much as I disliked punching time clocks, I hated passing up a party even more. I lived in fear of missing a good time, of being left out. The responsibility of being gainfully employed meant nothing to me.

Many of my buddies began forging their futures. Some went to work for their fathers, joining family businesses. Some furthered their education. Others entered the trades as their dads and brothers had before them, becoming plumbers or steamfitters, carpenters or electricians. But we all had one thing in common; we were ripe for the military draft.

I'm not proud of my service to country. I served. I did my measly part. I didn't run away to Canada. I was of age, healthy, out of school and as suitable for the military draft as a young man could be in 1965, as the conflict in Vietnam was kicking into high gear. As the draft board loomed closer, my father suggested that a practical alternative to being called up might be the Army Reserves. It was one of the few times I took his advice about anything. I was a teenager. What did he know?

When I got to the recruitment center I discovered that hundreds of guys had signed up ahead of me and were on a waiting list. Here I was doing something prudent for a change and all these other assholes had beat me to it. If the recruitment official in charge of that enormous list of weekend warrior wannabees hadn't been our next-door neighbor, I don't know what I would have done. In less than a week my name mysteriously appeared at the top of that roster, along with that of my good buddy Alan.

I would serve my military term and be released from it honorably—their choice of words, not mine—six years of weekly four-hour meetings, four months of active duty in California and Washington, and five two-week summer camps at various Army posts. With the exception of my eight weeks of basic training I was fried to the gills for all of it.

Preparations for my 7 p.m. Reserve meetings entailed stopping at my hangout on Winton Road and downing four bourbon manhattans in half an hour, and smoking a bowl of wacky weed on the way to the armory. About the time I pulled into the armory parking lot the pot and bourbon came together like an Indian summer sunrise, and I walked in the door wearing the best pressed uniform and most glittering shoes, shiniest brass and glassiest eyes, and a primo buzz guaranteed to get me through the dreadful duty ahead. Behind the seat of my car was a warm six-pack for backup, in case my head cleared unexpectedly during the ordeal.

I was a clerk typist in the orderly room of headquarters company, rubbing elbows with the officers and NCOs that most of my comrades tried their best to avoid. But there were advantages to working in the hub of the unit. I was cozy with the first sergeant and company commander and always knew what was going on. When my hair got too long to pass the scrutiny of the more fastidious higher officers, the captain covered for me. I was anything but the most enthusiastic soldier in the ranks, but I maintained the sharpest uniform and no one else could man the typewriter as I could. Military forms and correspondence that clerks customarily milked for whole meetings I dashed off in minutes.

Army draftees and enlistees filled the active duty military ranks in those days. (The Selective Service System established by President Roosevelt in 1940 ended in 1973, when the U.S. converted to an all-volunteer military.) A few select Reserve units did in fact serve in Vietnam, but as a paper-shuffling headquarters company, my outfit's likelihood of seeing battle was minuscule. We were designated combat-ready nonetheless, though half the guys hadn't seen their feet in years, and none of us had been subjected to any semblance of field training since basic.

I started my professional writing career at a weekly suburban newspaper and in time was allowed to write my own column. The publisher felt that I'd approach matters of interest in the community from a hip young man's perspective, which for the most part I did admirably and even won a national award. But I unwisely used the column to express my displeasure with the Army Reserve system a couple of times. Thousands of young men were being dismembered in Vietnam while we played soldier by going to silly meetings and processing paperwork.

In one column I ranted about the deplorable conditions at our summer camp one year at Fort Dix, NJ, where, for two weeks of alternately playing soldier and partying, we'd been subjected to the inexcusable unpleasantness of having cockroaches in the showers and mess hall. Immediately after publication of that column my editor received and in the next issue ran a response from a Vietnam veteran recently returned from the war. He tore me to shreds. He wrote of sharing flooded fetid foxholes with insects the size of mice, suffering constant exhaustion from being too terrified to sleep, enduring interminable monsoons, seeing friends and comrades get blown to pieces in front of him, forgetting when he'd last had a hot shower or an enjoyable meal, fearing for his very life every waking minute, doubting that he'd ever see home and his loved ones again. I didn't write about the Reserves after that.

And as I saw my closest boyhood friend Jackie Maxwell return from Vietnam with a look in his eyes that revealed he'd seen a hell I would never know or could even imagine, those weekly Reserve meetings seemed all the more ludicrous and useless. When Phil, another neighborhood kid who'd been a friend since kindergarten, came home in a bag, his remains escorted by Robert, another dear friend whose experiences in the military nearly drove him to a breakdown, I cursed and damned the military establishment all the more. But never did it occur to me to be grateful for the fact that the Reserve program I so abhorred had saved my self-centered butt.

Friends died in that war. Others returned disabled for life. Some had earned combat medals. Some still suffer the traumatic emotional effects to this day. A few years ago I watched my boyhood friend Hammy die slowly and horrifically from non-Hodgkins lymphoma as a result of his exposure to agent orange as a Marine in Vietnam. I had marched on Washington, sung protest songs, served my country in a state of drunken oblivion, and bitched about what an impact my half-assed patriotic duty was having on my hippie lifestyle. I should have been awarded a medal for hypocrisy above and beyond the call. Indeed, even as I write this, Reservists are serving, and dying, in Iraq.

11

Bailing

In my early twenties there were indications that I was dangerously close to settling down to job and home and making something of myself. They were short-lived. Settling down meant responsibility. Responsibility meant establishing sensible priorities. I never quite got the hang of it. Hedonism was my priority. Everything else was secondary.

My career as a journalist fell into my lap despite my having no college degree or formal training. My credentials amounted to nothing more than those of possessing a tolerable ability to piece words together, and being the son of a locally well-known newsman who had mentored the publisher of my paper when the latter had embarked on his own career in the business.

While still maintaining my preferred vocations as hippie freak and aspiring troubadour, I settled into my so-called professional niche as an up-and-coming reporter and newswriter, and for a couple of years I actually took the opportunity enthusiastically, though not always soberly. I became adept as a photographer, knew my way around a dark room, and became skilled at layout in the composing room. I was learning it all and excelling. Soon I was assigned editorship of two of the company's several newspapers and had started my weekly column.

My father could not have been prouder. My mother found a clipping of the first feature article on which my father had been given a byline as a cub reporter, and I had it displayed with my first byline story in a handsome frame, and gave it to him for Christmas. He was overwhelmed. He told me that my first story was better than his, but it wasn't.

I married my awesome high school sweetheart, a remarkable girl who was an honors student and college grad and a hell of a lot of fun. She would pay dearly for loving me. I'd been crazy about her to the extent of being excessively possessive, but in truth I believe I loved her only as much as I was capable of loving any woman then, with an affection driven more by my inexorable need to be pleased and revered than any genuine devotion in return, as if my allowing her to accompany me was reciprocation enough. I knew how to please a woman in the bedroom. I knew how to show her a good time. I hadn't a clue about how to respect her or recognize her needs.

Abby gave birth to a baby girl whom any man would call a gift from Heaven, but who, like her mother, quickly became an impediment, another ingredient of the ho-hum home life that I had begun to find so suffocating. I loved that little girl, but as a parent I was only going through the motions, as I had been going through the motions of marriage. I was no more prepared or willing to be a family man than I was to cross the Atlantic on a raft, and in the roles of husband and father I felt hopelessly at sea and unfulfilled. There had to be more to life.

We had moved into a new townhouse in a neighborhood bordering the suburban town of Brighton. By all appearances we were a typical young family, full of promise and eagerness, and we had essentially started out that way. Abby might even have tolerated the heavy drinking and late arrivals home from work indefinitely. She'd known all along how much I liked my cocktails and the company of my drinking and drugging buddies.

But Abby herself was shifting priorities and I was too immature and narcissistic to understand why. Everything changes when a baby comes, and I didn't like the changes. Now we couldn't crank up the stereo. Now we couldn't make love every night, and certainly not on the sofa. Now we couldn't have parties. Now Abby drank little and wouldn't touch pot. Now I was expected to be home at night. Now we couldn't even turn up the TV for fear of waking the baby. Now I couldn't bang on my guitar all hours of the night. Suddenly it seemed I'd been relegated to the back seat in my own home, and I didn't care for the view.

I wasn't making much money to begin with, and I routinely cashed my meager paycheck at my usual hangout, where most of it went to cover the bar tab I'd already run that week. A good part of what remained went over the bar that very night, and I'd make it home with barely enough left for groceries. I frequently spent it all and wrote checks that I knew would bounce. I didn't care. I had always followed a policy of taking what I needed to satisfy my hungers and worrying about the consequences later. If the funds for an overdue bill were what I needed for a bag of pot, there was never a choice in the matter. Priorities.

One day I received in the mail my very first credit card, which I immediately maxed out on a brand new twelve-string Guild acoustic. When I proudly brought that shiny new guitar in the house and told Abby how I'd come by it, she was anything but thrilled. We had no spare money whatsoever, principally because I insisted on managing our finances. Our furniture was hand-me-down, worn and mismatched. I had one sport coat that I wore every day and two pairs of rumpled slacks. Abby hadn't had any new clothes since college. We were driving a battered old VW that was on its last legs. We were behind in our rent and utilities, and Abby didn't even know about my drug debts and the hefty tabs at several saloons. Yet I couldn't understand why she wasn't ecstatic over that beautiful new guitar.

It was just that kind of attitude that was making my marriage so bothersome and unrewarding. I needed my pot and my music and my booze, and I thought she understood that. As one who considered himself a charter member of the flower generation, I felt like a phony going to Army Reserve meetings and dressing up for work in an office like a typical cop-out upright citizen dickhead; and my drugs and alcohol and music were all I had left to retain my balance and dignity. I'd already sold out enough by getting married and having a respectable job.

Add to the mix a little honey who had cast her spell on me in my high school days and who suddenly appeared on the staff at the newspaper. I was enticed immediately, and took to her as instinctively and powerlessly as I did to my stimulants. She was all the incentive I needed to sabotage my family and career, neither of which I was devoted to anyway. I routinely came home after work only long enough to eat, and went out almost every night until the wee hours. And on those nights when I did stay home with Abby, the comfort was missing from our relationship and the passion from our sporadic lovemaking. I was too unperceptive to understand why, and too indifferent to care. Abby had come to realize that I was only home as a last resort, and that it was she who had become the woman on the side.

I was now drinking so heavily that I had begun chugging warm beers stashed in my car on the way to work in the morning to relieve the mind-numbing hangovers, and awaiting the noon hour and the end of each work day as a kid awaits the bell at school. At the age of twenty-three I was drinking morning, noon, and night, and in the throes of full-blown alcoholism.

The promising young journalist who had won awards for the paper, and whose future in the field seemed wide open, now missed assignments and deadlines. I failed to attend vital meetings and interviews, left the office to cover stories and spent the time in saloons and motel rooms and returned empty-handed, submitted copy poorly written and often factually inaccurate. Following lunches spent in a bar room, I often stared drowsily at my typewriter and contemplated whether someone had played a trick on me by rearranging the keys. And though I had once been much appreciated by the typesetting staff for producing the cleanest copy, I now turned in pages fraught with typos and cross-outs.

It is believed that alcoholism is merely a symptom of a deeper, far more encompassing misery. Call it what you will—genetic malfunction, allergy, chemical imbalance, manufacturing flaw, defective wiring, loose screw, improper maintenance, negligence, God's work on an off day—it didn't really matter whether booze had robbed me of reason and turned me into an egocentric bastard, or if I'd been a faulty product to begin with who had instinctively and inescapably turned to booze for salvation. Either way, at the core of my conscience I felt no allegiance to anyone but myself, and I felt no shame whatsoever. The purpose of life was to feel good, to have a good time. When Abby finally suggested that if I was so miserable at home perhaps it would be better for both of us if I found another one, I readily agreed—with no consternation at all over the fact that she was pregnant again.

At the same time my stint in the Army Reserves came to an end and I was released at last from my six years of military obligation. The publisher of the newspapers, having already given me several warnings, summoned me to his office and said that my drinking and irresponsible behavior were persistently impacting my work and jeopardizing the paper's reputation and that I was thereby dismissed. What's more, having learned that I'd abandoned my wife and child and lost my job, my parents washed their hands of me, again.

And I was utterly jubilant. This was not the bottom falling out of my world; it was the world opening up to me. I could drink and drug and play my guitar and retire forever my dress shirts and ties and grow my hair and crash where I wanted and with whom I wanted and pursue full throttle at last the freewheeling bohemian life I thoroughly believed I was meant to live—now that I'd got all those monkeys off my back.

I felt as if an enormous weight had been lifted from me, as if my feet had been tied to a ponderous anchor that had been pulling me under again and again, and from which I had loosed myself just in time. I had harbored a fascination for that alluring little package at the office for years, and although it's difficult to say now whether she became the catalyst or the excuse, she was definitely, in my eyes, the prize worth pursuing at any cost. Beautiful women can do that to a man, and this one came equipped with an understanding of the artist within me, an appreciation for the stifled creativity that had been screaming for release.

I took up residence with her in a studio apartment. She had previously been fired from the newspaper for being such a distraction to me. The boss had felt that by removing the distraction I might get back on track, but the train had already derailed.

On the morning of Palm Sunday my doorbell rang. I snuck I peek through a curtain and saw my mother on the porch. I had no idea how she knew where I was living, but I didn't need her to find out that I was shacked up with another woman. I ignored the bell until she went away. I kept a hash pipe in the ashtray in my car, and when I went out later I found it on the dashboard, with a strand of palm leaf tied in a bow around it. I thought it was a nice touch, actually.

When Abby's new baby came one of my friends tracked me down and told me that Abby had gone to the hospital. I thought the least I could do was make an appearance. She had already given birth by the time I got there. Abby's mother was in the waiting room. I didn't know what to say, except "I'm sorry." She said, "So am I," and turned away. I was the last person Abby wanted to see anyway, and the last person to whom she wished to show her new son.

12

Nashville

Nashville beat me. She lured me, teased me, embraced me, and then blew me off like untold thousands before me who had either similarly failed to grasp that the music business is a business, or who just couldn't make the grade. I saw her as the country music version of Hollywood, with a path to fame and riches meandering through a minefield of temptations and exploitations, where opportunities abounded if you watched where you stepped, and all manner of enticing and perilous alternatives if you didn't. I figure she saw me coming from four states away.

It was there that I headed after dropping out of a marriage, a family, and a profession, seeking my fortune while oblivious to the fact that I had just wholly flushed one down the dumper. In the time I lived there, while attempting to infiltrate the ever-fickle world of working songwriters, I befriended a dozen locals with whom I drank and drugged and caroused, and within a year after I left town every last one of them was dead. I heard that one loving couple did a handful of reds and dozed off together most peacefully. Three overdosed unintentionally in various other ways. One was killed in Vietnam. Another died of cancer. Two were lost in a car wreck. One suffered a heart attack. One got run over by a bus. And another was shot outright.

They had accepted me into their wild and crazy southern circle of misfits, at least as much as they could accept any Yankee hippie wiseass who'd cruised in from upstate New York with a Sicilian princess on one arm and a geetar hanging from the other.

The city's omnipotence in the music industry hovers in all her buildings and hangs out on all her street corners. She can make you a household name overnight whether you sing like Linda Ronstadt or Jimmy Durante. Or she can bring you to your knees and make you walk home on them. A more ambitious and committed newcomer might have sought out acquaintances whose company better served his musical aspirations, but as usual my primary yearnings steered me instead to the nearest resources of drinks and drugs.

Naive pickers and vocalists of every bent gallop into Nashville thinking they've got the fresh new sound those country hick music execs are looking for, provided they ever get one to listen. They rarely do. I did, inexplicably, and abused the opportunity with my usual indifference and blindness. It is one thing to fail when the odds are acutely against you, and another when you've been given chances reserved for a special few and you screw them up royally anyway.

I truly do not remember what circumstances enabled me to get my foot in a couple of essential doors on Music Row. I met songwriters who'd been in Nashville a good part of their lives and had been pounding on those same doors unsuccessfully for years to get an audience in a top publishing house. But I got in, and played and sang songs for high-level producers in two prominent publishing firms, whose lavish offices were festooned with gold record plaques and portraits of country music legends. They weren't doing somersaults over what they heard from me, but they kept asking me back.

I hadn't the means to record proper studio tapes and was forced to present my material live, an always excruciating ordeal. I had regular appointments with an executive at Tree International who insisted on seeing me at eight in the morning. She was a forty-something snooty blonde, easy on the eyes, and she seemed to thoroughly enjoy my agony in those sessions. I'd stand before her desk, sing and play a song, and she'd customarily stop me cold halfway through the first verse and ask what else I had. When I'd exhausted my newest batch of ditties she'd say, "I don't hear anything. Bring me something next week." I wanted to lean over the desk and slap the bitch. I reckoned that if she'd let me at least get into the song she might like it. But if it didn't grab her early, it wouldn't grab the listening masses either. She didn't get where she was by not knowing her stuff. Trying to wow her with my limited mastery of the twelve-string didn't move her much either. I was in the land of the best pickers in the business.

In essence the songmongers humored me. They expressed interest because I had the tools and talent to become a source of sellable tunes. If and when that potential blossomed, they didn't want it to happen in someone else's studio. So they endured my frequently sloppy auditions and threw me a song contract once in a while, an investment in the possibility that one day I'd walk in with a hit. I wrote about a hundred and fifty songs in the year or so I was there, nearly all of them album fillers without hit potential. I was given studio time to record demos of those that were deemed borderline possibilities. I had regular sessions to present new material, and I was rewarded with assurances that I was on the right track, and with just enough encouragement to keep me coming back. For an outsider who'd had no previous connections in the business whatsoever and had only been in town a few months, I was sitting pretty. Any day I might produce, as if out of the blue the way so many great songs come, the hit that might launch my career.

I met a free-lance songwriter who belonged to a stable of contributors on standard contract to a publisher. He was paid a salary to spit out mindless three-chord country ditties that would be pushed to the popular mainstay singing stars of the day and invariably end up on commercial radio—the bubblegum country ballads about cheatin' hearts and broken cowboys. This guy lounged around a grubby apartment behind closed yellowed draperies, its rooms littered throughout with empty beer and liquor bottles and overflowing ashtrays. He spent his days hammering himself with Jack Daniels, downers, and weed while grinding out three or four songs a month.

On the ladder of achievement in the music industry this guy was sitting on the bottom rung in his gray underwear, and I envied him. What could be sweeter? He got paid to write songs and didn't even have to get dressed. Unless he came up with an enduring classic his shot at fame and fortune didn't amount to much, but he didn't seem to mind. And though I had first considered that to be about as swell a job as a nobody songsmith could hope for in that brutally competitive industry, I in fact could have found myself in much more advantageous circumstances if I'd only had a morsel of perseverance.

You can pursue the prospects I had in different ways. You can plug away at it, respecting that having a foot in the door is the pivotal element, for without any link to the music-marketers you and your songs aren't likely to go anywhere. If you have the right people listening to your stuff, the song you write tomorrow could be the one. Hang in there.

You can take your act to the streets to get a realistic idea of their appeal, try your material on different audiences at the clubs, strum and sing your heart out to a roomful of leery strangers, endure some cool responses, swallow the dreaded dead silence at the end of a song, warm to occasional smatterings of polite applause. Try another place, another night, another crowd, another batch of songs. You never know who might be out there in a dark corner: a producer, a scout, an established star willing to give you a leg up. Stick with it. In the end it will undoubtedly be a matter of being in the right place at the right time, but the right place and time will never materialize in a smoky apartment with a guitar in one hand and a bottle of sour mash in the other.

Another avenue is to stop busting your butt spitting out new songs because you're tired of being rejected day after day. Those spiffy rednecks wouldn't know a good song if they stepped in it. This popular tactic requires kicking up your alcohol and drug consumption yet another notch in order to cope with the depression, of course, but it affords you the freedom to spend more unproductive time with other drunk, spaced-out and depressed failed songwriters who are more than willing to drag you down with them.

Eventually, the publishers and club owners tire of smelling booze and reefer on your breath and hearing what sound like the same songs week after week. Soon the regular appointments with the publishers dry up, along with the nightclub dates, and when you come around hoping for an open ear, the music suits and club managers aren't in the office just now.

Meanwhile one must sustain himself. I did so as a cook in a popular restaurant, where I met many of my hard-drugging friends whose proclivity for walking through life in a purple haze was as prodigious as mine, and where I of course got cozy with the bartenders. We were forbidden to drink before or during our shifts, but I had an arrangement with the barkeep to have a concoction prepared when I walked in. When no bosses were watching he'd slide me a tall iced tea glass of refreshment to guzzle as I walked down the bar toward the kitchen. There were at least ten ounces of booze and no ice at all in the glass, an incredibly effective elixir of 151-proof rum and 110-proof green chartreuse liquor. They went together as delectably as Nyquil and kerosene, but the pick-me-up could amply power a sizeable turbine or restaurant grill man for a good three hours without refueling. After my shift, during which I'd inhale at least one more of those devastating bombs along with assorted beers—clandestinely delivered from the bar in exchange for underground fried shrimp—I'd tone my intake down considerably by switching to slightly less potent bourbon manhattans.

The relationship with my wondrous woman had been gradually deteriorating. She'd grown tired of my coming home drunk and smelling like hamburger, and I was getting tired of her being tired of me. I might have kept her if I'd mended my ways, but of course I didn't see the need for renovation. She ditched me in favor of a well-heeled southern pseudo-aristocrat twice her age whose first name was Harland for God's sake, and when I was asked to remove myself from our shared domicile I forfeited our shared mode of transportation in the bargain.

I was on foot and heading home from work at three in the morning to the upstairs apartment I now rented by myself. I was thoroughly boiled and coming down from a two-day-long peyote ride, rambling down the center of a side street. There in the road was a run-over rabbit, or at least a third of him had been run over, the third that was wafer flat. When I walked by he looked straight at me. There was a glint in his eye. He was still alive. And I, compassionate fellow critter of the Almighty's creation, wasted on organic mescaline and byproducts of grains born of His good earth, could not allow that noble animal to endure that awful death. God would expect me to end his suffering.

When the car headlights came up behind me and stopped I was sitting in the middle of the street, my legs outstretched, strangling the life out of what was left of that rabbit. I wrung its neck and still he glared at me. His fur was soaked with blood and the disgusting, slimy goo that a terrified dying animal secretes and that reeks so bad it can wilt magnolias. It was all over my hands and forearms, shirt and lap, gummy and sickening, and still I squeezed until my hands shook because I needed to show this animal mercy. I shook its neck fit to snap his head off, crushed and yanked and twisted still harder, and finally resorted to bending it double and hammering its head on the pavement. Still it glared at me, refusing to die.

The cop tapped me on the shoulder and asked me what the hell I thought I was doing, and as soon as I started to explain he realized that this marble-mouthed longhaired drug-addled hippie punk was also a Yankee. Marble-mouthed long-haired drug-addled hippie punk Yankees didn't sit well with old-school southern constables, and even in my state of diminished intellect I knew I was in deep shit. No way in hell could I invent a story that would mollify this guy, who of course was built like a steam boiler, so I told him the truth—that I was only trying to put the poor animal out of its misery—with as much solemnity and courtesy as I could muster. I was only two doors from my apartment and wasn't really guilty of anything beyond public idiocy and bunny abuse, so he told me to go the hell home. Maybe he just didn't want to touch me or put me in his car smelling the way I did. I thanked him repeatedly and tried to hand him the limp rabbit, asking if he wanted to take it to a clinic or something. He shook his head and walked back to his car, and I threw the ungrateful rodent on someone's lawn.

On the landing of my door it occurred to me that if I put my scummy hand in my jeans pocket for my key I would never get that smell out of the pants no matter how many times I washed them. It didn't matter. My clothes were saturated with the slime anyway. Still I thought I'd break out just a corner of the door window with my elbow in order to reach in and flip the lock, and of course the window exploded into a bazillion pieces. I got inside and flicked the light on, shuffled across the room and sat on my bed, and promptly passed out.

I don't know what kind of bugs they were. Huge bugs, like locusts, attracted to the light and the smell, too, I suppose. They had come through the broken window by the hundreds, and when I woke up in the night I was covered with them, encased in a squirming, humming body suit of repulsive creatures that were inside my shirt and all over my face and arms and in my hair. When I opened my eyes and took in the scene I screamed, "Sweet Jesus, I've got the DTs," and immediately passed out again, quite likely from shock. In the morning the bugs were gone. The smell wasn't. I would have sworn that rabbit was still alive.

***

Elizabeth was a sleek, redheaded beauty with a spectacular ass and a voice you could cut lead pipe with. She was one of those chicks you could hear above everyone else at a raucous party, or a train crash for that matter, and in the throes of a shrieking orgasm she could shatter a bathtub. Elizabeth had given me a standing invitation to stop at her apartment after work in the early morning hours. She asked only that I not get too drunk before coming, but she never got her wish.

She lived in the first floor front unit of a huge antebellum mansion that had been divided into apartments. It had wide front steps approaching a deep veranda from which could be seen her living room through a large picture window. One night after I'd pounded on her apartment door in the cavernous vestibule without an answer, I went out on the veranda and saw her asleep on her living room sofa. I hammered on the window but she never stirred. I was too drunk and horny to give up the cause, so I went back inside and got on my knees and tried to trip the lock on her door by jamming my own key in it. I never heard the door to the apartment behind me open, so I almost painted my undies when I got a tap on the shoulder. When I turned my head the business end of a double-barreled shotgun dropped slowly down and came to rest on the bridge of my nose. The tank-topped Elmer Fudd at the other end was a fat ol' boy with a crimson face, bloodshot eyes, and candy corn teeth, and as he cocked both hammers his only words were, "Y'all wanna leave in one piece or fifty?"

In spite of my befuddled condition my fight or flight response was functioning just fine. I bolted out the door, and just as my feet hit the ground after launching me from the porch, that bastard blew both barrels of that blunderbuss into the air over my head, and in the dead of night ten sticks of TNT could not have been louder. As I rounded the street corner I heard a car engine start up and tires squeal. Roger

Bannister may have been the first to break the four-minute mile on foot, but I bet he never did it shit-faced.

Could I have made it in Nashville? As a songwriter, possibly. As a performer, doubtfully. I had a pretty good voice before the cigarettes and booze began to take their toll. I put heart and soul into my songs, but as for performing live I lacked the most important gift of all—balls. Some of this stemmed from common stage fright, but most of it was symptomatic of the insecurity and fear of rejection that had plagued me all my life. Not since high school had I performed on stage in any state short of stupor.

After a while the thrill of the hunt was gone. My pursuit of fame and fortune faded into the background of a familiar and comfortable routine of working and partying and chasing women. The whole environment had begun to depress me. The more depressed I became about failing to make the grade, the more I drank. The more I drank, the more defeated I felt.

> *First the man takes a drink,*
> *then the drink takes a drink,*
> *then the drink takes the man.*
> *- Japanese Proverb*

I find it ludicrous now that if someone had approached me then and offered on a silver platter the world I thought I wanted so much—a hit song, platinum album, fame and riches—and all I had to do in return was stop drinking, I would not have accepted. I would not have thought even that implausible dream could justify sacrificing an enjoyment I was convinced was as much a part of my constitution as my skin and bones. Drink had proven time and again to be my most reliable ally, the one steadfast friend who never judged or ridiculed, who never refused me, who was always there to comfort me, who always let me think I was better than I was. I could hardly abandon the one true friend who refused to abandon me.

In the span of a year I had evolved from cocky yet clueless greenhorn in the country music capital of the world, to aspiring songwriter with potential and possibilities, to burned-out grill man in a nightclub kitchen. Count me not among the ineffectual dreamers that the Nashville machinery had chewed up and spit out, but as one of the chosen few who'd been given a precious chance and who shot himself in the very foot he had in the door.

The ambition and enthusiasm were exhausted. Nashville for me had gone from hub of hope to just another place to use drugs, drink, and women. My associations on Music Row and any lingering relationships having evaporated, I did what I had always done when the going got tough. I quit. It was time to move on. The news that Abby had been banged up in a car accident awakened a lingering if measly guilt within me, and I headed back to Rochester with my hair on my shoulders and my tail between my legs, and with a fragment of hope that it was not too late to mend our relationship.

I damn near got to leave my mark in Music City USA. I could have been jailed there too, and I was indebted to the gent who had swiped the princess. He was an attorney, and on one occasion I blasted into his office and threatened in a drunken rage to break both his legs if I saw him near her again. The outburst was witnessed by five other gentlemen, all of them lawyers. Another time when I saw him pulling away from her apartment in his big shiny Lincoln, I tried to smash the driver side window with my guitar. Thank God for hard-shell cases. The Guild suffered only a minor bruise. In both incidents he could easily have had me arrested.

As for her, in the waning days of our relationship I'd given her a colossal case of crabs. I didn't know from whom I'd gotten them myself, but we'd been through so much together I felt the need to share, and to call her a few choice names for having given them to me.

Leaving Nashville, I couldn't help thinking I was escaping with my life, if not wholly unscathed. I had retreated, surrendered, deserted. I could return to Rochester with tales of how I'd bucked the Music City system, but in truth I had used my collapse to justify finding solace in a bottle yet again. All I had lost was another great chance at a promising career and the love of a woman, tossed away like worn out shoes.

Abby took me in, circumspectly, aware that my stripes were probably indelible, yet holding onto a shred of hope that was as skimpy as my commitment. She may have been blinded temporarily by the consolation of having my shoes under her bed again, but she must have known as well as I did that our expectations were doomed from the start. I was still devoid of sincerity and any sense of responsibility, and my paltry attempt at reconciliation succeeded only in torturing her further and breaking her heart even more. Not even my gorgeous little girl could inspire me to make a serious go of it, and my son was a stranger to me, and I to him. It seemed as if I had moved in with a woman who had kids from a previous marriage. We were trying to rekindle a fire that had already been reduced to ashes. She put me up for a while, but the while came to its inevitable conclusion.

13

Slipping

I was on the streets again, hop-scotching from one low-rent studio apartment to another, from one part-time restaurant job to another, earning just enough to get by on, or get high on, take your pick. I was rarely able to accumulate enough money to pay my rent on time, let alone funnel any toward my family, although at one point I managed to scrape together five hundred dollars to buy the batmobile. It was the coolest sled I've ever owned, a black '66 Thunderbird that I lived in for a month while bumming a shower wherever I could. It was comfy enough for sleeping, despite my having to share it with everything I owned, but it didn't handle all that well off road.

Since I was an artist, at least by my definition, I was entitled to a *period*. Picasso had his blue period. Dylan had his folk rock period. I had a farm period. A horsewoman who'd had more than a few sidekicks in her day got sweet on me and offered me shelter in the house she rented on a farm out by the county airport. At one of Big W's famous Halloween parties on Park Avenue, I wore a saddle and came in on hands and knees with her on my back, which pretty much illustrates how that relationship was going. I'd been with her a few months when I came home blitzed one freezing winter evening and missed the turn into the farm road doing about eighty. When I flattened the first fence post the batmobile got tangled in electrified barbed wire that twanged loose from a dozen or so other posts in succession, popping a few clean out of the ground like toothpicks. The brakes and steering were useless. The car sailed across a sea of snow and finally came to rest fifty yards into the pasture, trussed up and sparking, buried halfway to its windows in slush and mud and horse dung.

I was afraid to touch anything lest I light up, but when I was fairly sure the circuit had shorted out, I left the car and trudged to the farmhouse. Annie Oakley asked me where my car was because she hadn't seen me drive in, and I told her I left it in the parking lot. It was the next afternoon before we found all the horses that had sauntered out. One was moseying around a shopping plaza two miles away doing a little window-shopping, and another was creating havoc at the airport.

The horse farmer had to drag the batmobile out of the pasture with a tractor. It took two days to replant all the fence posts and string new wire. After that it wasn't long before Annie started bucking and snorting over the fact that my sole function appeared to be that of strumming geetar around the ol' homestead while guzzling bourbon and smoking locoweed that she seemed to be the only one purchasing. Maybe I should have punched a cow or soaped a saddle or something. The relationship became so strained I was forced to move to another farm.

Some buddies had bought a farmhouse in North Rose, NY, in such ramshackle condition that snow drifts accumulated in the living room through cracks in the walls. A well pump and a three-seater were in the back yard but there was no indoor plumbing. These were the waning days of genuine hippiedom, before that glorious and inimitable utopia withered away from abuse—sabotaged from within by those who began to prey on the trusting and submissive nature of their brothers and sisters—when for a while our world was as right to us as we thought it could ever possibly be, and probably was. The aspiring farmers took their new endeavor seriously, while the rest of us treated the farm as a commune. Hail to Queen Mother Earth, bring your axe, sleep in the barn, you can ride that fat mare but don't make her run, Boone's Farm apple and Strawberry Hill, fresh foods from the fields, every freak a friend, folk rock, rock rock, country rock, acid rock, bathe at the well or in the rain, homegrown weed, fresh eggs from the hen house with shells like armor, fuck Nixon, music fests in the hay loft, try a hit of this, man, don't turn your back on that ornery goat, love the wine your with, and with it all a religion of sharing and brotherhood that we thought we invented and with it could save the world.

These days too saw the prevalence of modern-day women's liberation, when flower-haired ladies expressed their discontent with ages-old sexual domination by us male chauvinist pig bastards by discarding their bras, thus enabling us male chauvinist pig bastards to see their nipples through their tops and what their guns really looked like without the structural aids—not to mention the easier access. We had to admit it was liberating. Their motives were authentic enough; happily, so were the guns.

I made the farm my home on occasion, arriving with my big-box twelve-string, some new songs, groceries and beer and wine as gratuity for their putting me up, and for putting up with me. The goods I would ordinarily bring from Rochester, but on one such trip I shopped in the humble hamlet of North Rose. I walked around the small local grocery for half an hour, tolerably sautéed in bourbon and some fine Jamaican I'd smoked during the hour-long drive, and exceedingly puzzled by my inability to find the beer cooler. I must have walked right by it on all six laps around the store. Finally I confronted the lone cashier about why they found it necessary to hide the beer on a hot summer day. She said they didn't sell beer; it was a dry town. The only dry town I'd ever heard of was Mayberry. She said I could buy beer a few miles down the road in the next town, which was not dry, and where everyone else in North Rose got their booze. Silliest damn thing I'd ever heard of. To my knowledge the town is still dry, and deserves to be.

One of my farmhouse buddies decided to go into the mechanical fruit harvesting business and offered me a job. It involved working on giant machinery that snuck up on an unsuspecting apple tree, wrapped huge iron jaws around its trunk, and shook the bejesus out of it until it dropped its crop onto a huge canvas mat that rolled the harvest onto a conveyor belt and into a bin. My job would be to help guide the mat as it retracted toward the receiving apparatus, lifting the mat so that the fruit wouldn't roll off before it got there. Full of apples, the mat weighed as much as a plow horse. I had no pressing obligations so I accepted the job offer, not fully understanding that what he proposed was very much like actual farming. He was in the orchards cracking the whip at the time of day I was accustomed to coming home.

But it was an opportunity for me to do some soul-searching, to cut back on my alcohol intake, and to apply myself to some serious labor that had me going to bed exhausted at night instead of passing out drunk. I certainly needed the break from hammering myself with the sauce so relentlessly, but of course it couldn't last. I could say that I just wasn't cut out for farming and that the bright lights and nightlife of the city beckoned me back. I could even say that I eschewed all that physical work, but that wasn't it at all. What beckoned me back, as always, was my liquid lover. I missed getting hammered. I missed my beloved Never Ever Land, that hallowed corner of oblivion to which I could always escape, where music sounded so fine, where my own music sounded so good, where time went away somewhere, in a land reserved for dreamers and losers, where accountability and reality could never ever find me.

At yet another farm one afternoon I got into the magic mushrooms, the real-deal organic psilocybin shrooms that are far superior to chemical LSD, and a little sneakier. In low doses it's not unlike decent pot. In larger doses it's like a very colorful excursion through the goofy house. My friends and I opted for larger doses, of course, though not necessarily intentionally.

Someone had a whole bag of the stuff. First we made some generously-spiked hot chocolate. After an hour or so we were commenting that we didn't seem to be getting off all that much, so someone made a huge pot of chili and threw in a handful more. After eating we sat around a living room that was overrun with mice and played guitar and laughed until our faces got sore. We still didn't feel as though the stuff was working all that well, but it seemed like a good idea to eat again, so someone threw another handful into a kettle of oatmeal. We were still waiting for the magical mystery tour to get underway when we decided the silo needed climbing.

I tried a dozen times to climb that thing. Iron footholds were placed about two feet apart all the way up, but every time I got to the fourth one the silo started tipping over. I'd scurry back to the ground, study the perfectly upright silo once again, and give it another try. Most of the other guys had reached the top without any problem, but I never did get up the damn thing.

I was still waiting for this organic acid stuff to start kicking in when I decided to take a walk out to the main road a good mile away. I lighted a cigarette and set out, returning about an hour later, and couldn't imagine why it was that the cigarette was still going and only half gone. Most strange. All in all it was a pleasant afternoon, though I was a little baffled to discover upon returning home that three days had passed.

***

I always had the restaurant business to fall back on. For a man on the move who only needed a means of paying the rent (occasionally) and buying necessities (stimulants) without taxing his cerebrum or saddling him with a long-term commitment, a restaurant gig was my ace in the hole wherever I roamed. I enjoyed working with food, though I was never qualified to be a master chef. I was a great prep man and short-order cook, and a chef of sorts in restaurants that would never be accused of offering epicurean fare. In other words, I could work my way up to head kitchen honcho in a neighborhood steaks and chops tavern if I stayed there long enough, but I'd probably never wear a toque in a top-notch eatery.

I might have been a good waiter if I'd had the tolerance for it. I once told a bigmouth trying to impress his guests by berating me for everything from the number of ice cubes in his water glass to the size of his croutons: "You know, sir, I think you probably knew that everything at your table was going to be wrong before you got out of your fucking car." Another waiter was assigned to serve them coffee and dessert. I was unemployed at the time. At another restaurant I served a pain in the ass a dessert of strawberry shortcake made with urinal cakes, and they weren't fresh from the wrappers either.

Everyone in the restaurant business knows that the customers who complain the most and treat servers like scum either suffer from the delusion that they are of a higher order of humanoid, or are merely cheap bastards who bitch about everything to justify leaving a lousy tip. It has always amazed me that these pseudo-sophisticates don't even possess the intellect to comprehend that the last people on earth you should abuse and publicly embarrass are those who have access to your food.

As a bartender I took a lot of abuse as most do, but I tolerated it by abusing myself first with liquid refreshments hand-selected from the array of medications at my fingertips. This enabled me to turn the tables and abuse the customers instead. Chefs sample foods to be sure they're fit to serve, and I always felt that refreshments should be monitored in like fashion, and frequently. You never know when the Wild Turkey or Grand Marnier might suddenly turn.

My best barkeeping gig was in a service bar cubicle so small that no matter how drunk I got there wasn't room enough to fall down. I could teeter to my heart's content and didn't have to deal with any customers. I only had to be unnecessarily rude to the waitresses, or at least the ones I wasn't trying to de-panty. After my foray into farming life I took a nighttime bartending job in which I was soon making enough cake to get an apartment and to enhance my mixology prowess and rate of personal alcohol consumption with snootfuls of cocaine every night. While a good part of what I earned went toward the pharmaceuticals essential to the job that was essential to support my need for the pharmaceuticals, it was an endless cycle but hardly a vicious one. I was having a ball. I spent my days walking barefoot from one end of Ellison Park to the other, smoking weed, conversing with nature, often dragging my guitar along and serenading from atop a boulder or hilltop, baking in the sun. I spent my nights pouring and sampling booze behind the bar of one of the hottest nightclubs in town, flirted with the ladies, and partied the night away after hours.

When the tavern expanded and added a sizeable new kitchen that the proprietors intended to lease out as a separate enterprise, I jumped at the opportunity to run the concession and start my own business. I put out some great food but I wasn't much of a businessman. I worked and drank about eighty hours a week. Every morning I found a rock glass full of Old Grand Dad waiting for me in the refrigerator to get my motor started, compliments of the lady who lived upstairs and cleaned behind the bar every morning, and throughout the day and evening a glass of bourbon was never out of reach.

At the end of each week, after paying my kitchen rent, the purveyors, and my staff, there was just enough money left to tuck away to cover sales taxes. I couldn't help wondering what was in it for me. There simply wasn't enough left to pay both the state of New York and myself, so the tax hounds would have to wait; and wait they did, right up until they seized my cash register and padlocked the doors. No sense of humor, those people. By then I owed the saloon keeper several months back rent, which I satisfied by turning over to him my entire inventory of stores, and I was jobless again with nothing to show for my venture into the world of commerce but an $8,000 debt to the tax department and an overtaxed liver.

After a period of licking my wounds and drowning my sorrows I sought out occasional bartending gigs. These were short-lived because the tax people started garnisheeing my paychecks, and I reasoned that the only way to end that nonsense was to stop working altogether. Every once in a while they hunted me down to remind me that I still owed them money, plus growing interest, and I was forced to tell them that I was out of work and you can't get blood from a stoned stone. When they pressed me to find a job, I told them I already had a job. I was a songwriter. It wasn't paying me a red cent, unfortunately, but it was still my job, and I didn't feel that their insistence on satisfying a piddling tax debt justified the ruination of a perfectly good struggling artist. And when they'd had their fill of that bull, I told them that I was an unemployable alcoholic, which happened to be a lot truer than I would have admitted at the time.

I performed at various coffee houses and small bars for little or no pay, sometimes with a partner who was by far the more talented of us. Sheva was a housewife and mother who never quite found the proper direction and discipline to pursue her craft seriously, but I have never known or worked with anyone who had more raw potential. A reckless native Texan with light red hair down to her waist and a freckled beaming face, she had a country-blues voice that could at times melt you with its sweetness and emotional huskiness, and other times astound you with its operatic clarity. She had the guts and the goods to walk into any Nashville studio and say, "Give me a microphone and five minutes of your time and I'll blow the windows clean out of this joint," and I doubt that the music agent existed who wouldn't snatch her up on the spot upon hearing her belt out a song.

A local agent whose services I had loosely procured lined up a few solo gigs for me to play and sing at some area saloons, though my act wasn't what you'd call Vegas caliber. The best he could do for me were roadhouse taverns out in the boonies that catered to bikers and truckers. One paid all of fifty bucks for a four-set performance, which was a bit of a stretch because I didn't have that much material. I also didn't have any sound equipment. On my first night I perched on a stool with my twelve-string, wailing away at a truly heartfelt rendition of *Mr. Bojangles* to a dozen beefy members of a biker gang, who were lined up with their backs to the bar looking as if they were watching a dead TV. At the end of the song they didn't move a muscle. I thought I'd really grab them next with a harmonica-enhanced styling of a favorite Dylan song that had them glancing at one another with a smidgen of interest, and I immediately realized that maybe *I'll Be Your Baby Tonight* wasn't the best selection.

After the first set, which received not an iota of response, I bellied up to the bar in need of a keg of bourbon. The woman who owned the joint served me a drink and wanted money. I explained to her that it was customary for the entertainment to drink for free, and she explained that it wasn't a customary kind of place. At the end of the gig she told me not to come back the next night because it obviously wasn't working out. She had evidently broken down and decided to hire some entertainment to enhance business, and had probably expected Elvis himself and a line at the door three miles long on opening night.

She reluctantly paid me twenty-eight dollars, all that was left of the contracted fifty after drawing my bar tab, and I packed up the guitar while the bikers watched. I had not been rewarded with so much as a solitary toe-tap the whole night. I meekly slid out, climbed in the

Batmobile, and headed on down the road toward the big city doing something like a hundred m.p.h.

During this period my drinking was at the highest level it had ever been. I drank every waking hour. My evening cocktail of choice was a manhattan made with Old Forester bourbon and a splash of Amaretto instead of vermouth. I drank them like they were shots. When your drinking has reached that stage you become oblivious to the volume you are consuming, and just as oblivious to the preposterous state of your daily life. You honestly do not see anything wrong with what you're doing. You keep telling yourself that you're having fun. At my favorite hangout it was routine for the bartenders to shoo the riff-raff out at closing time, lock the doors, and get down to some serious drinking with close friends. We ordered up to a half-dozen drinks at last call, and we'd hang out and gamble and drink.

For me the absurdity of this routine was that in the course of a day and evening I had already consumed enough alcohol to kill a walrus, yet I would order up to four more manhattans at closing time because at two in the morning I didn't feel as if I'd drunk quite enough. There were many nights when I just couldn't get any drunker, but I'd keep drinking anyway. I was never one to pass out or fall down, so it was like pouring water down a drainpipe. I don't remember ever quitting because I thought I'd had enough. I quit when there was no more to be had, or when I ran out of money or people to bum from.

Characteristic of my volume of consumption was a night when I'd already been drunk and napped it off twice in the course of the day, and I sat at the bar with my buddies and drank five of those bourbon manhattans after ten o'clock. At last call I ordered four more to drink after closing. That would amount to a fifth of bourbon in that sitting alone. While the bartenders were cleaning up and waiting for the other customers to leave, I went out to the parking lot to smoke a joint in my car. The pint of vodka I always kept under the seat was half full, and in the time it took me to smoke the joint I finished it off. After already drinking suicidally for fourteen hours, with four more bourbon manhattans waiting for me inside, I couldn't even take ten minutes to smoke some pot without accompanying it with half a pint of white whiskey. And I saw nothing odd about that at all. The vodka was there, so I drank it.

It was after one such all-day, all-night drinkarama that I found myself walking the aisles of a local supermarket in search of a thick steak to take home and cook. After roaming around for half an hour I finally located one in the meat department of all places, a marbled beauty that was too expensive for my liking, despite the fact that I had the cash to pay for it. To protest what I considered the unreasonably high cost of beef, I stuck it under my shirt and was on my way out when I was stopped by a small, gray-haired woman who poked my stomach to verify my cargo and told me to freeze. I would have slipped by her and beat feet, but behind her stood a stocky stock boy who was apparently earning extra money between seasons as an NFL fullback. He wore big sneakers, big arms, and a big grin.

Apparently there was this silly law I wasn't aware of, whereby adults who steal things aren't slapped on the wrist for shoplifting but are arrested for petit larceny. A policeman led me out of the store in handcuffs and tossed me in the pokey with a few dozen other unfortunates. The accommodations were pretty dingy and they didn't serve steaks. In the morning I was led to a holding room off the courtroom along with everyone else. There were no chairs, and floor space apparently was by reservation only. One guy got up to take a piss. When he returned to find someone else in his spot, he knocked his teeth out. I elected to stand. A couple of hours later I stood smelly, hungover, and bedraggled with a public defender before a judge who, because I had no previous record, released me with an unconditional discharge. "I trust," he said, "it was at least a sirloin." I assured him that it had been.

***

I got an under-the-table cooking job in the kitchen of my usual hangout. I smuggled bottles of vodka in and hid them in the basement. The boss and my fellow workers were well aware of my drinking habits, but I had always been able to keep my wits about me. I was a good drunk, as they say. I showed up every day and did the job.

I'd been having trouble with a God-awful rash on my shins that itched so intolerably at night I dug at it in my sleep, and woke up with bloody fingernails and torn open skin. I went to a dermatologist, but he was more concerned about some big red blotches on my chest. He wanted to know if I was a drinker. When I told him I relaxed with a toddy on occasion, he told me my occasional toddying had to cease. What my drinking had to do with my itching legs I couldn't imagine, but he didn't seem all that concerned with my itch.

He told me to stop drinking immediately and gave me a plastic gallon jug in which I was to collect every piss I took for twenty-four hours starting the next morning. Then I was to drop the jug at his office the following day so it could be analyzed and to come back for another appointment in a week. This meant taking the jug to work with me in a paper sack, which I hid in the basement where I usually stashed my vodka, appropriately enough.

I somehow managed not to drink at all the next day and dutifully used the jug. After my night shift I was headed out the back door when the proprietor stopped me and wanted to know what I had in the bag. Nothing of interest, I told him. We'd been friends for years, but he said he couldn't have employees carrying sacks out the back door at night.

"You don't want to know what's in here," I said.

"Yes I do."

"OK, it's a jug of urine."

"Open the bag, wiseass."

I took out the jug.

"What the hell is that?"

"I told you. It's a jug of urine. What'd you think it was, a box of shrimp? Next time don't be so fucking nosey."

I cut my drinking down considerably that week, hoping the blotches on my chest might miraculously fade away so that the doctor could treat my itching legs instead of my lifestyle. But when I confessed at my next appointment that I'd had a few drinks he threw me out. He said he couldn't help me if I refused to follow treatment. I was confused. I was still tearing at my legs. I went to a dermatologist and he made me stop drinking. Where was I supposed to go to stop the itching?

The bar I was working in changed hands and I was unemployed again. The kitchen I had leased in the other joint was taken back by the proprietors, who hired my younger sister Maris to run it. She worked in the restaurant business but the management of such a busy kitchen was a bit over her head. I had barely settled into another sabbatical when the owners asked me to come back and help her, with a promise of paying me under the table.

I then took on two part-time bartending jobs in which my pay was garnisheed again, so I was working days in the restaurant kitchen and nights behind the bar at two other joints, a schedule for which it became necessary to augment my energy level with an intensified regimen of hydration. I walked in the kitchen one day and my sister immediately called the doctor. She said I was orange. She said people weren't supposed to be orange. The doctor took one look at me and knew I had hepatitis. The urine sample I gave him was the color of coffee. He said that not only did I have hepatitis but that the disease was presently peaking and I should probably be hospitalized. He wanted to know how I could possibly be that sick and not know it. My answer was that I didn't feel any sicker than I had the day before or the day before that, and that I'd felt like crap for so long I had nothing to compare it to.

He said I was not to even smell a cork for at least six months. I went out and got very drunk, and then went home to my apartment. My sister and her husband Lou came to find me and had to break in. Maris told me later they'd found me unconscious. I was bedridden for three weeks and about as sick as a man could be. By the sixth week I was drinking again.

I had not paid rent for my apartment in so long that I was finally booted out and was taken in by my sister and brother-in-law. Lou was so easy to get along with that we quickly became fast friends. He would prove to be more of a brother to me than my own had ever been, and remains dear to me still. He didn't even get mad at me when I ripped the sink off his bathroom wall.

I'd had a toothache for some time and hadn't been to a dentist in years. I finally arranged an appointment with a colleague of my father's dentist who told me I needed a root canal. I hadn't the means to pay for it, of course, so we made an arrangement by which he would eliminate the source of my pain by doing half the work—that of drilling out the tooth and putting in a temporary filling—and I would pay for his services on my next visit when he'd complete the procedure. But, since the pain was now gone and the temporary filling seemed to suffice nicely, I didn't see any need to go back.

It wasn't long before the tooth became infected again and the subsequent pain unbearable. That damned tooth would almost literally be the death of me. Even after the better part of a quart of bourbon and a handful of Tylenol the pain wouldn't subside, but things were looking up when I came across a bottle of codeine painkillers in my sister's medicine cabinet. I washed a couple of those down with plenty of bourbon, but nothing happened, so I took three more and drank some more. An hour later the pain was the same so I took five more. I decided I'd take a walk, thinking that maybe getting my circulation going would get the pills working better. Then I decided I was really sleepy and thought I'd lie down and take a nap in a field at the end of the street. It was a warm summer day and there was a lovely breeze and the long grass felt silky and inviting. All I wanted to do was close my eyes, but it struck me that I didn't appear to be breathing.

There haven't been many times over the years that I've been close to death, but I believe that was one of them. It was as if I'd been tapped on the shoulder just then and informed that I now had two seconds to live, that as soon as I fell asleep I was a goner. I somehow became aware of that reality and understood what was happening. I rolled over on my stomach and started doing push-ups as fast as I could. I got up and ran in place. I ran around in circles. I had to keep moving. I ran back to the house and ran up and down the stairs. There was no one else home. Finally the danger passed but I didn't dare even sit. I kept walking around the house. Then the pain came on like a freight train. I looked in the bathroom mirror and saw that a swelling in the roof of my mouth was the size of half a ping-pong ball. Somehow I had to relieve the pressure of that infection, like jam something up through the temporary filling so that the tooth could drain.

The lower G on my twelve-string looked about right, so I yanked it off the guitar and started jamming the end of it up through the tooth. I got about an inch of it rammed in there pretty good and sure enough some awful looking bloody goop started oozing out. The drain on the bathroom sink had always been sluggish but now it didn't seem to drain at all. As I spat into the sink and ran water, the water kept rising with the crud from my infection swimming on the surface, and the more water I ran the more it rose. I couldn't leave the sink filled with that sickening mess for Maris or Lou to find. I had to free up the drain, and for some reason the concept of disassembling the trap in the plumbing didn't occur to me. The only logical alternative was to rip the entire sink out of the wall, plumbing and all. The subsequent mess wouldn't have been nearly as extensive if I'd thought to turn off the water under the sink first, but I was delirious at the time and couldn't think of everything.

I stood there holding the sink, water gushing from the pipes where I'd twisted them off, an array of crumbled plaster and broken wall tiles on the floor, the guitar string still stuck in the tooth and dangling out of my mouth, and in spite of that somewhat awkward circumstance I was pleased to notice that the pain had abated a little. It finally registered to me to shut the faucets on the piping to stop the geysers, which I did right after the sink accidentally slipped from my hands and crashed on the floor into several chunks. I was sitting at the kitchen table when Lou came home. After exchanging greetings I said, "By the way, the drain in that upstairs sink isn't clogged any more."

I got a job as a service bartender at a restaurant in suburban Pittsford, and it was there that I met Kay. She was only twenty-one, a decade younger than I, a natural blond beauty who I would come to learn hadn't a pretentious bone in her lithe lovely frame. She wanted to be part of my life, such as it was, and she would spend the best years of her own life watching mine slip away.

14

Cowboy

One Saturday morning when I was a child, watching a western movie on TV with my father, I was fascinated by a cowpoke who upended a bottle of whiskey in a saloon and took several long gulps as if it were a soft drink. I asked if a man could really drink straight liquor like that. My father said it wasn't really liquor but something else in the bottle that looked like it, because the man was just acting. He didn't answer my question. I knew that whiskey was strong, awful-tasting stuff because I'd sampled my parents' drinks. And whenever I watched them or their friends drink cocktails they sipped them.

Still I wondered if a cowboy could really guzzle straight booze that way. Some years later I found out on my own. The answer was yes, and at eight o'clock in the morning, too. I now get a kick out of seeing a cowboy in an old movie stop his horse in the desert to survey the horizon, five weeks on the trail and two hundred miles from the nearest town, as he pulls out a pocket flask the size of a sardine can and takes a dainty sip as if he's been nursing that diddly-squat ration of hooch all the way from St. Louis. I'd have polished off that puny flask back at the bunkhouse before I could find my boots.

Like nearly everyone who spends half a lifetime in a bottle, it never occurred to me that as a young man I could have chosen not to drink. But I saw my parents drink every night. They didn't entertain any friends who didn't drink. People in restaurants we went to drank before dinner, congregating at the bar amid great chatter and laughter. People in the movies drank. I always knew I too would drink, and as soon as I possibly could.

After a typical teenager's thirst for beer—lots of beer—I developed a fondness for manhattans that probably took root when I was treated as a toddler to maraschino cherries from my parents' aromatic concoctions during their nightly cocktail hour. Alcohol counselors want to know when you had your first drink and what it was. The information helps in their studies of alcohol abuse patterns and gives them a clearer picture of your history of addiction. But when you're dangling at the frayed end of your rope at your last rodeo you don't care much about their data. Scraping a drunk off the floor and trying to ascertain the derivation of his problem by learning when he had his first toddy won't make his circumstances one bit rosier. But since the counselors insist on asking, my answer is five years old.

When our parents had late-night parties, my brother and I surveyed the aftermath in the morning and finished off what they and their guests had left in their glasses. The remnants were watered down from melted ice and a few had cigarette butts floating in them, but we managed to find enough to satisfy our curiosity and didn't understand that we were getting whacked in the process. One day Jim was sent home from school because he didn't feel well. He was plastered. I had a pretty good buzz on myself that morning, but I was in kindergarten and slept it off during naptime.

I was born an alcoholic, which is to say that I was born with the tendencies that enabled me to become one. What causes alcoholism or any addiction in one person and not another has been debated by medical science for decades. But there is little doubt now that addiction is a disease, and current studies are proving that it is neurological in nature. Scientists are zeroing in on exactly what occurs in the brain of an addict and why he is helpless to restrain the urges that compel him to consume more and more of his drug of choice even while being cognizant of its negative consequences.

The brain is programmed to warn us when we are playing where we don't belong, and also to recognize when we are being satisfied. Drugs interfere with our ability to tell the difference, and create an accelerated sense of craving that in addicts is uncontrollable. But some of us are simply more prone to addiction because of a combination of genetic and environmental factors with which, appropriately, I had been vastly over-served.

Everything in my upbringing—my childhood craving for attention in a volatile family, the incessant feelings of inadequacy and guilt, the thirst for the kind of contentment I thought only other people enjoyed, the need to be something or someone I wasn't, the instinct to entertain and clown around to camouflage my lack of self-esteem—combined to generate an addictive personality that would dominate my entire life and leave me a sitting duck. Moreover, since I was probably behind the garage shining my rocket when the will power and perseverance were being passed out, my destiny was sealed; although it is widely accepted that sheer will power alone is as effective against addiction as it is against diarrhea.

I was a borderline alcoholic by the time I was sixteen. For every beer a buddy would drink, I'd drink three or four. One morning I awoke with the side of my face cemented to a pillow, glued there by the puke that had erupted in my sleep and dried overnight. My father stood over me telling me to get up. When I raised my throbbing head the pillow came up with it and remained attached like a great white earmuff. He knew by the odor what had made me so sick and demanded to know how much I'd drunk and where I got it. I told him that a couple guys I worked with at the supermarket had some older kid buy us a six-pack after work, and that I'd drunk a can and a half of it and boy was I sorry. My father said he hoped I'd learned my lesson and he'd speak to me when he got home from work. The truth was that the co-workers and I had managed to get served at the bowling center lounge across the street from the market, and I'd chugged at least fifteen beers.

The drinking age in New York State was eighteen then, which meant that we were sneaking into bars at sixteen. Most of us carried phony ID, and if a bartender accepted us as old enough to be served, he cared not a lick how many drinks we had, as long as we didn't tear up the place, or whether we were driving. A DWI arrest in those days was unheard of. If a cop pulled you over and found you to be drunk, he'd escort you home to make sure you got there safe.

Once when I was fifteen my friend Jackie Maxwell and I were at a girl's house while her parents were out. We alternated missions, one of us trying to pick the lock on the liquor cabinet while the other tried jimmying the one on her precious Jewish panties. The lock that eventually yielded rewarded us with an unopened quart of gin, which I stuck in my pants and covered with my sweater.

We were hurriedly saying goodbye when the front door opened and in walked her mother. She spotted the bulge in my pants and said,

"Either you have something that doesn't belong to you, or you're a very big boy for your age." Jackie and I bolted. We stopped running and laughing five blocks away, where we opened the bottle and had our first encounter with the juniper. Our adolescent brains reasoned that we certainly couldn't take the bottle home and that it would be an awful waste to abandon it, so there was no other choice but to drink it. We stood right there in someone's front yard and drained the bottle in less than an hour.

You'd think that throwing up as many times as I did on the way home would pretty much cure a kid of ever wanting to mess with the hard stuff again. Such is part of the mysterious insidiousness of alcohol, and of other addictive goodies. Father Joseph Martin, known among recovering alcoholics for his no-nonsense AA lectures, spoke of the inexplicable attraction and subsequent fixation we develop for substances that we initially could barely get past our lips. The first time we inhaled a lungful of cigarette smoke we damn near choked to death, but nevertheless became slaves to two packs a day or more. Few of us can deny that our first swallow of coffee wasn't about the vilest thing we'd ever put in our mouths, yet we can now scarcely start a day without it. And that first swallow of hard liquor might just as well have been flaming gasoline, yet we can grow accustomed to drinking it by the half-gallon.

For many years my fluid of choice, after beer, was bourbon, and eventually vodka—the last being the preference of so many in the end when they're trying to conceal how much they drink. It starts with the misconception that vodka doesn't smell on your breath. It does. It smells like alcohol. When you drink as much of it on a daily basis as I did and your liver starts to have trouble dealing with it, you sweat it out and start smelling like rotting, fermenting potatoes. You drink vodka because you can mix it with anything, like your orange juice first thing in the morning. You may have started out on smooth and trendy expensive stuff, but as your intake increases taste and quality are no longer factors. You can hole up with $6-a-quart turpentine-tasting panther piss, secure in the knowledge that you've got the cheapest drug addiction on earth, and you can get another fix anywhere.

When you drink martinis they are very dry, partly because you're sophisticated, but mostly because you don't want vermouth taking up precious vodka space. Then you say to hell with the vermouth. Eventually you realize you aren't getting a big enough bang for your buck in the restaurants and taverns so you do a lot more drinking at home, first in rock glasses, then in water glasses, then without the ice, then often without the glass. Now you hide bottles because you're drinking a lot more than you want anyone to know—under sofas, in attic rafters, in your golf bag, above basement heating ducts, in the bushes outside in a foot of snow, in bookcases, beneath the tool bench, and under the seat of your car, where you always keep a pint in case you get stuck someplace where you can't get a drink, like at a stop sign.

You used to drink only after work and on weekends. You started drinking at lunch. Then *for* lunch. You drank more after work every night. Going to bed hammered became routine. The mornings got rougher so you started bracing yourself with a pick-me-up, just enough to get the gears working, to clear the fog. That was not the sign that you had the beginnings of a problem. It was the sign that it had been a problem all along, and that it had now taken over your life. You drank now because you had to, and you would never be the same.

Alcoholics develop a preternatural ability not only to hide their drinking and their drinks, but also to find drink—not unlike a hungry rodent in search of a few crumbs. Knowing I'd chug it all, my wife hid booze that she kept for friends in obscure spots around the house she considered the last places I'd look. I'd find them in minutes. Kay bought a fifth one day because we expected our dear friend Joan, who likes scotch. After Joan left I heard Kay go up to the attic. As soon as she left for work the next morning I hit the stairs. She had laid the bottle on its side under rolls of Christmas wrapping paper that were standing upright in a tall stereo speaker carton among a hundred other boxes and assorted crap. I scanned the attic and zeroed in on it immediately. Six of the rolls of wrapping paper were standing three inches higher than the others.

At the height of my dependency I was drinking close to two quarts of vodka every day, or the equivalent thereof. When you are hiding your drinking and having to sneak swigs when no one is looking, you make damn sure you take enough of a hit when you do get a chance in case another opportunity doesn't materialize soon enough. And you find yourself turning up the bottle and taking several long swallows of raw alcohol as if it were a soft drink.

Yeah, a cowboy can drink straight liquor like that.

15

Sliding

I was seeing Kay on a regular basis, but when she asked me to move in with her I was seriously disinclined. Full commitment to another woman was the last thing I wanted. I'd screwed up every relationship I'd had since leaving Abby, as each woman in turn discovered as Abby had that no amount of love could keep me home, or satisfied, or faithful. Each had suspected what she was getting herself into, but believed nonetheless that she was the one who could turn me around. I was content now to keep my relationships casual and physical in nature, but two factors made it difficult to think of Kay that way. She accepted without reservation the understanding that what she saw was exactly what she was going to get, and she was the most unassuming woman of such remarkable looks I'd ever met.

We rented a small house near the restaurant where she worked. Its contents included a Formica table and two dinette chairs in the kitchen and a dilapidated armchair in the living room. We added a waterbed and called the place furnished. Two weeks later we threw a New Year's Eve party for thirty friends. We ate veal French while sitting on the kitchen floor. Very chic.

I had been in and out of work at various taverns before landing a daytime bartending job at a newly opened upscale restaurant twenty miles outside of the city. It was a necktie and vest gig that required being polite and accommodating to a clientele of the well-heeled who owned horse farms, belonged to private clubs, and tipped as if the very act of leaving coins behind disgusted them. But it was a pleasant job in which I managed to maintain a semblance of coherency, principally because my shift was over before I got too noticeably hammered.

After about a year I was lured away by the owner of the neighborhood tavern I had frequented all my adult life. A nighttime position had opened up. This bar was four deep with hardcore drinkers every night. Their reciprocation for generous pouring made it the best bartending job in the city at the time. On a good night the bartenders made hundreds in tips, and they worked for it. I was as experienced as any of them and just as skilled. The job called for stamina, footwork, and a high degree of tolerance. It required waiting on the most difficult and demanding of customers, my own friends and people I'd known most of my life. I simply was not up to the task, and I should have known better.

To prepare myself for the day job in the country I routinely bought a pint of vodka to drink on the way in the morning and slammed back a couple quick vodkas when I got there, so that I already had a fine glow going by noon. I drank all day and copiously after work as well, of course. On Fridays I was required to work into the evening, and the additional hours of sampling the goods behind the bar made for a long day. Kay waitressed nights and I customarily went to her restaurant after my Friday shift for several more cocktails I didn't need at that point and a steak dinner I did need. We had just bought a new Monte Carlo. Driving it into the city from my late shift one winter night I smacked a curb with enough force to blow out both right tires. I parked the car off the road and set out on foot toward Kay's restaurant. The temperature was near zero with a numbing wind and driving snow. I had no hat or gloves, and I wore a medium-weight jacket and dress shoes. If I'd been sober I'd have known enough to give up the journey after a hundred yards, but I kept telling myself that the restaurant was just a little ways further. When I arrived I was near hypothermia and, worse, stone cold sober. I had walked five miles through a full-scale blizzard. I told Kay that I'd been run off the road by a Mustang full of crazy kids who'd probably been drinking. It was many years later that I admitted to having been derailed by a herd of pink elephants.

I was tiring of the drive to the gig in the country, and of the meager tip jar, and the job offer in the neighborhood tavern became difficult to decline. But for months it had been my habit to arrive home in the early evening blind drunk from my day shift. How could I expect to handle a nighttime job as demanding as the one I would now undertake?

I embarrassed myself any number of times over the years because of my drinking, but that new job proved to be one of the most humiliating. The other bartenders were themselves heavy juicers, but they knew from experience not to dip into the hooch until later in their shifts. I was already drunk when my shift started, and as my inability to cope with the demands of the job increased, so proportionately did my drinking. It became my custom to get half whacked before I even started my stint. It soon became obvious that I could not hold up my end, and I was let go. My fellow bartenders were among my closest friends. One of them, Corvette Jimmy, just recently told me about one Saturday when I'd worked the day shift, and was so hammered by two in the afternoon that I had to be carried out. I don't remember ever having been that drunk while working. Then again, how would I?

It was the early 1980s now and my father faced retirement. After his career in newspaper and television, he had become a senior editor with a prominent public relations firm, and upon retiring from that position he proposed forming a partnership with me in which we would operate a two-man, freelance public relations agency of our own. I had spent the past several years in the restaurant business, and I'm sure my lifestyle and lack of direction concerned him deeply. Aside from my musical aspirations I had done nothing of a professional or creative nature since leaving the newspaper business. He hoped that the partnership would get me back to the keyboard. Our targets would be minor accounts, doing the sort of publicity projects for which small companies and organizations would find the services of big PR outfits too costly. Our drawing card would be speed and reasonable prices. We'd do in a matter of days what a large agency would take weeks to produce, and at a fraction of the cost.

My father's name alone garnered us any number of accounts. Soon we were producing newsletters for several organizations, print ads for small companies, public relations campaigns, magazine articles, product profiles, brochures, scripts for radio commercials, speeches, even personal letters. We earned a reputation for being fast and reliable, and we made it our policy to charge fair rates for the time and effort we devoted to a project. Our hourly rate was substantial, but our invoices were never padded.

I continued to work part-time in various restaurants as cook or bartender, stayed just coherent enough to attend client meetings in suit and tie and produce the goods on days when we had assignments, yet still managed to maintain a career as full time sot. The old man and I never scheduled morning meetings with clients. We met at a tavern to prepare sufficiently for conferences and returned to the tavern after the meetings to celebrate landing another account and to warm our creative juices.

It was during this period that we got word from Uncle Tom of Migget's death. She had suffered considerably in her final months. My father and I had gone to Auburn to visit some months previously and had found her to be anything but the plump and jovial Mig we'd always known. She was frail and gaunt and it was all she could do to get out of a chair. She had given up smoking a few years before and had confessed to having even lost her taste for beer, an indication to us that her end must surely be at hand.

My father was deeply saddened by her death. His cousin had been his sole relative. Tom was now in poor health himself and wanted no services for Mig. I phoned him to express my condolences and to ask if there was anything I could do. He was grateful for my call. He'd been crazy about her. She was a lazy slob, smart as a whip, funny as hell and an absolute joy to be with, and beneath her stout breast had beaten a spacious heart in which there lived an inextinguishable love for a grand blue river.

As for the cottage, my siblings and I now owned half of it, the half that had been bequeathed to us by our grandmother after Mig's life use. Mig had willed Tom the half that had been hers in her own right from her mother, so any claim we had now remained in limbo as Tom continued to use the cottage himself, if sporadically. The opening and closing of a cottage and its routine maintenance are a lot of work that Tom was surely not up to, but any help he may have required he did not seek from us. All I knew at that point was that I owned a fourth of half a cottage that I had no access to anyway.

As my father and I continued to work together he gradually turned over to me a responsibility he had maintained for most of his professional career, that of Rochester correspondent for Fairchild Publications in New York City, producers of the most influential fashion and retail trade publications in the business, whose titles include *Women's Wear Daily, the Daily News Record, Brides, W, Details, Menswear, Jane, Vitals, Home Furnishing News, Footwear News, Supermarket News*, and others. They paid top dollar per column inch of copy submitted, and since Rochester still preserved at least some of its once-renowned status as a vital clothing manufacturing and retailing center, assignments came regularly. My father took great pride in his association with Fairchild. The assignments began coming my way as he groomed me to be his successor, with Fairchild's blessing, preparing for the day I would take over for him.

After my father died it took me all of about four months to totally ruin the lot of my professional prospects because of the interference they posed on my recreation. Without the old man around to keep me half-focused, I neglected my Fairchild assignments until they ultimately stopped coming. In a matter of months I destroyed an association my father had nurtured for twenty-five years. And, without my father's good name to sustain our little business, requests for my services dwindled away to nothing, especially after I began showing up for meetings with a noticeable bag on.

A top PR agency farmed out to me an assignment that called for five short articles on design concepts being considered at Eastman Kodak Co. These were to be general information pieces for one of

Kodak's own in-house newsletters—nothing of a technical nature that required research or specialized knowledge. All I had to do was briefly interview some low-level executives and produce reports on the proposed innovations that involved a total of only six or eight pages of double-spaced copy.

The interviews and writing would require ten or twelve hours in all, for which I was paid $500 in advance—a handsome wage for a part-time freelancer in those days. I had completed two interviews and had not yet scheduled my next when I was summoned to the director's office of the PR outfit that had engaged me. He told me that one of the department heads I had interviewed had called to report that I'd shown up for our 10 a.m. session stinking drunk. I was dismissed on the spot. I had embarrassed him and his company. He told me to get help for my obvious problem, and to keep the $500. It was a personal gesture. He had been a good friend and professional associate of my father's, and a fellow member at his golf club for twenty-some years.

As my father struggled in his final days, I faced the inevitability of his death with my usual cowardice, drinking it away and pretending it wasn't happening. I regretted all those years during which the gap between us had been so immense, and I cherished now the past few years that we had at last been father and son.

He was editor of the local Auto Club newspaper, the next issue of which would be his last. As his strength seeped away and his discomfort escalated, he was adamant about finishing that final issue. He wouldn't leave it mid-stream for someone else to finish, and with my help he got it out on time. The very next day his pain became so fierce that he consented to go to the hospital, though we had no idea that his life would end in a matter of hours. They hooked him up to an array of equipment but said there was no hope. The cancer was everywhere, including his spine. How he had endured his last few weeks was beyond me. Anyone else would have said to hell with the newspaper. Knowing as I did the dedication he had always devoted to his craft, I supposed he had never missed a deadline in his life, and had refused to miss his last one, even while aware that he was dying.

As the morphine carried him off to another world, we were informed that we were welcome to stay with him if we wished, but nothing could be done to save him. There was no telling how long he might hold on. We might just as well go home and get some rest, they said. I didn't need rest. I needed drink. I had to handle that awful chapter the only way I knew how. When the hospital called to report that he was gone, I thanked God for taking him quickly. I wanted his suffering to be over, so that my suffering could be over. I would later view my selfishness then as one of my most inexcusable transgressions. The need to drown my own sorrows had been more imperative to me than that of being at my father's side when he died. Six months later I was in Pennsyltucky, splashing soup down my front, and wallowing in regret.

When I picture my father now it is often as I so frequently found him on summer evenings when I was a teen. Mother would routinely retire early, leaving the mess she'd made in the kitchen preparing dinner. My father cleaned the kitchen and did the dishes almost every night. Then he would settle on the screened side porch and play solitaire, a radio and a Genny Cream Ale at his side, and listen to the broadcast of the Rochester Red Wings playing baseball at Silver Stadium. The sound of the announcer's voice, the background noise of the stadium crowd, the crack of the bat were like music to his ears, like the clickity-clack of his Underwood typewriter.

Mother once surprised him with a word processor for his birthday, long before the advent of home computers. He asked what she expected him to do with it. It had a spell-check built right into it, she told him. He asked her when he'd ever been known to misspell a word. It even had a thesaurus built into it, she said. He reminded her that there wasn't a word in the English language for which he wasn't already aware of every possible synonym. She said that it printed out pages of copy. So did his typewriter, he told her. She said that the greatest thing about it was that it didn't make any noise. He was already convinced that the contraption was useless to him, but that sealed it.

It occurred to me one day after he died that in spite of all the rotten choices I'd made in my life, and all the times I'd disappointed him, and the jams he'd bailed me out of, and the embarrassment I must have caused him, and the strings he'd pulled to arrange opportunities I'd frittered away, he had never once told me he was ashamed of me. He seemed to have had a bottomless wellspring of hope that somehow, some day, I'd turn things around. I had no idea where all that hope came from, because I had no idea what it was like to be a parent.

16

Sally

When I graduated from the Pennsyltucky detox ward on my eighth day I had amassed enough coherency to believe that I was going to live and was now strong enough not to take any more guff from these evangelists. The counselor to whom I was now assigned for rehabilitation with about fifteen others was a pudgy hay-haired woman about my age named Sally, who dressed like the Michelin Tire man. She was a rosy-cheeked bubbly sort who impressed me as someone whose idea of raising hell had been sneaking a second ladle of fruit punch at the prom. She seemed to know already about my tumultuous upbringing, no doubt from reports of my counseling sessions in detox, and focused on it immediately.

I should have known my mind wasn't right when I became infuriated by her derogatory remarks about my loving family. Her reference to my mother as an "obviously very sick woman" brought me to my feet. How dare she attack my dear sweet mommy like that? She threw some jabs at my father and siblings as well, characterizing me as a classic middle child in a highly dysfunctional family who was destined to grow up feeling neglected, left out, and unwelcome. Actually, that's exactly how I had always felt, but where did she get off telling me so? I was struck by one comment in particular, however, when she said, "If it's any consolation, you didn't stand a chance."

As a new recruit I was typically clueless about alcoholism in general and the process of recovery in particular; but before I could allow any intelligence on the subject to worm into my brain I had issues to resolve with this counselor. Frankly, I didn't care for her attitude. I'd only been her guest for a week before I'd had my fill of her endless recitations from the beloved Big Book, the AA bible, the teetotaler's torah, which she seemed to have memorized even to the extent of knowing exactly what passage appeared in which paragraph on every page. I asked a question and she answered with a page number. She seemed incapable of engaging in any sort of casual conversation that wasn't AA-approved or rehab-sanctioned, and no matter what I said she had a perfect response cocked and ready to fire as soon as I opened my yap, accompanied invariably by the *you poor lost little boy* smirk on her face.

Whenever I had occasion to deal with other counselors I discovered they weren't any different. It seemed like the entire staff had been brainwashed. Since I am inquisitive and analytical by nature and take offense at being put in situations where I am not allowed to voice an opinion or share an observation, I was tagged a wise guy and a troublemaker from the get-go.

Drug and alcohol rehab is like military basic training for the mind. In the Army I had learned that the theory behind running recruits into the ground during boot camp was to wear them down physically to the point of exhaustion, then methodically to build them back up to peak strength and endurance. In drug and alcohol rehab, they do the same thing with your head. If I'd been able to employ the same degree of acceptance in rehab that I had in the service, my vacation in

Pennsyltucky would have gone a lot smoother.

When a drill sergeant had told me to give him twenty push-ups for no apparent reason, I'd learned to shut up and give him the twenty, lest it become fifty. But when a rehab counselor insisted on playing mind games that appeared to serve no other purpose than to yank my yams, I needed to know why. I figured I had that right. I had in essence hired these people at considerable expense to provide me a service, and I was entitled to question their methods. I felt as though I'd been tricked, caught off guard in a confused and demoralized state, and captured by a ruthless band of know-it-all, been-there-and-done-that psychology candy-stripers who relished feasting on my fears and weaknesses and treating me like some sort of low-life.

At one point I told Sally I didn't like being bullied.

"How are you being bullied?"

"What would you call it? I'm in a no-win situation. I'm wrong as soon as I open my mouth. You can say whatever you want about me and if I don't agree it's because I'm in denial. If I question some facet of the rehab, I'm being belligerent. If I don't do exactly what you decide is best for me, I can get thrown out of here. No matter what I say gets twisted around to prove your point. I can't make a comment without being treated like I got brain damage."

One night it got so cold in my dormitory room that I couldn't sleep. When I asked Sally about it the next morning I heard that I needed to work on my acceptance, that I wasn't focusing on my sobriety, that I needed to let go and let God. She gave me everything I needed to hear except a simple answer. I found out later that the furnace had broken down, and when I next saw Sally I confronted her about it.

"Why couldn't you just tell me the furnace broke down?"

"Why is it so important to you?"

"I just wondered why you couldn't give me a straight answer about a simple mechanical malfunction that would explain why I froze my butt off all night."

"Why can't you just let it go?"

"Why can't you just answer the question?"

"Why are you getting so angry about it?"

"Because I don't understand the runaround. Why is it so taboo to answer a simple question about a furnace? Because broken furnaces aren't covered in the Big Book, so we're not allowed to discuss it?"

"Why don't you try the serenity prayer?"

"Never mind. Forget it. I'm sorry I brought it up. It wasn't cold in my room. It was really rather toasty. I must have been in denial."

"Now you're being childish."

"No, I'm being bullied."

She smiled.

When Sally eventually revealed that she was herself an alcoholic, I thought she was putting us on. I soon learned that most of the staff members were recovering addicts. The blind leading the blind, I thought. Terrific. But in time this knowledge would lead me to a basic truth about the recovery process: that the people who know best about what you're going through are those who have been through it themselves. I would also hear for the first time, if not yet believe, that alcoholics remain so for life, no matter how long they manage to stay sober. How encouraging.

You meet all kinds in a rehab: potheads, skin-pokers, coke freaks, crack and crystal heads, speed-junkies, juicers, pill-poppers—everyone addicted to something and some of them to everything, though in varying degrees. I met a young woman in her mid twenties so ravished by long-term heroin use that she'd already lost all her teeth, and a boy of seventeen whose parents sent him away because they caught him smoking a joint. Some were only there to appease a spouse, an employer, a judge. Some risked losing everything if they didn't straighten out. Some had already lost it.

This rehab was top shelf, with a reputation as one of the finest facilities in the country in terms of the quality of its staff and accommodations. Compared to many it was a country club with landscaped grounds and comfortable quarters, terrific food and modern amenities. But the pleasant surroundings did not offer its guests a better chance of success. Those who were fortunate enough to land here would benefit from the tutelage of exceptional counselors and therapists, and find their journey to recovery more pleasant than in other venues, but not one iota easier, and with absolutely no guarantees.

A few patients had arrived in their own cars, which were stored in a barn on the grounds. It was winter, and their owners were allowed each week to run their engines for a while so the batteries wouldn't go dead. These visits were conducted as a group and closely monitored, though the vehicles had already been thoroughly searched for drugs and booze by a team of staffers that probably knew of more potential hiding places than a DEA agent or border inspector.

One guy always seemed to sport an upgraded attitude and suspicious breath after visiting his car, so he earned special scrutiny. Each time he went to the barn he'd start his car, open the hood, poke around in the engine compartment checking this and that and goosing the throttle, but could not be observed putting a bottle to his face. After each visit staffers searched the car but still couldn't find anything. Finally they got him. He had filled his windshield wiper reservoir with vodka and they caught him sucking it out through a straw.

One young woman, though her room and belongings had been searched like everyone else's, also seemed to be wearing a glassy eye on occasion. The staffers knew she was getting something somewhere. Eventually the gift shop proprietor reported that she routinely bought a couple of cans of hairspray every other day, which she ultimately admitted to having emptied into a glass and drinking for the alcohol content. A vodka gimlet it wasn't, but in the desert a drink's a drink.

After two weeks of rehab, during which we in Sally's group had begun revealing ourselves to her and to one another, Sally began employing strategies of Gestalt therapy, a technique of anger management that focuses on awareness of emotions and behaviors in the present rather than in the past. Instead of continuing to suppress old emotions, the patient is encouraged to bring them to the fore in an effort to resolve long-suffered issues by meeting them head on and dealing with them. The result is often not pretty.

Sally determined that my foremost problem was the guilt I suffered over, among other things, the abandonment of my children. Her remedy was for me to write a letter to my daughter Wendy, who was then in college at Potsdam NY, telling her where I was and why.

"I will like hell," I said.

"Why not?" asked Sally.

"Because my daughter, last I heard, is doing very well in school without my help and without knowing anything about me. I haven't seen or talked to her since she was a baby. Leave her out of this. I've tortured her and her mother enough. I'm not going to disturb her schooling and try to weasel back into her good graces at this stage of the game, telling her the bum father who walked out on her and her brother is at a drunk farm and needs her sympathy. I won't do it."

"I didn't say a thing about asking her for sympathy. But you need to open up to her about where you are and why you're here. It's imperative to your recovery."

"*My* recovery? What about *her* recovery? She's spent the last sixteen years forgetting that I exist. Now I'm just gonna pop in with my sad-ass story after all this time? Leave her alone."

"I strongly recommend it for your treatment."

"And I just as strongly disagree. I'm sorry. I won't do it, and you have no right to make me do it. This is a personal affair."

Sally then asked the rest of the group what they thought, and of course they all agreed wholeheartedly that I deserved to be drawn and quartered and to suffer an inordinate amount of emotional pain by writing my daughter, because nothing cheers you up in a rehab quite like seeing some other poor slob get slapped around.

"Let's try an experiment," Sally said in her best kindergarten manner. She put two chairs facing one another in the center of the room and told me to sit in one. She told me to close my eyes and picture my daughter, then to hold the vision for two or three minutes. She told me to open my eyes and pretend that my daughter was in the other chair facing me. Then she told me to talk to my daughter and tell her what I was feeling.

"I want you to say to her exactly what you would say if she were really sitting here, all the things you'd like her to know, all the things you've never been able to tell her."

I tried to imagine talking to her.

Sally said, "Out loud."

"Out loud? In front of everybody?"

"In front of everybody. Do it."

I did, haltingly at first, embarrassed. And then out it came, as if from an obscure compartment of my soul that I didn't know existed. Sobbing, shaking, crying out as I had wanted to in the detox shower stall *I'm sorry I'm sorry I'm sorry*, and wilting into a fetal position with my arms around my knees. Before a roomful of strangers I sat center stage whimpering, quivering, mentally and physically spent, my face dripping. I had carried on for a good ten minutes and had experienced what may have been a full-fledged breakdown.

After a long pause Sally said softly, "Now I want you to write that letter, and say to your daughter what you just said here. When it's finished you will read the letter to the group, and give it to me to mail so that we'll all know exactly what you wrote. And then, when your daughter writes back, her letter will be given to you here in group, so that you can open it and read it for the first time, out loud, in front of the others."

"Come on. This isn't fair. I can't believe you're making me do this. I can't believe you made me do what I just did."

"Listen to me. That was the first display of honest emotion you've shown since you got here, do you know that? You didn't question it or analyze it. It just came flying out. It was your true feelings coming to the surface, maybe for the first time in your life. Nobody here forced that out of you. Now I want you to understand something. This is exactly why we're here. We have a tremendous amount of work to do in a short time because you have a lot of baggage to unload. We have to seriously concentrate on that for you to have any chance of recovery. We can't be wasting our time worrying about why you weren't properly informed about a furnace breaking down. The furnace was fixed. It was already fixed by the time you came in here ranting about it. It wasn't worth worrying about. You're complaining about a stupid furnace and your very life is on the line here. You understand what I'm saying?"

"I guess. Why do I have to read her letter in front of everybody?"

"Because now we all know what you're feeling and what you need to do to fill this huge void in your life. You've shared that with us, and you need to share the outcome with us."

"She won't write back."

"Yes she will."

"What if she doesn't?"

"She will."

Over the next several days I saw others in our group similarly brought to their knees. Sally seemed particularly proficient at scavenging for soft spots and coaxing them out of hiding. While growing up, one guy had been beaten by his father. He said he'd been consumed by resentment his whole life. Sally told him to imagine his father in Wendy's chair. She gave him a bataka bat, an anger stick, and told him to tell his father how he felt. He didn't say a word, but he beat the shit out of that chair. Sally had to jump in and stop him when he discarded the club and started beating the wooden arms with his bare knuckles.

I don't remember now exactly what I wrote to Wendy. I don't even remember where I got her address, but probably through Kay. I remember telling Sally that I was having trouble with the letter because I couldn't get the wording right, and her telling me that I was fighting myself again, trying to say things the way I thought they should sound instead of just saying them. Let the volcano erupt, she said, and stop worrying about the lava.

Wendy wrote back immediately and I read her letter in front of the group. She told me how happy she was that I was getting professional help. She told me she understood that I had a problem. She told me she was sorry that I had to go through this but that it was surely for the best and that I was in good hands. And she told me she loved me. I had not laid eyes on this child, this young woman, or spoken to her since I walked out of her life before she was three years old, and she told me she loved me.

As I sat in group, sobbing like a kid and staring at the letter, reading it over and over to myself, Sally said, "Welcome aboard. I see a ray of light, and I think you see it too."

17

Hero

At the conclusion of my rehab I was given a send-off in a gathering of fellow patients and counseling staff in the large foyer of the main building. Departing guests were expected to share with the congregation their gratitude for everyone's support and hope for everyone else's recovery. The ceremony culminated in a spirited group chorus of Manfred Mann's *Do Wah Ditty Ditty* while I made the rounds collecting hugs and good wishes. When I came to Sally she hugged me warmly, looked straight into my eyes, and said, "You're not going to make it."

I assumed she said that to all her departing charges as an incentive, although she had remarked many times that I still suffered a great deal of denial, which I had repeatedly denied. I had consented to seek professional help for what I recognized as a genuine drinking problem. I had yielded to their endless rules and regs and adhered to their precious policies. I had honored the all-important first step of the twelve-step program by admitting that *I was powerless over alcohol and that my life had become unmanageable.* I had completed thirty-five days of rehabilitation during which on several occasions I'd been wholly stripped of my dignity and reduced to a whimpering puddle of tears, baring my very soul to strangers and sharing secrets of my life I had never before revealed. What exactly was I denying?

In the final week I had been required to have a tête-à-tête with any staff member with whom I chose to do the fifth step of the AA program: *We admitted to God, to ourselves, and to another human being the exact nature of our wrongs.* This is where you get to spill what if anything is still left of your guts. I had chosen to do the step with Sally and had mentioned in passing my relationship as a teenager with Roy Pratt, and what I believed to be his murder. I had never been troubled by my relationship with him, but the way he'd died still bothered me. How shameful it now seemed that the last time I had seen Roy, a week before his death, he had asked me if I'd swiped a bottle of whiskey from his liquor cabinet and taken it to a party, as witnessed by another of his young friends who had obviously squealed on me. I denied it, of course, so the last thoughts he'd had of me were that I was a liar and a thief.

Sally had said, "You mean to tell me you were sexually molested from the time you were twelve until you were fifteen and you never thought this was important enough to bring up in group? You've been carrying this baggage around all your life?"

"I didn't figure it had anything to do with my drinking."

"You were molested for three of your most formidable years by a homosexual pedophile, and you didn't think that had any lasting effect on you?"

"I never thought I was molested. I thought it was like a baby getting his balls tickled. I didn't care who was doing it. It felt good."

It wasn't that Sally was shocked about that chapter in my life. I never thought of it as being all that shocking myself. But she evidently viewed my casual reference to it so late in my rehab as an indication that there still remained within me some unopened cupboards and dark corners that would deter my recovery. I think she had also suspected that I just wasn't with the program yet, that I hadn't fully surrendered.

In spite of her doubts I felt like a million bucks. I had gained a dozen needed pounds from having adhered to a steady, nutritious diet that included a hearty breakfast served at the proper time of day for that meal, not at 3 a.m. in a greasy diner on the way home from closing the saloons. I had not had a drop of alcohol or a drug in five weeks. I had hope and energy and a wealth of confidence. I felt like superman and I had no desire to drink. I was ready to test my wings.

Throughout my vacation Sally had insisted that I was cross-addicted. I had entered detox hooked on Xanax and, she claimed, as addicted to pot as I was to alcohol, an analysis with which I had vehemently disagreed. Her theory was that since I invariably smoked pot when I drank alcohol, and visa versa, I was obviously powerless over both. But in my mind it wasn't marijuana and hashish or my sporadic affairs with coke and a variety of other pharmaceuticals that had cost me a family and careers or was ruining my present marriage or destroying my liver or rendering me unemployable. I'd been smoking pot nearly as long as I'd been drinking, but I could take it or leave it. I had gone without it many times for extended periods when it wasn't available or I couldn't afford it. Sally remarked that the fact that I repeatedly went back to pot after refraining from it was evidence enough of an addiction, and that the ultimate goal was absolute abstinence—clean and sober, not just dry. But that was for the saints. I went to rehab to keep from drinking myself to death, not to become a Mormon. In any event, my reluctance to see the light in this regard was evidence to Sally that I could only recover on my own terms. At least she got something right.

Another concept I had difficulty swallowing was that of continuing involvement with AA after rehab. Once I returned home it would be mandatory to attend weekly after-care sessions with a therapist for two months, and on top of that to attend ninety AA meetings in ninety days, just for starters. I had never excelled in math but that sounded very much like a meeting every damn day for three months. Who were they kidding? I had just devoted five weeks of my life to their relentless AA propaganda through God knows how many lectures, movies, demonstrations, readings, therapy sessions, discussions, and group fun and games, listening to horror stories from people I couldn't care less about, enduring their tearful accounts of beating their wives, swallowing handfuls of pills, falling out windows, embezzling funds, burning down houses, robbing convenience stores, slicing their wrists, muling coke from Colómbia, forgetting where they lived, walking naked down Main St., hiding bottles in trees, waking up in strange countries, hemorrhaging from multiple orifices, losing millions of dollars, smashing up cars and boats, tearing up taverns, throwing up on the Christmas dinner table, spending weekends in drunk tanks, pawning their wives' jewelry, whoring themselves out for drugs, sleeping in dumpsters, tripping down stairs and breaking their legs, losing $200,000-a-year jobs, molesting their own daughters, poisoning the neighbor's dog, stealing fire trucks, punching cops, and being abducted by aliens. And the counselors thought I needed ninety more straight days of that drivel.

What's more, beyond the ninety days, I was expected to continue attending meetings on a regular if not daily basis until the end of time, or until I dropped dead from an overdose of maximum strength boredom, whichever came first. I personally felt that I had devoted quite enough of my life to this particular project and it was high time to move on.

I had told Kay that under no circumstances was she to throw any sort of party for me on my return. Even in the hopeless state of denial in which the counselors insisted I still wallowed, I had the sense to realize that a party with the friends I'd spent twenty years drinking and drugging with wasn't a good idea. Besides, I didn't want the attention. Despite feeling revitalized, and proud to have completed my tour of duty, I had been humbled like never before and needed some time to find my legs.

When I came through the airport gate in Rochester and embraced my beautiful Kay, I felt like I'd been released from ten years in prison. When we got home I was greeted by a "Welcome Home, Hero" banner Kay had strung across the kitchen doorway. The second thing I did was make love to my wife. The first thing I did was smoke a joint the size of a ballpark frank.

***

Probably foremost in the mind of a hero returning from the trenches of rehab is his bewilderment over how he will be accepted and treated by friends and loved ones. While he may feel physically rejuvenated and blessed to have been given a new lease on life, he nevertheless considers himself an outcast who had to *go away* to treat his weakness, and he feels anything but proud of it.

But that is a fear fabricated in his own mind by his own paranoia and uncertainty. It will fade in time as he adjusts to his new lifestyle, provided that he or she in fact continues to pursue a new lifestyle by following a program of preventive maintenance. The real difficulty that faces him, however, lies not in his loved-ones' acceptance, but in their ignorance. They have no more knowledge or understanding of his disease than they did before he went away.

Most rehabilitation programs also offer AlAnon sessions and other counseling services to educate family members affected by an addicted loved one, but too few families take advantage of them. After all, *they* aren't the ones with the problem; why should *they* need counseling? And though the addict may have learned a thing or two about his disease, his loved ones generally have not. Upon his return, they consider him fixed.

When I had departed for Pennsyltucky I had directed Kay to say nothing to anyone about where I was, particularly her family. Her mother and siblings—themselves moderate social imbibers who belonged to that incomprehensible genre referred to as normal drinkers—were certainly aware that I enjoyed my cocktails with a good deal more gusto than most people, but I doubted that the prospect of my being an alcoholic even occurred to them. I'd been in rehab only a day when I received a lovely note from Kay's mother wishing me well. This was followed by letters and cards from longtime friends, a couple of whom had recently embarked on a life of sobriety themselves. So much for my big secret.

When I saw Kay's family for the first time after coming home they were as warm yet reserved as always. To avoid embarrassment for either them or me they spared me questions about my ordeal and chose to act as if nothing was different, thankfully—unlike most people who don't know what to say and inevitably say too much or try too hard to be accommodating, and in doing so make the situation much more awkward than it need be.

The first social outing Kay and I attended was a league bowling banquet at a restaurant. Kay asked if I wanted a beverage and I said ginger ale. She went to the bar while I took a seat at a table. Then I heard her calling to me across the lounge, "Would you rather have coffee, or a lemonade or a 7-Up or a club soda or a coke or a cup of tea or ..." I barked back, "Ginger ale is fine, dammit! Thank you very much."

When she brought it to me she asked why I was so annoyed. I said, "Because it isn't necessary to recite the entire fucking list of every nonalcoholic beverage known to man. I told you what I wanted. Ginger ale. Ginger ale is fine. If I'd wanted something else I would have said so. They didn't remove my brain."

Touchy? You bet.

A week later I picked Kay up at her restaurant and saw her fellow workers for the first time since rehab. I sat at the bar briefly while she finished her shift. The bartender was afraid to approach me. I thought, what is this, a test? Is he waiting to see if I'll order a cocktail? Finally I said, "John, could I get a ginger ale?" John sprang to life, saying "Ginger ale, you got it, Buddy. Let's see, we also got cola and iced tea or I can get you a coffee or we got V-8 juice and orange juice and grapefruit and Perrier and ..."

"John," I whispered, "just give me a goddam ginger ale. Thank you." Kay told me later she'd heard me and thought I'd been rude, that John was only trying to help. I told her that if John wanted to help all he had to do was ask if he could get me something like he would any other customer who walked through the door, not treat me like a leper.

Kay's family could not be more contrasting to mine. Kay lost her dad to an aneurysm when she was only fifteen and her mother raised five kids on her own. It is clear to me where Kay got the unpretentious and straight-shooting manner for which I love her so much. I have yet to hear her mother raise her voice. In her home or in any of Kay's sibling's homes I have never heard a malicious remark. All families have disagreements and arguments, and no family escapes difficulties along the way. But in Kay's family I had never witnessed the kind of vindictiveness and vengeance and anger that had always been almost routine in my family. When I'd first started seeing Kay I thought of her family as being so unperturbed and quiet and respectful of one another as to be downright abnormal. It took me years to understand that that's the way families are supposed to be.

It's quite possible that the extent of my addiction hadn't escaped Kay's family after all. I'd given them reason to find my sanity somewhat suspect to begin with. Early in my relationship with Kay, on only my second visit to her mother's for a family cookout, I'd been put in charge of grilling the pork chops. Kay and her mother had gone to the store for incidentals, and I'd been left with her two brothers and two sisters and a large rambunctious dog that spent half his life locked in the cellar when no one was home, and the other half demolishing the house and anything else in his path. I'd been into the vodka pretty good and was headed out the back door with a platter of chops when Trigger appeared out of nowhere and tried to beat me to it. He'd knocked my feet out from under me, I'd launched the pork chops skyward as I crashed through the glass of the storm door, shattering it, and had landed sprawled in a pile of broken glass with my arms dripping blood from several sizeable gashes.

I'd run the dog down, cornered him against the house, grabbed him by the loose skin of his stomach, hoisted him over my head, and was in the process of body-slamming him to the ground when Kay's younger brother, then about thirteen, had appeared. I'd thrown the dog down so hard that he'd bounced off the patio about two feet and I'd punched it in the mouth a few times while Mickey looked on in horror.

Incidentally, never punch a dog in the mouth.

I'd caught a lengthy canine tooth between two knuckles and imbedded it in my hand about half an inch. The dog had been rendered unconscious by my beating or sheer fright or both. My arms had been awash in blood, with my impaled fist beginning to spew.

When Kay and her mother had returned from the store they found me hosing myself off, a river of red trickling down the driveway, and the younger brother in the back yard sobbing and trying to revive the dumb mutt. After the dust had settled I'd thought it best to console the kid as best I could.

"Mickey," I'd said. "Do you understand what happened here today?"

"Sure I do. You got drunk and tried to kill my dog."

***

The scene was a little different at my mother's house upon my return. My brother and sisters had been invited over to welcome me home. When I walked in I could see that they all had drinks, but there was no liquor out on the kitchen counter as usual. Everyone had hugs and kisses and compliments about how well I looked, though my mother was as aloof as I thoroughly expected her to be.

We sat in the living room as my siblings asked about what they'd done to me in rehab. I was full of newly acquired knowledge about alcoholism and recovery that I shared like an expert on the subject, which I surely felt I was. Every once in a while one of them would get up and go to the kitchen and I'd hear glasses clinking and ice cubes rattling as another drink was made. It was going to be a long haul. I envisaged a lifetime of hearing liquid gurgling and cupboard doors closing faintly in the background, of listening to bartenders and hostesses recite long lists of beverages I was allowed to have, of knowing that I was dry but that nobody else seemed to be, and of swallowing the reality that the chaotic, depressing world had not changed at all. I still had to live in it with no place to hide. Dodge City was as dangerous as ever, and my gun had been taken away.

18

Reborn

Two months later, as Upstate New York began to awaken from another dreary winter, I completed my post-rehab therapy and was on my own to lead a sober life, or at least as sober as I intended. I was still smoking pot but had not taken a drink. AA meetings were a compulsory part of my aftercare program and I'd been required to report each week how many I'd attended. My therapist was herself a recovering alcoholic who frequented area meetings, so I couldn't fool her for long if I lied about what meetings I'd been to.

With that obligation behind me now, I felt secure in my sobriety and couldn't see that the AA meetings were doing much for me. After all, if I were overwhelmed by a desire to put my lips to a martini, no AA meeting was going to keep me from it. The only reason all those other people went to meetings was that the gatherings obviously provided the only social life the poor bastards had left. I had no intention of spending my evenings in stuffy church basements sipping decaf and *sharing* with a bunch of boring losers who desperately needed that kind of camaraderie.

One day that spring when I visited my mother she surprised me with a letter she'd received from Uncle Tom's lawyer. Tom, now in too poor health to use the cottage any longer, had apparently elected to put his half ownership of the cottage on the market and was giving our family first crack at it, since my sibs and I already held claim to the other half. This came as quite a blow. Tom had told me personally that he planned to bequeath his share of the cottage to me because I was the only one of the children who had visited and communicated with him or Mig over the years or had shown an interest in it. That prospect notwithstanding, we had been led to believe back when Gramma died that we'd end up with the property because Tom and Mig had no other heirs.

Mother reasoned that he evidently needed the money, what with his mounting medical bills and his having to hire help to care for him and his home in Auburn. Therefore, since she was sitting pretty with the entirety of our father's sizeable estate and knew that none of her children had a pot to piss in, she offered to purchase Tom's half in order to keep the property wholly in the family. We weren't about to refuse her offer. The necessary legalities were immediately undertaken, starting with an appraisal of the property.

The cottage is a two-story post-and-beam, board-and-batten structure with vast wrap-around front porch, living room and dining room, good-sized kitchen, four upstairs bedrooms and a sleeping porch, on a lot of 9,000 square feet with fifty-six feet of shoreline. It is prime waterfront property to be sure, in what is proudly referred to as "the heart of the Thousand Islands." When the appraiser submitted a figure of only $64,000 we found it preposterous. I phoned him to question the appraisal, and he explained that $56,000 of that figure was for the waterfront footage alone. The cottage itself was worth a mere $8,000, such was the extent of its deterioration.

The appraiser added that the structure was in such poor shape that it could realistically be considered more a liability than an asset because the property was in essence more valuable without it. Should the cottage go on the market, a new owner would be inclined to eye it in terms of demolition costs, since removing it entirely and building a new structure would be far more practical and feasible than repairing and upgrading to code a building that was already a hundred years old and in such deplorable condition.

Mother subsequently purchased Tom's half for $32,000, and no sooner had the ink dried on that transaction than she made an offer to my brother and younger sister that they couldn't resist. Maris then lived in Michigan with her second husband, with no plans to move back east, and didn't foresee having much opportunity to enjoy the cottage. When Mother offered her $8,000 for her eighth share, Maris grabbed it. My brother Jim, always in need of cash to support the country club lifestyle he could scarcely afford, accepted Mother's offer just as readily.

With those transactions completed, there could be heard a faint and distant wailing that most certainly issued from my grandmother as she rolled over in her grave. Ida Jean now owned a controlling three-quarters of the property, which was precisely what Gramma had hoped to prevent by bequeathing her share to us grandchildren. But I was not then concerned with these details. All I knew was that as a family we now owned the cottage in its entirety, and that we were free to open and enjoy it as soon as weather permitted. It would need a lot of work and we were anxious to begin.

Suddenly my new life had taken on new life. I had shaken off the demons that had controlled me, and now I stood on the threshold of realizing a thirty-year-old boyhood dream of summering on the river again. I pictured raising the flag in front of the pavilion. I saw myself selling penny candy to children from behind the counter in the little store. I could hear the back screen door whapping shut. I pictured leaping into the cold clear deep and sunning peacefully on shoreline bedrock. I thought of lazing in wicker rockers on the wide screened porch, watching the great river slide to the sea. I could smell the swaying pine trees and hear the hooting freighters. I could almost taste molasses cookies and warm apple pie.

***

For several years before the cottage came into my life again, Kay and I vacationed with friends at a resort in nearby Alexandria Bay each summer. Along the shore was a large Victorian cottage with individual rooms for rent like a bed and breakfast. Our group of eight or ten reserved the entire cottage and partied unremittingly, boated and sunbathed and fished, picnicked on unoccupied islands, cooked on grills in the yard, inhaled cocktails and passed doobies on the veranda, stayed up half the night playing board games and carousing, and boisterously patronized area restaurants, a couple of which asked us not to return.

Kay and I always stopped by the cottage to see Mig and Tom. They would insist we stay for dinner but we'd graciously decline. A look at the kitchen and a whiff of the prevailing aroma were all the deterrents we needed. She and Tom kept a herd of seven or eight rotund cats. One named Lancelot weighed thirty-eight pounds. The animals were fed nothing but raw calves liver that was cut up on the kitchen table throughout the day and apparently served there as well. The tabletop was decorated with an unforgettable montage of dried bloody liver stains matted with cat hair that had apparently never been molested by a sponge. The whole cottage smelled like a litter box because the whole cottage *was* a litter box. I have long wondered whether Mig was really that much of a slob or just kept the cottage that way to discourage visitors, her own kin among them. The cottage had certainly never been like that when Gramma was alive.

On our first excursion to the cottage as a family after acquiring it, then, we were not unprepared for a considerable mess. We suspected that Tom had put as much effort into the routine maintenance as Mig had put into housecleaning, so it came as no surprise to discover at first glance that it was in dire need of painting, screen replacement throughout, a new roof, and myriad repairs large and small. Gardens that had once been thick with blooms were indistinguishable. The back lawn was overgrown and strewn with fallen twigs and branches. The front yard by the river was six inches deep in pine needles. At least four towering evergreens were dead and would have to be removed. The enormity of the work ahead was obvious before we even opened the cottage door. What awaited us inside, however, was beyond even our most liberal expectations.

The cottage had apparently been abandoned for the last couple of years. The odor of cat waste had been replaced by a damp sour mustiness like that of a closed-off dirt-floor cellar. The living room and dining room were filled with dust-coated debris that looked like it had been amassed to be discarded but never made it that far: broken lamps and worthless knick-knacks, desks and tables missing legs, chairs with seats busted through, a dilapidated sofa with chewed upholstery, piles of rotting clothes and rags smothered by fur, countless boxes and bags of assorted trash. What we saw was the way they had lived, in the midst of an indoor junkyard.

A single bed had been pushed against a back window facing the yard away from the river. Yellowed sheets and a dingy blanket had been left in disarray. Evidently this is where Mig had slept during her last cottage season, presumably no longer able to climb the stairs to a bedroom. It was a sad sight. Either Tom had never been back after she died, or he had never bothered to remove or at least smooth out the soiled bedclothes.

I could picture Mig in her final days looking forlornly out the window at the squirrels she had once tamed to eat from her hand when she'd still been able to venture into the yard with her bottle of beer and a can of peanuts. In time, as our new neighbors got to know us, they would relate how they'd often seen her in the yard sipping suds and feeding her squirrels, and how they'd stop and chat and join her in a brew but would refrain from calling on her in the cottage itself, such was the overwhelming smell.

In the filthy kitchen the table and counter tops were as disgusting as I'd remembered them when Kay and I had visited. There were dirty frying pans on the stove, crusted dishes in the sink, packages of dry goods on shelves with their sides and bottoms chewed out, and so many droppings on every surface that the movie *Ben* might have been filmed there. The boarded-up screen-enclosed front porch facing the river was a veritable junkyard of more broken furniture beyond repair and rusted dead appliances. I spotted what looked like bones behind an old dresser, and when I pulled it out I found two skeletons that might have been raccoons or groundhogs or maybe even cats, and which were devoid of any tissue from having been there so long, or from having been picked clean.

On the second floor we found rumpled beds in rooms that probably had not been used or cleaned in twenty years. The bottom corners of solid wood bedroom doors had been chewed through by something with a ferocious set of choppers. Even the face of a dresser drawer had a fist-sized hole gnawed through it. Rodent and cat shit and fur were everywhere. Our biggest fear, as we opened cupboard or closet doors or moved a box or pile of ragged blankets, was that whatever critters had invaded the place were still in residence.

Throughout the building the electrical configuration was such that it was truly remarkable the structure was still standing. A lone double-outlet fixture set in the floor was the sole source of power to the living room. A three-socket adaptor had been plugged into each port, and into these were plugged six different extension cords, some connected to additional cords, feeding an old TV, several table and wall lamps, a rusty fan, a device for rotating a rooftop TV antenna, and two antiquated electric space heaters that probably sucked enough juice to dim the entire eastern seaboard. In the kitchen a lone outlet was overloaded in like fashion, with a spaghetti-like network of extension cords tacked to the walls and leading to assorted lights, toaster, toaster oven, electric frying pan, coffee-maker, microwave, and refrigerator.

The tiny bathroom off the kitchen had a sliding wood door so out of kilter that no matter how you tried to close it there remained a two-inch gap, enabling its occupant to exchange pleasantries with anyone who happened to be in the kitchen. It barely accommodated a toilet and small sink and a gray bathtub filled with snow tires generously bedecked with cobwebs and dust. One corner of this enclosure seemed to sag precariously, and an inspection outside revealed that it was supported by a paint can that had buckled from the weight.

Discouraged and disgusted we set to work, with Mother predictably taking command and making the daunting project exceedingly difficult and exasperating, which was, after all, her reason for living. Rudy, ever the model of efficiency and expediency, would have preferred the use of a small bulldozer with which to plow the entire contents of the cottage through the back door and out to the road, save for a few pieces of furniture worth refinishing.

Mother, however, examined at excruciating length every item, setting aside and saving a nine-inch hunk of splintered molding that she said might make a perfectly good fourth of a picture frame, an odd furniture leg that with some sort of top and three more legs would make a perfectly good table, a perfectly good tool handle minus the tool, a perfectly good frying pan minus the handle, a perfectly good clock with one hand, a perfectly good knob that obviously belonged on something important, a little metal doohickey that was undoubtedly a vital mechanical component of God knows what, a perfectly good lawnmower wheel rim, a foot of two-by-four that would be ideal for whittling into something, half a wooden coat hanger that would be perfectly good for hanging up half a coat, a piece of broken TV antenna that would make a perfectly good fishing pole for a nitwit, a rusted metal waste basket with no bottom that might make a cute planter in the yard, an oven rack that did not fit in the oven but which would be perfectly good after a darn good scrubbing, a foot-square piece of rusted screen that would be great for sifting something, a totally corroded flashlight battery that was probably thirty years old but just might have a little life left in it, and on it went. The nightmare was underway. All we wanted to do was get the colossal accumulation of junk the hell out of there so that we could find the floor, while Mother demonstrated at every turn that she was unequivocally in charge and that nothing would be discarded or moved without her approval.

My first project was to hook up the electric water pump. With no municipal water service available, cottagers pumped water from the river for everything but drinking. Drinking water was available from a spring a few miles away. I found myself under the cottage staring blankly at a vintage pump that didn't appear capable of sucking wind. I knew as much about operating a water pump as I did about landing a lunar module. I hit it smartly with a hammer, nothing happened, and I drove into town in search of a plumber.

As the season progressed, much as we wanted to hang the ship's captain from the yardarm, we were thankful nevertheless that Mother was willing to finance several renovations that Rudy and I simply could not afford. We had sought the advice of a contractor, who told us that we had rescued the cottage just in time. Had it been left unattended for another season or two it would surely be ready for a wrecking ball. An inspection of the structural work underneath revealed that the building was on the verge of collapse, with sagging beams and rotting, askew support posts. Substantial foundation work needed to be done. An entirely new and larger bathroom was certainly advisable, as well as reconstruction of the stairs to the second floor that were so narrow and steep as to be hazardous and barely navigable. A plumber strongly suggested a new water-pumping system. And though these were expenditures that Mother readily offered to cover because they were so vital, her willingness represented a rare show of generosity for her. It also served to substantiate further her status as supreme ruler, and we knew from long experience that anything she did that seemed to come from the heart invariably came with strings.

Soon we encountered conflicts not unfamiliar to those who have shared ownership of seasonable property. Who gets to use it when? In some families, in which everyone gets along and the more the merrier, it wouldn't have mattered. In our family it mattered a lot. Rudy and her kids wanted to be there as long as Mother wasn't, since the children soon learned that their grandmother not only didn't make apple pie and molasses cookies but put them to work and orchestrated their every move. Kay and I preferred to have it to ourselves whenever possible and to entertain our own friends. But anything either Rudy or I planned at the cottage was forever at risk of being upstaged by Mother if she chose to be there at the same time.

We were not ungrateful for what she had spent on the place. Nor had we forgotten that she had *saved* the property for us by buying Tom's half and keeping it in the family. But the sanctity of the haven to which we had always escaped as children was disintegrating before our eyes. The enemy was among us, masquerading as savior, and carpeting the floors with eggshells.

One sweltering weekend in July, Maris was visiting from Michigan with her husband and two grade-school stepsons, his children from a previous marriage. I had driven Mother to the cottage. The kids were jumping in and out of the river and having a grand time in the front yard and on the sea wall along the shore. I sat on the porch as Mother stood at the screen overlooking the activities, and there occurred an exchange between us that serves to describe how my mother could create a full-scale typhoon from a mere wisp of wind, and how I could so easily find myself in the path of it.

She said, "Just look at that front yard."

I said, "What's the matter with it?"

"Well, just look at how everything is just every which way and strewn all over."

"What exactly are you talking about?"

"The lawn chairs, for Pete's sake. They're all over the yard facing different directions, with wet towels and clothes hanging off them, and sneakers and sandals scattered all over, and an air mattress no one is even using just thrown on the lawn, and fishing poles and a dirty old bait bucket lying around. It looks just exactly like, like some …"

"Like what, Mother? What exactly does it look like? Like there's a bunch of kids playing in the water on a hot day? Like every shore on every lake or pond or river everywhere in the country on a day like this? Is that all you can come up with to bitch about, wet towels and sandals and lawn chairs? Why don't you pull up a rocker and sit your butt down and watch the river go by and enjoy seeing your grandchildren have a good time and chill the hell out for a change?"

I was then, and always had been, incapable of letting her slide when she got like that. The intelligent response would have been for me to agree with her wholeheartedly and let it go. But I could never do it. I could never resist jacking her up when she had it coming. I knew perfectly well that ignoring her attempt to manufacture friction would be a fruitless effort anyway. She would only find some other fire to light. If she was aching for a confrontation, I was happy to oblige. Once again I had seen the pile of dog doo and stepped in it anyway. In so doing, I had given her all the ammo she was looking for to make a scene, to get pissed off at me and everyone else in turn, and to wield her mighty sword the rest of the day. Mission accomplished.

What grandmother wouldn't beam with pride and contentment and gratitude that those kids could enjoy that cottage experience on such a spectacular day along the majestic river? She wouldn't and couldn't. The kids were having fun on their own, without her direction, without her control, like that incident in my childhood when I'd been playing cars with my friend Dave and she'd asked me to take out the trash. Tranquility must be sabotaged. We were allowed to be happy when she felt happy. If she was down, she took us down with her. By the end of the day she had lit into those kids so unmercifully that Maris and her husband packed up the family and went back to Michigan.

I found Mother on the seawall after they'd left.

"You want to talk about what just happened here?" I asked.

"There's nothing to talk about."

"How long has it been since you've seen Maris? You invite her and her family to the cottage all the way from Michigan and then treat the kids like such crap that they pack up and leave. You see nothing wrong with that?"

"Those kids are the most spoiled, irresponsible, disrespectful children I've ever seen in all my days."

"Mother, that's Maris' problem, not yours. I realize they're a little unruly, but you were terrorizing those kids. They were scared to death because they didn't know what the hell they were doing wrong."

"This is *my* cottage, by God, and no little snips are going to come here and act like those kids did, I can tell you that."

"*Your* cottage? I don't believe this. You honestly think of this as *your* cottage? What happened to *our* cottage? Remember Rudy and me, the other owners? Tell you what. Since you consider this *your* cottage, you can have it to yourself. You obviously can't stand to have any underlings around, so I'll leave you to rule your kingdom. I'm outta here. You win. Have a nice time. Stay the rest of the summer.

Stay the rest of your life. Want me to leave you a baseball bat or a scatter gun in case any little bastards wander into the yard and turn a lawn chair the wrong way?"

And I left her there, stranded, and drove back to Rochester. Rudy went up two days later to fetch her. Rudy told me later that when she'd entered the cottage Mother had cheerfully struck up a conversation and acted as if nothing at all had occurred. I would not have expected anything else.

Within a week I'd made peace with her, but as the season progressed the general discord continued to escalate. Rudy lived thirty miles outside of Rochester. Since I lived in the city I was saddled with having to take Mother to the cottage whenever she wanted, and with feeling obligated to invite her whenever I was going. I relished the occasions when she chose not to go. Rudy and Mother had always been at odds, and Rudy made no secret of her objection to Mother's domineering ways at the cottage by making her feel uninvited at every opportunity. I tried to accommodate the old girl with the hope that she might miraculously mellow, but we nevertheless clashed frequently. Soon she was threatening at every turn to sell the cottage and be done with it. It was her ultimate weapon, and she began to wield it ruthlessly.

One day in her kitchen in Rochester, when she again threatened to dispose of the cottage, I got in her face.

"Okay, Mother, let's get this out in the open once and for all. Explain to me why, since you certainly don't need the money, you would even think about selling an irreplaceable piece of cottage property like that? Explain that to me, because it makes no sense whatsoever."

"Because we do nothing but fight about it."

"And who starts the fights, Mother? Who can't spend two minutes there without finding fault? Nothing is ever right. You're never satisfied. You don't go there to enjoy yourself. You go there to find fault and wield your authority. You don't know *how* to enjoy yourself. Why don't you just give us the place and be done with it? Turn it over to us."

"Why the hell should I?"

"Why the hell should you? Well, let's see. Because our grandmother, who owned it to begin with, wanted us to have it? Because you know how much it means to us? Because it was always meant to be ours? Because we've waited thirty years to get the place? Because you want us to have it out of the kindness of your heart so your children and grandchildren can enjoy it? Because it's what any mother in the world would do for her children if she could? How many reasons do you need? What the hell was the purpose of buying Tom's half so you could keep it in the family if you're going to turn around and sell it?"

"I would never have spent a penny on that cottage if I'd known how you and your sister were going to treat me whenever I set foot in the door, you can bet on that. You've made it perfectly clear I'm not wanted."

"Mother, we've told you any number of times how much we appreciate the money you've put into it. And you're wrong about not being wanted. We'd like more than anything for you to enjoy the cottage like the rest of us, but you can't do that. You have to run everything. Everything has to be your way or else. You're never happy unless you've got everyone squirming under your thumb, which is exactly why Gramma left the cottage to us instead of Daddy in the first place."

"What on earth are you talking about?"

"You know damn well what I'm talking about. Daddy told me about it years ago. Gramma didn't leave her half of the cottage to him because she didn't want you to get your mitts on it, for the very reason we're talking about right now, so that we kids could end up with it and have it to ourselves without you running everything and everybody, which is exactly what you're doing. And you *knew* that's the reason she did that and you've been pissed off about it ever since."

"Your father told you this?" She was livid.

"Years ago. I've known it all along. It's been a thorn in your side since Gramma died. You can't sell the cottage anyway. Rudy and I own part of it too, in case you've forgotten. Just give us the rest of the cottage. Please."

"Not in your wildest dreams."

"Jesus, Mother. This is what you've wanted all along, isn't it? To get your mitts on that cottage just so you could dangle it in front of our noses. It was supposed to be ours free and clear and that just drove you nuts, didn't it? You were deprived of the place and you couldn't stand that it was going to be handed to us on a platter. Now you've got nothing else to do with the last years of your life except screw your own children out of that place so you can satisfy a grudge against a mother-in-law that's been dead for thirty years."

"What are you *talking* about?"

"You know what I'm talking about. No one stabs you in the back and gets away with it. I've seen it a thousand times, Mother. One way or another you get even, and you don't care who suffers in the process.

When you don't get your way someone has to fry. Gramma stuck it in your ass thirty years ago and you're going to get even by sticking it in ours."

"That's the craziest thing I ever heard of."

"You got that right. Crazy as a shithouse rat."

With that she stomped out, went to her room and slammed the door, ending the discussion the way she had always ended discussions. And suddenly it dawned on me. If she couldn't sell part of a cottage, then Tom couldn't have sold his part ownership either. Something wasn't right. Even if Tom did try to sell he'd have contacted us kids. Mother hadn't any rights to it at all.

The more I thought about it, however, the more I realized that whatever had happened was a done deal. Mother owned three-quarters, and that was that. She got over our clash and we again returned to a façade of family togetherness. It was only a month later that we learned of Tom's death. He must have been sicker than any of us suspected, except perhaps Mother.

In June the River flows so cold,
only a boy of ten
would dare to plunge into her heart
time and time again

Soaring from a boathouse peak
I crashed into the silent deep,
as free as I would ever be of fear

Bobbing in the deadly currents,
mothered by a loving sun
when waking was the whole of my career

It seems a hundred years since I
knew every inch of shore
as far as I could see down river
from the cottage door

Now I feel old, afraid of cold
and scared by where I've been,
and think the ageless river
must have known me better then

19

The River

The cottage stands just forty-five feet from the magnificent St. Lawrence River, on the north side of Houghton's Point. It is a quiet community of forty modest cottages, most of them built in the 1880s. They face the shipping channel in the American Narrows, on the New York mainland between the majestic International Bridge and Alexandria Bay in the storied Thousand Islands. Across the channel sits Wellesley Island, at four by seven miles one of the largest, splitting the great river like a boulder in a brook.

I swam across this channel when I was eleven, alongside a safety boat manned by buddies who jabbed me with oars by way of encouragement, as buddies are wont to do. The river moves along at a pretty good clip on its journey to the sea. Depending on where you want to hit shore on the other side, you have to start out quite a ways upriver. I couldn't swim the channel now.

The river is fifteen miles wide at its source at northeastern Lake Ontario, but this channel, the main thoroughfare, is just 350 yards across here at the Point, where Great Lakes cargo ships up to 730 feet long and deep-draft freighters from nearly fifty nations groan by a stone's throw from our shore, as close to the mainland as they get anywhere else in the narrows. Their passing is a sight one never tires of.

From an elevated porch we have front row balcony seats for a constant parade of vessels that includes anything man has devised to float, from canoes and kayaks to ramshackle houseboats and luxury cruise ships, whining jet skis and multi-million-dollar motor yachts with on-board speedboats for dinghies, battered scows and exquisite schooners, bulky barges and puffing tugs, multi-deck tour boats and vintage mahogany runabouts, dented aluminum rowboats and thundering off-shore racers, restored pirate ships and roaring hydrofoils, tiny sailboats and great naval cruisers, sleek silent skiffs and screeching bass boats, even a submarine and a replica of the Niña.

But the most prominent and endearing are the freighters: the long-hulled lakers, scraped and scruffy, plowing low through the water as far as Duluth; and the colorful salties from across the seas, riding high and imposing, their towering bows seemingly near enough to touch, their monstrous diesel engines sending vibrations through the water and bedrock. The ships carry past our cottage some fifty million tons of grain, coal, stone, iron and petroleum products in the course of an eight-month shipping season.

With gray in our hair and our boathouse leaping days long behind us, still we instinctively call out "big boat!" when one approaches. We wave at deckhands leaning on gunwale railings, and watch the behemoth glide by to see the name painted on its rump, to learn what faraway and sometimes unfamiliar land it hails from. Their resounding whistle blasts still make us jump. In the night they seem to hoist us a foot from our beds and set us back down again, and scare the hell out of unaccustomed guests. And in the occasional thick fog their incessant hooting reminds us of how narrow the channel is here, how little space for error there is, how closely together two ships must pass, how easily one can find trouble. When the Exxon Valdez hit bottom off Alaska on Good Friday, 1989, it was several miles out of the shipping lane. Any number of ships have run aground here, including a tanker just upriver from Alexandria Bay in June of 1976 that spilled 140,000 gallons of oil into the river, having strayed from the shipping channel a matter of yards.

What a remarkable transformation this marvelous area has undergone. The Thousand Islands are what remains of a geological progression that has seen the region change from sea floor to mountain range, from Ice Age glaciers to part of the most extensive fresh water system on Earth, as long as the Atlantic Ocean is wide, stretching 2,300 miles from Minnesota to the sea, and encompassing nearly 100,000 square miles of navigable waterways.

We sit atop the solid granite of the Frontenac Axis, a fifty-mile-wide mountainous ridge that links the Precambrian rock of the Canadian Shield with that of New York's Adirondacks, and which once confined glacial waters to the west in what would become the Great Lakes. Erosion over millions of years allowed the waters to break through and flow to the sea. The Thousand Islands are what we now see of that ridge, the peaks of the mountain range poking out of the water and numbering some 1,850 in all.

And for every one there are perhaps three others that do not quite break the surface, and which have consequently splintered or caved the hull and mutilated the prop of many a wayward vessel large and small whose captain was unfamiliar with these waters. Such shoals can lurk a thousand feet from shore, where the water is otherwise a hundred feet deep and where no such shallows ought to be. Some of these shoals are marked with buoys. A good many are not. If you're outside the channel markers, you're on your own.

The first humans here belonged to the Laurentian Culture and arrived some 4,000 to 7,000 years ago, depending on whom you talk to. Around 1400 A.D. came the Iroquois, who paddled these waters among the islands in birch canoes and called it Manitouana, Garden of the Great Spirit. In 1535 European explorer Jacques Cartier took credit for discovering the river as far inland as what is now Montreal, though his large ship could not traverse the ferocious upriver rapids further inland. Later, smaller ships from Europe were able to navigate the waters and reach the Great Lakes region. The explorers apparently considered it irrelevant that the region they were discovering was already occupied by local residents who were watching them discover it. Samuel Champlain, who first ventured up the entire river in 1603, was the first to establish permanent French settlements along the shore, principally that which became Quebec, and was followed by Daniel de Rémy de Courcelle in 1665, Comte de Frontenac in 1672, and Jean Desbayes, who first charted the region in 1687 and named it Les Milles îles, the Thousand Islands.

Its obvious geographic significance played a major role in military strategy in the various wars that determined our country's destiny and that of Canada in the eighteenth and nineteenth centuries, providing a vital route for warships, personnel, and supplies, while the myriad islands and hidden channels became a virtual playground for pirates. Later, smugglers during Prohibition devised ever-changing routes to outsmart the Feds, and it is said that some could be heard unloading their Canadian cargo at night right here at Houghton's Point. There may be a fortune in Canadian whiskey sitting on the bottom of the river to this day. Smugglers sometimes hauled their booty in nets towed behind their boats, which were cut loose if authorities approached. If the cargo went down in relatively shallow waters, the smugglers came back and dived for it. If it went down in the center of the channel, it may still be there, entombed in silt.

Outlaws and fugitives of all kinds have hidden among these islands, from flamboyant river scoundrel Capt. Bill Johnson in 1838 to reclusive political activist Abbie Hoffman, who took his own life here several years ago. Someone thoroughly familiar with the immense network of islands and water routes might outwit pursuers in this region for years, much as pike and bass and perch and pickerel have been doing since sportsmen discovered here some of the best freshwater fishing on Earth. A world record muskellunge of just short of seventy pounds was caught in this river, as was a six-foot, 235-pound sturgeon.

It wasn't long before people of note learned of the spectacular region: politicians from presidents on down, European royalty, business tycoons, movie stars and entertainers galore. The ultra-rich like railroad magnate George Pullman, financier John Jacob Astor, and Waldorf-Astoria owner George Boldt built castles on the islands and called them summer homes. Celebrities found refuge and seclusion here, including songwriter Irving Berlin, whose descendants still reside in his unpretentious summer home, named "Always," just upriver from Houghton's Point.

The population is made up of the locals who in winter brave sub-zero temperatures along the half-frozen, soundless river, and of the seasonal people, some of them with elaborate mansion-like retreats, but most of them content with humble cottages and fishing camps and a satisfactory slice of heaven, and who tend to believe that this is where God summers too.

Often a sunrise stages an extravaganza over the water made all the more glorious by the absolute stillness of the surface, a circumstance sunsets are rarely treated to because of evening breezes and boating. Even this swift river can be as smooth as polished marble on windless dawns. When the tangerines and scarlets and violets bleed across the heavens, you can watch the awesome masterpiece unfold in kaleidoscopic replication, at least until the first bass boat screams by, unzipping the mirror like running a finger through a still-wet painting, shattering the dreamy quietude with the impudence of an alarm clock.

Sometimes on such mornings a cargo ship will beat him to it, sneaking around the bend by Alex Bay, pointing her big nose upriver, gliding past the cottage toward the International Bridge, the whole of the gigantic freighter's reflection sliding quietly by, a new morning's sunbeams dancing on its hull. Once any motorboat ruffles the surface the mirror is gone for another day, but the ship is always forgiven.

The quart bottle of vodka, nearly full, stood on the kitchen counter. Mother was holding court on the porch. Every time I walked in the kitchen that bottle leered at me. I had been sober five months. So accustomed had my family become to my apparent cure that they had long before stopped hiding liquor. I had tried to ignore it, but it teased me now, like a pretty girl playing, testing her allure. Curiosity kills the cat and countless alcoholics. Counselors have all sorts of explanations for what makes a recovering addict fail, but on the surface it was for me nothing more complicated than simple curiosity. What would it taste like after all this time? There is a one-way switch in an addict's head, a trigger. Once you pull it the bullet is gone, irretrievable. Like the last rock that supports you on the brink of a cliff. The rock dislodges and breaks away, and there is nothing else but the falling.

I turned up the bottle and took a short swig. It burned like fire and made me gag. I couldn't believe I used to drink that gasoline by the half gallon every day. I must have been crazy. I took another hit and it still burned a little. By the third swig the burning stopped and the delightful warmth took over, the hot creamy soup I now remembered so well. I took another swig, the damage done, and I still called it curiosity. In a matter of two minutes so much of the vodka was missing that someone would surely notice. I took three more good swallows and replaced what was missing with water. The little nip of curiosity had blossomed into almost a pint. As much as I felt guilty and ashamed, I slowly began to feel magically and gloriously intoxicated, rewarded and fulfilled, a long-muffled lullaby now sweet and divine in my ears. Welcome home, my love. Where have you been so long?

For the next two days I willed myself to believe that nothing was wrong. I had merely tripped up and it wasn't a problem. There was no way I could get back to drinking like I had before, so an occasional refreshment surely couldn't hurt. I contented myself with snatching a beer here and there and guzzling it when no one was watching. But the curiosity had now been replaced by hunger. I thought almost constantly about the next beer or slug of hooch I'd sneak as I succumbed to what quickly became a perpetual and familiar pattern of monitoring everyone's movements, waiting edgily for them to go down to the seawall or out to the yard, rearranging beers in the refrigerator so that another wouldn't be missed, stashing empties under the work bench on the side porch, squeezing toothpaste into my mouth to cover my breath.

When the others left two days later and I had the cottage to myself, I bought a six-pack. The next day I bought two six-packs. The next day I bought a six-pack and a pint of vodka that was gone by mid-afternoon, so I bought another. The next day I bought a quart. Within a week of that first small curious swig I was buying a quart of white whisky every day. Back in the saddle again.

There is no such thing as a slip, they say. Addicts don't stumble. They don't fall off the wagon; they leap. The failure isn't deliberate, but it is unconsciously premeditated. When they turn that corner and welcome back into their arms the long-estranged lover, it is because they had left on the table an open invitation. Drop by any time. No need to call. It is a matter of when, not if. Everything happened that the rehab counselors had told me would happen if I took my fragile sobriety for granted. The potential for relapse would cling to me like my shadow, and without a regimen of fortification I would be helpless to defend myself. If I believed I couldn't possibly revert to drinking as much as I had before, I was profoundly mistaken.

In the months preceding rehab I had struggled to conceal the ludicrous extent of my drinking. Now I was forced to hide not only that I was drinking as much as I ever had, but that I was drinking at all. It takes a magician and superb actor to drink that much alcohol without anyone knowing it. But I had always been a stupendous performer in that particular medium, and for a while I pulled it off, living in a secret and unremitting hell, maintaining apparent abstemiousness around others, while sinking into despair and drunkenness whenever I could be alone.

I tried to keep my escalating downfall in check, but the shadow had engulfed me. So many times I left for the cottage on my own, planning to spend several days there drying out. I could suffer there in peace and get another foothold on sobriety. I preferred traveling the Seaway Trail, Rt. 104 to Rt. 3, roughly following the shore of Lake Ontario. It is a three-hour ride. About a half hour into it there was a liquor store in a small plaza by the highway. Just one pint. A couple swallows to take the edge off, maybe a hit or two later in the day, a couple at night, save the rest until tomorrow, taper off slowly. In Oswego, halfway to the cottage, another pint for later. The first pint gone. At the cottage, unload the car, settle on the porch to greet the river with a much-deserved official arrival cocktail, in an actual glass with ice. Enough vodka left for just one drink. Back in the car, off to town for another pint. That one empty by bedtime. Tapering off. Drying out. Getting another foothold. A quart and a half of white whiskey in nine hours, after intending not to drink at all. No more curiosity. No more false fulfillment. Just the drug for the need of the drug. The next day to hell with pints, get a quart. Gone by 7 p.m. Back for a pint. Day after day. Flailing.

I continued to put up the front that all was well. I still don't know whether I was really that great of an actor or if Kay was just too blind to see. An alcoholic may be clever at finding and sneaking drinks, but he is otherwise guilty of some incredibly stupid behavior that would certainly alarm any loved ones if they weren't so consumed by wishful thinking. How could Kay not find it peculiar that I now frequently appeared with so many mints stuffed in my cheeks that I looked like a chipmunk? Or that in one afternoon I thought it necessary to check the condition of the spare tire in the trunk of the car half a dozen times? Or that I heard the water pump under the cottage make funny noises and needed to investigate every hour? Or that I needed something at the hardware store that I apparently hadn't needed the last three times I'd gone to the hardware store that same afternoon? If she suspected I was drinking, she may simply have been willing herself to disbelieve it. I would discover later that a few of our friends were pretty sure I was at least sampling, and that one had even told Kay. Kay had insisted it wasn't true.

One day at the river when Kay headed out on an errand, I scurried to one of my hiding places under the cottage and guzzled the best part of a pint of vodka, one of several I had stashed there. I was strolling back up the hill to the rear door of the cottage when I saw Kay pulling in, apparently having forgotten something. I had just enough time to mosey casually inside and race to the refrigerator for something to hide my breath. The only thing I could put my hands on as she came in the door was a raw onion. I took a mighty bite like it was a succulent apple, and stood there chewing contentedly with tears pouring down my face, as Kay looked at me dumbfounded.

"I love a good onion," I said.

20

Flailing

One of several mistakes I made to put my tenuous sobriety at risk was to take on a new job a couple of months out of rehab. Counselors had warned against making any major changes in my life or taking on stressful new challenges. Don't run for president, have a sex change operation, buy the Buffalo Bills, things of that nature. But the new gig seemed innocuous enough, working part-time for another publisher of weekly newspapers covering towns in a neighboring county.

The pay was paltry and the work uninspiring, but it was a way to get back in the game and get my professional writing juices flowing again. I was given editorship of a small weekly paper that covered rural communities wholly foreign to me, and I can't say that I made much effort to learn much about them, especially after I'd started drinking again. I was required to put in three days a week, but for the ludicrous paycheck even that was expecting a lot. Town board meetings necessitated lengthy evening drives, and while the usually protracted sessions covered issues of importance to officials and a handful of residents, they didn't mean squat to me and I regarded them accordingly. Like I gave a flying wazoo if a town engineer had inadvertently run a sewer conduit through some jerkoff's patio.

I could easily put the blame for my failed sobriety on any number of factors, the constant turmoil at the cottage under my mother's consuming dictatorship in particular. But nobody bound me hand and foot and crammed a siphon hose down my throat and force-pumped me full of vodka; nor had I stumbled accidentally into some unforeseen abyss from which there was no other escape. I had seized that bottle firmly and deliberately by the neck and taken it captive. Certainly the act had involved an irrefutable powerlessness that is at the very core of addiction itself, but the decision to drink or not to drink had been plainly laid before me after months of abstinence. I had made my choice in a state of total awareness, and I was guzzling whiskey from a quart bottle as if it were a soft drink again, regardless of the where, what, and why of it.

That the encounter had been inevitable no longer mattered. That I had exposed myself to the enemy with no means of defending myself was now irrelevant. I had not taken seriously the insidiousness of my disease, and I had eluded most of the measures my counselors in rehab had insisted were crucial to sobriety, attending AA meetings especially. That the counselors had been absolutely right did little to diminish the fact that I nevertheless found myself slumped in the car on a side street or parking lot at ten in the morning, my head on the door sill, an empty bottle in my lap, too drunk to go to work, too drunk to go home, too drunk to drive, too drunk to walk, too drunk to care.

By fall, having closed the cottage for the season, I narrowed my already abbreviated work schedule considerably. I was expected to spend all day Monday gathering stories in the field at town halls and schools and anywhere in the rural countryside that an earth-shattering event might occur, all day Tuesday in the office writing and processing copy and taking calls from folks who expected the editor of their hometown newspaper to be at least occasionally accessible, and most of Wednesday submitting final articles to the typesetters and laying the newspaper out in the composing room.

The crippling workload had become a strain. I'd found it increasingly difficult to remain lucid for extended periods, like entire mornings, and I soon omitted Monday altogether. I arrived mid-morning on Tuesday, took a two-hour lunch, and departed by three. I sauntered in mid-morning on Wednesday and threw the paper together as best I could with articles from the meager supply I had amassed and any I could swipe from the paste-ups of the other town newspapers the company published, and exited as soon as possible to avoid the bothersome business of getting a jump on the following week's edition by working on new stuff. Sometimes I'd find notes on my desk from the managing editor, asking that I please be in the office more often.

One Tuesday morning in November I shuffled in at eleven, barely able to hold my head up. I was welcomed by two state troopers who were there to complain about an article in my last issue in which I had put a couple of their colleagues in a bad light regarding an incident at a town rally. I had not attended the rally myself, due to a scheduling conflict involving the intake of fluids, and had stolen the tidbit from an article by an overzealous reporter for one of Rochester's daily newspapers. The episode concerning the troopers evidently had not even happened. They were at the office merely to ask that I be more careful with my facts, an admonishment with which the managing editor wholeheartedly agreed. Incapable of leaving well enough alone, however, I felt the need to comment on the troopers' neckties, which I considered an exceptionally gaudy shade of purple. One explained, pretty tersely I thought, that the color was a long-standing New York State Police tradition, symbolic of their loyalty and unity as demonstrated by the ancient Roman Praetorian Guard, whose revered troops had worn royal purple in their uniforms. The troopers wore the color with a great deal of pride, they said, to which I responded that wearing ties like those was probably the reason they had to carry such big guns.

After the humorless troopers left I slouched at my desk and stared blankly at my keyboard, which seemed to have a lot more keys than usual. I had yet to submit any copy at all for that week's paper. I had attempted that morning to pick up material at one of the two town halls I was expected to visit each week but had fallen asleep in the parking lot. Upon waking, I had driven out without getting the material, pretty proud of myself for having made it to the town hall at all. For weeks the managing editor apparently had been receiving calls from various town officials, wondering why there hadn't been anyone from the newspaper at the board meetings lately and why there hadn't been any articles in the paper about town business. The gig was up. The editor looked at me sprawled in my chair and didn't know quite what to say, so I said it for him.

"I think I'm in trouble," I said.

"Yes, I think you are," said he.

"I don't think I can get the paper out."

"I don't think so either. Go home. Get some help. You have a problem. You're no good to us here. Maybe after you get squared away. Take care of yourself." Nuff said.

That evening Kay found me curled up in a ball in bed. Like the old days. Like nothing at all had changed. She was heartbroken. In spite of the hell she'd already gone through, she was still largely ignorant about the force my disease held over its victims, and remained at a loss to understand how I could have failed so catastrophically. I tried to assure her that this was a minor setback and that everything would be fine. I just needed some time to regroup and start over. She probably knew that I was drinking, but not that I was indulging so much that I had returned to the sick and sorry physical state she hoped never to see again.

The trouble was that flawed liver I'd been issued. Damn thing never did work right. You'd think that a device whose very function is to process toxins could have done a better job of dealing with a mere half-gallon of raw alcohol every day. Mine must have come faulty from the factory because it always seemed to begin malfunctioning just as I was assaulting it with massive amounts of poison and needed it most. I'd even given it five months off to pull itself together, and now it was turning on me again.

I told Kay I could manage this on my own. I knew the ropes now. After all, I'd had so much of that recovery propaganda crammed down my throat that I could be a counselor myself. I'd taper off and get back to square one. Too bad about losing the job, but it was crappy work, way below me, insulting salary, deteriorating my talent, waste of time and brainpower, probably what drove me back to drink in the first place, hick-town bush-league papers, perfect for those typical journalism school grads I'd had to work next to, who'd drool at a chance to blow the lid clean off that misrouted sewer conduit caper, but certainly not for a journalist of my caliber.

During the next few weeks I made a half-ass attempt to curb my drinking, but in truth my consumption was limited only by a meager source of supply. I had no means of acquiring money and Kay made sure I didn't have any extra cash. My best friend and former drinking partner lived just two doors away, and I frequently called him and asked that he sneak me three or four fingers of hooch to take the edge off. I'd stop at my mother's, particularly when she wasn't home, to steal whiskey that I'd smuggle out in fruit jars I found in the basement ("You can burn my house, steal my car, drink my liquor from an old fruit jar …"—*Blue Suede Shoes)*.

I blew off Kay's substantial collection of Susan B. Anthony coins, riffled her purse for five bucks whenever I could, rolled pennies, dipped into the coin jar reserved for our vacation, dropped by the homes and apartments of former drinking buddies who welcomed me back into the fold, raided the liquor cabinets of friends we visited and guzzled whatever I could get my hands on when no one was looking, and ordered soft drinks at my old watering holes and swiped drinks off the bar when people turned their backs.

Some days, when the usual resources were unfulfilling, I found myself plotting some pretty strange escapades. You know you're in a sorry state when you start thinking about robbing a liquor store for the liquor. Kay would give me just enough money for gas and cigarettes. I'd put five bucks worth of gas in the car, buy a pack of Kay's brand of cigarettes, stop at my mother's and steal a pack or two of Winstons for me, and have enough cake left over for a bottle of vodka. Every day I had to come up with another set of schemes with which to snatch enough sauce to get me through. Plotting where and how to get your next source of drink is a full-time job. Some days I made out pretty well. Other days I suffered.

A buddy who was a master furniture-maker tried to help me out by hiring me for a project he'd taken on. He wanted me at his shop at nine in the morning. I usually got there about twenty minutes late because I had to wait for the liquor stores to open to get a measly half-pint of vodka to get my motor started. A lousy half-pint. Barely enough to brush my teeth with, but enough to get me to work. My God what long days those were. One day I vowed not to drink no matter what. I'd suffer as much as I had to but I would get through that workday if it killed me, and it damn near did.

I got through the day, despite laying the heel of my hand open with a utility knife. On the way home I experienced the most horrifying ride of my life. Five minutes into the trip, in the center lane of the expressway, I was suddenly overcome with what can only be described as a horrendous attack of withdrawals. It was like I'd been dipping into angel dust. The three lanes of the expressway ahead kept crossing one another as if tying the highway into a braid, while my eyes danced every which-way in an attempt to focus. I had no idea what lane I was in. My shoulders cramped from my grip on the steering wheel. I didn't dare pull over because I didn't know where over was. Cars whizzed by me, horns blared, the lane lines kept crisscrossing, huge globs of blackness floated across my vision. I thought I was passing out. I shook my head, slapped myself in the face, screamed, came to my senses a little, and saw that I was doing twenty miles an hour and weaving from lane to lane totally out of control.

The feeling finally subsided. I managed to get home, all the way thinking that if a cop were behind me I'd be pulled over for drunken driving, and I'd have to explain that I wasn't driving like that because I'd been drinking, but because I hadn't been. How ironic can you get?

Three stiff cocktails would render almost anyone too impaired to drive, but I had no business behind the wheel of a car without at least that many in my gut.

Kay preferred a large Christmas tree that cost at least forty dollars every year. Two weeks before Christmas she gave me the money to get the tree while she was working one night. I shopped at a farm market and found a shapely specimen for thirty-seven bucks. The kid working the lot hauled it to my car and tied the trunk lid down and handed me a ticket to take into the store to pay for the tree. It occurred to me that the cashiers had no idea I had a tree in my car, so I meandered around looking at wreaths and candles and such and moseyed on out the door.

Down the road I cruised with the stolen Douglas fir hanging out of my trunk and forty clams in my pants, singing *O Tannenbaum* at the top of my lungs, and headed straight to a liquor store to stock up for the holidays. I bought seven quarts of cheap vodka that I calculated could get me at least through Christmas if I imbibed judiciously. They were gone in four days.

On the morning of December 30, a day before New Year's Eve, when I was asked to sign my name to admission papers at the Park Ridge Hospital detox ward, my hand shook so that Kay had to hold my wrist down. The signature was no more mine than William Shakespeare's. I gave Kay a feeble hug. Someone helped me down a long hallway. I was very tired. It was time for my coma.

***

My crusty eyes opened on a strange and blurry room. I knew exactly where I was. There was no bewilderment, no sudden shock of awareness. Just a whole lot of disgust, and the all-too-familiar God-awful sickness. It was another whole day before I pulled myself together enough to join another set of others in another dayroom. A ponderous rattling smoke-eater was suspended from the ceiling directly over a worn sofa. If it somehow vibrated itself free of its brackets it would drop like a refrigerator and likely kill anyone seated below, which is why I chose that very spot to sit. The poor slob, people would say. Struggling to rediscover his sobriety, courageous enough to admit himself to a hospital again to seek the proper treatment he so badly needed, to bravely face his Goliath head on, only to meet his end in a freakish accident, killed instantly by a 300-pound rectangular meteorite.

I was engulfed by déjà vu. How could this be happening again? Was this rock bottom at last? The real McCoy? Then what in hell was that near-death experience the first time around in Pennsyltucky? Introduction to Rock Bottom? Rock Bottom for Beginners? Rock Bottom Basics? From utter disgrace and physical collapse to Superman, from refurbished hero to waste of skin again via a single moment of weakness, a single curious swig that could not possibly have led anywhere else but to another swig.

I would not have thought it possible to feel worse physically than I had in my previous meltdown of nearly a year before, but I did. I had dropped twenty pounds. When the blood tests from my physical came back they revealed that I was suffering from severe malnutrition. It was not uncommon. Addicts don't eat much, and their ability to absorb nutrients is impaired by the alcohol or drug's relentless affect on the liver, pancreas, and other components designed to do that sort of work. And, because it is the liver's job to make cholesterol, my impaired equipment had apparently produced low serum cholesterol levels that the doctor called appalling. When he'd returned with the test results he told me that my cholesterol was extremely low.

"That's good, ain't it?"

"Low cholesterol is good," he'd said. "Your HDL reading is about thirty milligrams per deciliter, which means you're practically starving. When was the last time you ate?"

"I had a grilled cheese sandwich a couple of days ago. How can I be starving? I'm not even hungry."

Each detox facility has its own procedures, but the overall techniques are universal. This detox would not vary much from my previous experience, except for the vitamin shot and the feminine products. There must been a menstruation epidemic here at some point. What appeared to be tampons were taped to the walls everywhere I looked. Very strange. I later learned that among detoxifying patients there is a chance of withdrawal seizure, which can occur without warning and in the throes of which patients have been known to bite their tongues clean through—hence the close-at-hand cotton plugs that are inserted between the teeth in such emergencies.

For some reason I felt the need to use one of my allowed phone calls to contact my mother. The news of my whereabouts was likely to reach her eventually, if not immediately, and I figured I'd better tell her I was okay. I should have known better. The conversation was more gap than gab. I told her I was in the hospital again, but doing all right.

Her response was, "I see. So we're back to this again, are we? I certainly don't know what you expect me to say."

"Nothing, Mother. I just wanted you to know I was okay."

"How considerate of you. And how long this time?"

"I don't know. As long as it takes, I guess."

"Well, I can't say that I'm all that surprised."

"Why is that?"

"Oh never mind. Just do what you have to do."

"I will. Thanks." I was so glad I called.

A nurse appeared. She looked nothing like Natalie. It was time for my injection of Vitamin B, in which alcoholics are usually deficient. This was a muscle hypo, injected in the top of the rump. It feels like a Phillips-head screwdriver launched by a crossbow. You could tell which patients had recently got their shots by the way they walked around dragging a leg behind them like Igor.

Otherwise the detox was pretty much the same, with the usual chats with counselors and therapists who had to know when I took my first poop and what color it was and what my mommy and daddy were like and how old I was when I first got drunk, and what I got drunk on and where I got it. But mostly they were interested in the fact that I had been to this show before and had obviously learned absolutely nothing from it, as evidenced by my divulgence that I hadn't found AA meetings all that entertaining.

What I needed now, they said, was another round of rehab. They wanted to send me away but I refused. We compromised with enrollment in an outpatient rehab not far from where I lived. I'd attend sessions there and would otherwise be free to maintain a normal schedule. It turned out to be ruthless. I was expected there every weekday evening for three hours. On weekends I was to attend at least four AA meetings. I also had two hours of reading and written homework to do every night. After a week of that drudgery I was convinced that the intensity of the curriculum would drive me to drink, so I quit. I'd rough it out on my own. Maybe catch an AA meeting here and there.

In the months that followed I continued to wage my personal war with no chance in hell of winning. Like the meager defenders of the Alamo, I could hold my own only so long before the enemy poured over the wall. I soon found myself muddling through a day at a time and a week at a time, on and off the sauce, still refusing to believe that I couldn't defend myself, getting a foothold on sobriety only to lose it again, forever bewildered by the inability to achieve a lasting abstinence.

I maintained enough to keep Kay thinking I was winning, but it became an endless cycle of drinking myself stupid when alone at the cottage and putting up a hell of a front when home. One night when I returned after several days by the river, I found a note from Kay informing me that a friend had blown into town and she had gone to meet her at the Stride Right Inn for a drink. Isn't that lovely, thought I. I had never asked Kay to quit drinking just because I couldn't drink, but her decision to go bar-hopping instead of being home when I arrived was all the excuse I needed to blow the lid off.

I went immediately to the saloon and when I found her in the noisy crowd I asked over the din, "Are you having a good fucking time? You think I'm supposed to stay home and pull my prick while you go out and juice it up with your fucking girlfriends? You know what? I believe I'm pretty thirsty my own self. I think maybe a cold beer would taste pretty good after a long drive and coming home to an empty house." When I asked the bartender for a beer he hesitated and glanced knowingly at Kay. I said, "Tell you what, Tommy, you can get me a fucking beer or I can climb over the bar and get it myself."

He got me the beer. It was beautiful. I was announcing to the world that yes, by God, I was drinking again, thanks to my beloved wife, who obviously considered a night out with a girlfriend more important than my well being.

Another incident will remain forever indelible in my memory. As Christmas approached I was having a particularly difficult time of it. The holidays are always a precarious period for recovering alcoholics, but in my case it was more a matter of my continual decline climaxing at that time of year. Kay's family traditionally opened their gifts on Christmas Eve at her mother's house, and while Kay was aware that I'd been suffering in recent weeks, I was putting up a passable front when necessary.

As I sat in the corner of the living room I would have given anything for a drink, several drinks, but it was out of the question in front of her family, who of course didn't know I wasn't still sober. I tried to tough it out but I just couldn't do it. I wanted to ask Kay to slip me a drink but I didn't dare. I was twitching, sweating, my foot tapping and shaking. Just as everyone was about to settle in the living room to open gifts I whispered to Kay that I was leaving. When she asked what on earth for, I simply said, "I need a drink. I'm outta here."

I left, just walked out. Other cars blocked mine in the driveway so I drove across the lawn, my tires spinning, leaving a serpentine trail of muddy ruts. I went to my buddy A.J.'s house, spent the evening guzzling vodka, and went home to an empty apartment. When I awoke in the morning, Kay was there. So were my gifts from her family. I opened my gifts in silence while Kay sobbed. There were some very nice things, as usual. They must have thought I was crazy. They surely felt that only a total bastard could treat Kay that way by drinking again after what I'd already put her through. They would never understand. I didn't know how I could ever face them again, and neither did Kay.

On the morning of December 30, 1989, exactly one year to the day after my previous arrival, when I was asked to sign my name to admission papers at the same Park Ridge Hospital detox ward, my hand shook so that Kay again had to hold my wrist down. My signature was similarly indistinguishable. I gave Kay another feeble hug. Someone helped me down the long hallway. Detox number three. Kay's parting words were that she loved me more than life itself, but that this was absolutely my last rodeo. If I failed again she would leave me.

21

The Turn

A few recovering addicts tell of having had a profound religious experience with all the bells and whistles. For many there is a spiritual arousal of some kind if not nearly so dramatic. But few of those who have been blessed with continuous sobriety would argue that at some point, in whatever form it took, dynamically or subtly, a corner was turned, a transformation occurred, and there appeared a sudden clarity of mind, remarkable in its strangeness to them, that was something like a window through which they finally saw hope.

It is a phenomenon that skeptics would have trouble accepting, though in their defense they would not have reason to believe it if they haven't had occasion to need it. For those who have, it provides an undeniable taste of evidence that a power indeed exists that is greater and stronger than they are, and more so even than the addiction to which they were so long shackled.

I saw no blazing lights or fireworks or apparitions of the Almighty. I heard no organ music or choruses of hallelujah. I was not suddenly zapped with religion by a thunderbolt. I didn't fall to my knees. I encountered nothing tangible that I recognized as a miracle, and no one spoke to me from the heavens. But I damn sure felt something.

When I awoke after my customary coma I opened my crusty eyes on a strange and blurry nurse who was only slightly larger than Charles Barkley. I lay on my stomach, my underpants having been already pulled down, as she towered over me holding that fearsome syringe of Vitamin B. She asked if I had a preference as to which cheek I wanted it in, and I said, "How about one of yours?" Then I saw a blazing light show. She jammed it home like she was spearing a carp, leaned on it fit to bury the entire apparatus in my ass, plunger and all, gave it a couple of extra thrusts for good measure and then, I think, sat on it. And despite nearly passing out from the attack, I found it somehow amusing as she walked away that she had a surprisingly delicate giggle for an Amazon.

When I emerged from my room after the usual forty-some hours of withdrawal hell, I took up residence on the same threadbare sofa as I had the year before and under that same rattling smoke-eater that I again hoped would fall on my head. Numbed into a zombie state that allowed me only enough awareness to realize how deathly sick I felt, I was oblivious to the idle conversations of the other space cadets around me as I stared at the floor, where two white-shoed feet appeared. I looked up to see that they belonged to a nurse I remembered from the year before. She remembered me as well, and she was shaking her head as if I'd filled my diapers again.

In the next few days I heard the usual lectures, watched the requisite movies, talked to therapists, doctors, nurses, and listened to members of AA who had been brought in to speak. It was the same old drill, and yet I seemed to be reading it differently. Maybe I was truly scared for my life. Finding myself in a hospital detox ward was a harrowing experience I'd gotten to know pretty well, but always there had been in the back of my mind the comfort of knowing that no matter what happened, I had Kay to turn to, Kay to lean on, Kay to love me, Kay to understand if I couldn't make it. But I remembered vividly the look on her face as she spoke of leaving me, and what terrified me now was that she'd be crazy not to, and that if I failed again I would kill myself.

I'd been close to it before. During one of my awful periods of clandestine guzzling, while Kay had thought I was doing fine, we had been babysitting a house for friends while they were on vacation. Her face had turned ashen upon smelling booze on my breath one morning. She'd hunted around and found a quart of vodka I'd hidden in a closet. She'd been devastated, not having known I'd been drinking at all, let alone hiding bottles and drinking in the morning again.

I'd known that my friend kept a handgun in a bedroom dresser drawer because he'd told me so. I, too, had been devastated, not simply because I'd been discovered, but because I had failed her once more. Typically, I hadn't thought in terms of having failed myself. I'd sat in the bedroom alone for some time, awash in self-loathing, heartbroken again that she was heartbroken again, feeling the world caving in once more. I had walked to that dresser like an automaton. I had put the pistol to my temple as casually as I'd lift a morning cup of coffee to my lips, my finger on the trigger. I understood now that if my intent had been genuine there would have been no hesitation. But I had paused just long enough to hear Kay on the stairs, and had put the gun away. I couldn't now say whether I'd given in to spare Kay the horror or because I'd just chickened out. But sitting in that detox dayroom, staring at one of those hideous cotton plugs taped to a wall, I knew without a doubt that next time around there would be no hesitation.

Then one evening I experienced first hand what the founders of Alcoholics Anonymous themselves discovered as the vital missing ingredient in their long-sought recipe for sobriety: that an alcoholic can stay sober by helping another alcoholic stay sober—a simple concept that is the cornerstone of recovery.

We went to an AA meeting elsewhere in the hospital, escorted by an AA veteran who preached like a Wild West parson as he quoted from the Big Book. Among us was an elderly man who admitted entering the detox only at the insistence of his family. He wanted no part of this circus and, like thousands before him, honestly didn't believe he belonged there. Before leading us away like kindergartners, our escort described to the novices what the meeting would entail, and when he mentioned that a couple of prayers were among the proceedings, the old man declared that he'd have no part of any religious gathering. He'd lived seventy-five years without the assistance of any god and he certainly wasn't in need of one now. He refused to go, and when a nurse explained that his participation was mandatory, he asked her point blank if she'd be the one to try dragging him there. If that Amazon had been on duty she'd have tucked him under her arm. He put up such a fuss that he was finally permitted to stay behind, and warned that further resistance to treatment would result in his getting thrown out, which brightened him up considerably.

For some reason I felt a need to give this guy a hand. I could see how bewildered he was and how much he hurt inside, and while I had not myself embraced anything close to an understanding of how AA worked, I felt that he needed tutoring and that I was the one to provide it. I don't think he had any intention of quitting drinking, but when I returned from the meeting and as the others prepared for bed, I sat with this man in a corner of the dayroom and attempted to spoon-feed him encouragement. I actually found myself advocating the merits of Alcoholics Anonymous, which under the circumstances was like Ray Charles giving golf lessons.

It reminded me of my youth at the river, when I'd taught dozens of kids how to get up on water skis for the first time, and yet had never gotten up myself. I had tried and failed so many times and had been given so many lessons that I'd been full of pointers for everyone else. Those who can't, teach. (I finally got up and in time became an accomplished enough skier to try a treacherous three-foot-high ski jump someone had jerry-rigged none too professionally. For anyone inclined to pursue this exhilarating stunt, I recommend that as you are just about to hit that ramp, make sure your ski tips go *on* the ramp, not under it.)

I whispered with that old man for over two hours. I told him about the detoxes I'd been through, the rehabs, my numerous failures, my deteriorating liver, my lost careers, my discarded children, my seemingly hopeless addiction. I talked about the terrifying proposition I now faced that if I didn't straighten out I was going to lose the only person in the world who mattered to me, and that if that happened I would die by my own hand. And I told him all I knew about the fellowship of AA, gleaned almost entirely from what I'd read and heard, but certainly not from much personal experience.

About one in the morning a nurse walked in and made us go to bed. The old man and I trudged off to our rooms. He thanked me for giving him so much of my time. I thanked him for listening. As I lay in bed thinking about our conversation, wondering if I'd said anything that might help the old boy out, I felt a sensation come over me almost like a warming, as if I'd swallowed some sweet tonic of serenity; and for the first time I felt a surge of bona fide optimism, and I saw that window of hope. Somehow my efforts to help that old man in his demise had served to help me feel better about mine. As I had tried to encourage him, I had encouraged myself. My eyes were wide open, staring into the darkness, and I said out loud, "By God I'm going to make it." I didn't realize it then, but the wording was perfect.

***

"Look," I said, "Can we dispense with the background nonsense?"

"It isn't nonsense at all. We need your history to help us develop a course of treatment."

Like every other counselor I'd encountered, she was all business—an attractive black woman about my age whom I sensed had enjoyed a buzz or two herself in an earlier life. She had started the session talking as though it was my first day in pre-school.

"I mean, can we cut to the chase here? I've been through this so many times. I realize that my sitting here is a pretty good indication that I haven't progressed very much, but I do know the ropes a little, you know? It just doesn't matter anymore how old I was when I first tried alcohol, or what kind of drink it was or where I got it. It doesn't matter anymore that my father drank or my mother was whacky or my family was dysfunctional or any of that crap. I'm not trying to be a wise-ass. It's just that this stuff doesn't matter anymore. I'm forty-three years old. I've been through the mill. I'm a three-time loser. I'm at the end of my rope. I gotta find out what the hell I'm going to do now, not talk about what happened thirty friggin' years ago."

In two days I was to be discharged, which meant that I had to be discharged *to* something. To them, using a detox solely as a drying out tank was like putting a Band-Aid on an amputation. But I'd had my fill of people deciding what was best for me and what treatment I required and where I should be *sent*. I understood that they could only prescribe what they considered the proper path to recovery for each patient. I also knew that they weren't always right, and that a patient, in a state of bewilderment and desperation, might agree under duress to whatever a counselor happened to recommend, simply because he believed that under the circumstances he had no choice in the matter—especially after being reminded repeatedly that drugs and alcohol had turned his brain into cottage cheese, incapable of intelligent reasoning.

"All right," she said. "Obviously you're not in a frame of mind to discuss these details. We can cover that when you're not quite so agitated. Meanwhile we have to begin thinking in terms of what rehabilitation to pursue."

"No rehab."

"I beg your pardon?"

"No rehab. I did rehab."

There came the smile, the standard issue smirk. She said, "Well, you may have been through rehab but it's pretty obvious that not much of it rubbed off."

"I guess not."

"My honest opinion is that maybe now you're ready to take rehabilitation more seriously. I don't see that you have any choice. Your denial is still getting in the way of ..."

"Listen to me, please. Excuse me for interrupting, but this is exactly what I'm trying to avoid here. The automatic textbook theories, like not wanting to go to a rehab automatically means I'm in denial. I'm not in denial. I'm beyond denial. I graduated from denial a long time ago. There's nothing to deny anymore. I have no delusions whatsoever about where I'm at. I understand what you're saying. I mean it's pretty obvious that I *didn't* take rehab very seriously. I just don't think that going through that process again is going to help. I got the best treatment available and I'm still sitting in a glorified drunk tank, and I just don't think that going back to rehab again and again until I get it right is the answer. I'm missing something. I don't know how to describe it. Okay, wait a minute. It's sort of like this. I don't know what made me think of this, but when I was in high school we used to go to these dances at the YMCA, and everybody was doing the pony. You remember it?"

Her smile said she did.

"There was that certain sliding motion with your feet and I just couldn't get the hang of it. I had a dozen girls trying to show me how to do it. They said do this, do that with your foot, then that foot, over and over, but I just couldn't get it. It wasn't something you could *make* your feet do, you know what I mean? Then one night I'm out there stumbling around like an idiot, and all of a sudden it came to me, and my feet just started doing it, like magic, like I'd been doing it all my life. And I ponied my ass off. I ponied every dance, I ponied all night, I ponied all the way home. You know what I'm saying?"

"Okay, so something's missing that you don't think you'll find in rehab. Where do you think you're going to find it? What do you think is going to just come to you all of a sudden like learning the pony?"

"Well, I've been thinking a lot about AA. It's been shoved in my face from the get-go, but I never really took it seriously. I guess I copped an attitude that it wasn't for me. I went to some meetings and they were boring as hell, and for the life of me I couldn't see what good they were."

"So what's changed?"

"I don't know. I just feel different. I never really gave AA a chance, you know? It's sort of like when you couldn't stand a certain teacher and then you started to realize maybe she wasn't such a bad egg after all. I guess I started thinking there must be a reason I don't know about that those people go to meetings all the time. I've got a couple friends who go, and they're staying sober. I've always hated the expression you hear a lot, 'Don't drink, go to meetings.' The old-timers say that. They never did a rehab. Their answer to everything is 'don't drink, go to meetings,' like that's all there is to it. I always thought what a stupid-ass expression that was. Like you ask somebody how to skydive and they say 'take a plane, jump out.' Anyway, when I leave here, that's my game plan."

"Don't drink, go to meetings."

"Yeah. Maybe I can become an AA addict. Fight fire with fire."

"Well, that's fine in theory. God knows a lot of people get sober without setting foot in a rehab, but the point here is can *you* do it?

"I don't know. I gotta give it a shot. It's the only thing I haven't tried."

"Well, I can't force you into rehab. And yes, AA is absolutely necessary with or without rehab. But I've got a responsibility to make the best recommendation I can for your recovery. I have a duty to perform here. I'm responsible for recommending a treatment that's going to work for you."

"So how are you going to feel if you put me through another rehab and find me back here again next year anyway?"

"I hope to God I never see you again. Nothing personal."

Two days later I was thrown to the wolves, released on my own recognizance, left to my own devices. Days spent in detoxes and rehabs count as sober time, of course, if only because you can't get a drink there anyway. But real sober time is earned on the street; all that stands between you and a drink is the time it takes to get to it. Upon my release late in the morning I went directly to a noon AA meeting. When the speaker asked if there were any sobriety anniversaries on the floor, I raised my hand. "I just got out of detox. I'm celebrating an hour."

22

Square One

I wrote personal notes to Kay's family and hand delivered them to each of their houses when I knew they weren't home. I'd be seeing them at a family gathering in a few days and I had to apologize for my behavior at Christmas. I tried to describe briefly the insidiousness of my addiction and my powerlessness against it, and I asked for their forgiveness. Kay thought it was brave of me to spill my guts to her family like that, but I thought it cowardly that I needed to cover my ass in writing before I dared see them again.

If a recovering alcoholic learns only one thing, it is that only another alcoholic knows what it's like to be one. I needed Kay's family to believe that my ruining their Christmas Eve had not stemmed from selfishness or heartlessness, but I realized that no amount of explanation could make them fully empathize. The only way I could truly recompense would be to never let it happen again, which I couldn't guarantee for as long as I lived.

I couldn't honor the recommended prescription of ninety meetings in ninety days for AA newcomers (and I was one despite having been in and out of the recovery process for nearly three years) because I was special. Special people are nevertheless allowed in AA, even if they tend to be treated like all the other people in the room who used to be special. I didn't go to a meeting every day for three months, but I did average five a week. I didn't become anything close to an AA addict, but I did follow with determination that advice I had always found so inane. I didn't drink, I went to meetings. And I began to absorb the tenets of the AA program as they were intended, with an open mind, a desire to learn, a willingness to change. I also began to understand that if I really wanted a sober life I had to work at it—something new and strange to this boy, who had always expected his sobriety served up on a silver platter.

The purpose of the ninety in ninety concept is simply to expose the rookie to as much AA as possible in the precarious first weeks of his or her liquor-less life. It is hoped that in the process he or she will shut up and listen and take things as they come and concentrate on keeping booze at bay a day at a time. There was more to my initial success this time than a greater perseverance and pure fear, however. My entire attitude seemed to have changed. No longer did I go to meetings simply to attend, or arrive full of dread about the inevitable boredom that awaited me. I now found myself going dutifully if not altogether elatedly, as one heads to work each day out of sheer routine. I began befriending my fellow members as soul mates instead of looking down on them as social outcasts who were only there because they had nothing better in their lives to do.

Kay remained reserved. She liked what she saw but had learned not to put much faith in me, regardless of my new attitude. She'd seen new attitudes before. A top-notch rehab and the best of treatment hadn't done it for me previously, but she was now at least guardedly encouraged. Maybe I was finally onto something.

Returning to the rooms of AA meant confronting a number of

people who had known me on prior quests and with whom I couldn't help feeling discomfited about my latest failure. My principal mentor in earlier efforts and a longtime friend, one of the few who could probably match me drink for drink in our heyday, welcomed me with a hug.

"I guess it's back to square one," I said.

"Better than no square at all," said Jim. "At least you made it back. A lot of people don't." He knew I'd been struggling and that I'd abandoned AA. When he asked why I hadn't been around, I said that I'd been embarrassed to come to meetings because I'd been drinking.

He said, "You dummy, what do you think the meetings are for?" I didn't then grasp his meaning, but I figured it out later. The doors of AA are always open for those who understand the need to continually reinforce their sobriety, but they were opened to begin with for those who have yet to find it.

I decided against pursuing any professional avenues for a while, save for occasional free-lance writing assignments for little more than pocket money. I took a part-time cooking job, and as the cottage season approached I looked forward to it with both anticipation and trepidation. The cottage would be a major test. Back in rehab I had been told that it was imperative for me to remove the cottage from my life because I had used it as a haven for my drinking. I could hole up there and drink for days on end without anyone knowing. It would prove to be too much of a temptation, they'd said. While in rehab I had witnessed or heard about people calling home and arranging to sell bars and restaurants they owned to separate themselves from the business, put boats on the market because they'd never left a dock without a cooler full of beer on board, relinquish memberships in golf clubs, bail out of successful musical groups, unload cherished box seats at the ballpark and season tickets for NFL teams, dump girlfriends or boyfriends that they knew would still be partying, even to find new places to live, all out of fear of temptation.

A newcomer in recovery is urged to change the people, places, and things of his former lifestyle that might pose a threat to his delicate sobriety. Some of these changes are easier than others, and some are simply impossible. In one respect they'd been right about the cottage. It was there that I hid when I started drinking again, and it was there that I had fallen off the wagon to begin with. But I had never entertained any thoughts about offing the cottage or even avoiding it, and I wouldn't now. I had waited almost thirty years for the right to call the cottage mine. It made no sense to me to spend the rest of my life running from every enticement and hiding from every influence. Sure, there were obvious situations I'd be stupid not to avoid. But where does it end? Do I sell out of an irreplaceable gem of riverfront property in the 1000 Islands that I'd waited a lifetime for, just because I used to drink there? I used to drink everywhere. What difference did it make?

I couldn't just switch off my love for the cottage and the river. I could never change that, so I had to change myself. And as I had come to view AA differently, so too would I change what the cottage meant to me—not as a haven for my drinking, but as a citadel for my soberness, the home office of my recovery. The concept seemed practical enough, except that it didn't include provisions for dealing with one thing I could never change—my mother. That she was intolerably domineering and nearly impossible to appease was as much a part of her makeup as my drinking had always been of mine. I'd just have to learn to keep dodging her bullets, because I knew that, like temptation, she'd never stop shooting.

I was at the cottage alone one day when Rudy called from Rochester to say that Mother had suffered a stroke, though it was believed to be a minor one. Now I felt terrible that we'd been so at odds of late. I hadn't seen or talked to her in weeks. I frantically shut the cottage up and I was on the road in a matter of minutes.

"Hello, sonny," she said merrily when I entered her hospital room. "What brings you to this neck of the woods?"

"I heard you might be dying," I said, "and I didn't want to miss it." I kissed her on the forehead. She had experienced a TIA (transient ischemic attack), a mini-stroke, which she insisted on calling an ear stroke because it had affected her balance, and because she couldn't have had an attack that anyone else ever had or that the doctors had ever heard of.

A doctor took me aside and said that they were mildly concerned because when asked if she knew what city she was in, she'd said Cleveland. I told the doctor she was fine. He'd have reason to worry if she'd said Rochester, though I toyed with the idea of running out and getting a Cleveland newspaper somewhere and slipping it on her bedside table.

She suffered no physical disabilities from the incident, though she was thereafter prone to occasional dizzy spells and fell a couple of times. She called one day to ask me to erect a railing along the back walk leading to the garage because she'd fallen in the rock garden on her way to the car. I told her that if she couldn't get to the garage without falling down, she had no business driving. "Oh I'm fine as long as I'm sitting," she said.

I pulled the plugs on the distributor cap on her engine a few times, but she called the Auto Club. Perhaps because of her age, or because she'd gotten a ticket or had had an accident we weren't aware of, her insurance company ultimately put her into a risk pool, but she gladly paid the exorbitant premiums.

Though now eighty, she was determined to keep driving, as many aging people are long after some of them might better hang up their keys. It represents their last vestige of freedom to come and go as they please, and they can't be blamed for that. Truth be told, she couldn't be any more of a menace on the roadways than she'd always been anyway.

For the next several months, hope as we did that she might begin to mellow in her twilights years, Mother not only continued to be the monumental pain in the patoot she'd been all her life, but began to take it to an even more infuriating level as if intent on going out in a blaze of glory.

Since Kay and I lived closest, it was easiest for us to stop by and see if she needed anything, to run errands for her or do chores around the house. Kay made the mistake of offering to take her grocery shopping. Carrying the old girl piggyback across the Alps could not have been more excruciating. Kay hoped that a woman of my mother's years would prefer a trip to the market to be as expedient and uneventful as possible. Kay should have known better.

Each grocery item had to be thoroughly examined and discussed at length. Butchers and bakers and greengrocers and stock boys were engaged in endless conversations. It took her two hours to half fill a cart. And—as if there could possibly be any doubt—she was not only among those women who never have their checkbooks ready at the checkout, she was the grand poopah of them all. Milk curdled faster than my mother could produce a check, and the longer the line of shoppers behind her and the louder they groaned and sighed in exasperation, the slower she'd fumble through her purse, the more time she'd spend reviewing the entirety of the cash register receipt, and the longer she'd take to write the check. And God help any poor slob in line who made the mistake of commenting aloud about her obviously deliberate performance, because she'd be delighted to devote even more time to verbally tearing him or her to shreds for chastising an elderly woman who was doing the best she could. Eighty years old and still rattling cages, while Kay made apologies in her wake.

One night I took her to dinner at a neighborhood restaurant. At the table next to ours a young couple were enjoying fish fries and the man kept looking at the ceiling. "What on earth are you staring at, for heaven's sake?" Mother asked. The couple turned to her, appearing baffled by her intrusiveness, but the young woman explained, "Oh, we were thinking about getting a ceiling fan in our dining room and my husband was looking at the ones they have here."

"Well it seems to me," Mother said indignantly, "that when a fellow takes a lady out to dinner he should be enough of a gentleman not to spend the evening looking at ceiling fans." When the couple shot me an inquisitive look I could only smile and shrug.

The more we strived to accommodate her, the further she stretched our tolerance. Because she knew precisely which buttons to push, such lenience inevitably snapped, serving to confirm her unwarranted conviction that we really didn't care about her at all, and kowtowed to her only because we were after her money. Given the way she had misinterpreted our affection all our lives, she could not have thought anything else. She still didn't know how to love, and she still didn't know how to *be* loved. In her mind, a family member who exhibited affection had to have ulterior motives.

I spent the next few months in and out of her favor, on and off her shit list, depending on her moods as they coincided with my level of patience on any given day. I'd stop by a couple times a week and as often as not we'd end up fighting and I'd go away wondering why I'd bothered.

As autumn approached, so too did the time to close the cottage for another season. The endless work of upgrading and maintaining a place as old as ours had proved to be good therapy for me, and I'd spent considerable time fixing the things I'd previously fixed while drunk. I had survived the summer, and while I'd suffered a few flesh wounds from my mother's incessant barrage of gunfire, she had at least not driven me to drink. Nor had anything else. I frequented AA meetings, and I had not taken alcohol in nine months. But I tried not to think in terms of how well I'd done or that in a couple more months I'd be celebrating a year of sobriety. Looking ahead is deadly, and taking success for granted even more so. Still, my confidence was intact and with each passing week came a higher level of resolve.

***

I snuck into the gymnasium at Penfield High School. My son Jake, now a senior, was playing varsity basketball and had a game that night. I didn't want to run into Abby or any of her family who might also be there, but I didn't see any of them in the bleachers. I had to ask a cheerleader which of the boys was Jake. I had no idea what he looked like.

He looked six-foot-three, broad in the shoulders, strong in the legs, long in the arms, and he had a handsome puss the girls would call cute. He was a stronger ballplayer than I had been. He was lanky and slightly unwieldy, befitting a seventeen-year-old who had probably grown from guard to forward practically overnight, as I had, but he had more meat on his bones than I'd had at that age. But aside from all that he had a ready smile and looked like a damn good kid, someone who'd make a father proud, and I was—proud of a son I didn't even know.

It would be a while before I got to meet him. I had no idea how I'd be accepted, if at all, but I knew I wasn't yet ready. I had accumulated more sober time than ever before, but in the grand scheme, I had barely begun.

I don't remember now how the arrangements came about a year later. Jake had started college at Geneseo State. Wendy was in her last year at Potsdam with her eye on continuing at Michigan State. I think I wrote Wendy, asking if Kay and I could meet her and Jake somewhere, maybe for dinner, when they were both home for Thanksgiving. Deciding that it was time and deeming myself ready and worthy at last to meet my own children represented for me a milestone in my comeback akin to striking the mother lode; and I was terrified.

The initial introductions were slightly awkward, though more for me than for them, I think. I remember that their hugs were sincere and that they took an immediate liking to Kay. They were genuinely interested in learning who I was. They already knew *what* I was. I remember that I found them to be nothing short of beautiful, infinitely well-mannered, bursting with personality and humor, smart and levelheaded, and that they emitted not a flicker of resentment.

I suffered for many years from the guilt of abandoning my kids and the fact that they had to grow up without their natural dad. It became readily clear that they had not only managed quite nicely, but had probably fared better than they might have, had they been reared by the selfish drunk I had been throughout their lives. I will be eternally grateful to Abby for not having filled them with hatred toward me. I would have considered her justified, but she had remained too honorable for that, too good a mother, and too fine a woman.

I saw the kids again at Christmas at Mother's house. I was still somewhat sheepish, but I was also still sober, or at least dry, with two years under my belt. Kay and I gave them gifts, the first time we'd been in a position to do so. I gave Jake a cassette carrier that held twenty long-playing tapes I'd spent many hours recording from borrowed albums. I knew he was into music and like every dumb dad assumed he'd like the same music I did. I'd also tucked some folding money into one of the cassettes, the first cash I had ever slipped to my college-age son.

Wendy moved to Michigan to pursue her master's and doctorate degrees at MSU. Jake spent his summers between semesters working at an uncle's golf course near Saratoga. But they had gradually seeped back into my life, and I into theirs, though there was much ground yet to cover and in my mind a great deal to make up for. I expected them to be more curious about where I'd been all those years, and why; but they already knew. It appeared that to them, the important thing was not where I'd gone, but that I had returned, and that I'd left my demons behind. It took me longer to feel the same way. Guilt is a worthless emotion, but difficult to discard when you wear it so well.

23

The Mouse

I didn't know the small plain woman seated at Mother's kitchen table when I stopped by one day. Mother introduced her as Connie Mann, a financial advisor. She appeared to be a little older than I, and she smiled as you might expect a mouse to smile. Mother didn't know squat about how to manage what the old man had left her. We children had no idea yet what his estate amounted to, but it was apparently sizeable enough to make her mad as hell that they'd been much better heeled than she'd been led to believe. With the exception of some household furnishings that he had inherited and wanted us children to have, he had bequeathed her the whole of his assets.

He'd always been secretive about his savings, possibly because he hadn't trusted Mother to handle money responsibly to begin with, but chiefly because he knew she'd be hard-pressed to care for herself financially if he died prematurely. The very concept of working for a living was foreign to her. She'd only had one job in her life, a brief stint as a waitress in the Adirondacks in her early twenties, which she claimed she'd been forced to quit because the cooks kept making comments about her breasts. How horrible it must have been for her. Maybe it would have helped if she'd kept them out of the steam table. She had commented at the family dinner table one night when we were younger that she had no working skills and that if anything happened to our father she'd be forced to become a streetwalker. The old man had said, "You'd still starve."

She'd been given a weekly allowance for household management. It had never been enough, of course, and she'd often complained about not having bought herself a new dress since they'd been married. She'd scrimped all her married life, saved green stamps, clipped coupons, often bought clothes for us kids at next-to-new sales, and could stretch a pound of hamburger into a meatloaf that could seat six.

One day, when I was repairing a railing on her cellar stairs, Mother informed me that the lawyer she and the old man had always engaged was stepping down because he'd been diagnosed with cancer. The prognosis wasn't good, and he'd advised Mother to designate a new executor and to put her affairs in the hands of another attorney. This she had done. Her choice for executor was Connie the mouse, and for her legal affairs, a lawyer named Ken Matlick that the mouse had recommended. When I questioned why she had made a virtual stranger the executrix of her will, she told me that she and Connie had in fact become very good friends and that she trusted her implicitly.

I said, "You could have made one of us your executor, you know."

She said, "Ha!"

***

A horrendous ice storm hit the area on the evening of March 3, 1991. By morning a coating of an inch and a half from an all-night freezing rain had accumulated on everything. Trees dismantled under the colossal weight, huge limbs snapping off like twigs with a frightening crack like gunfire. Utility poles and lines came down, and several hundred thousand homes and businesses were left without power, some for up to ten days, others for two weeks or more.

The occurrence seems trifling now against the appalling loss of life and property suffered in devastating natural disasters elsewhere in the country and world of late. For a region unaccustomed to anything more problematic than a foot or two of snow, however, it was a calamity that caught us by surprise, and one for which our local utility company found itself alarmingly unprepared. On my mother's street, one side of the road was powerless for over two weeks, while the other side had not lost juice at all. We offered to take her in but she preferred to stay closer to home and chose to move in with a neighbor across the road. The relocation, however temporary, may have taken a toll on her.

She was understandably set in her ways, accustomed to eating what and when she wanted, sleeping in her own bed, having her own bathroom, watching the TV shows she preferred. Though she got along fine with the neighbor and was being comfortably cared for, she was out of her element, separated from her own stuff, and, worse, not in command. The experience must have been more traumatic for her than we realized at the time, for thereafter she seemed more out of sorts than usual. It may have been that she'd begun to suffer some dementia and that the storm had put her over the edge, but with her one never knew. It had always been next to impossible to determine which of her miseries was real or affected, and she'd gone over the edge so many times that the edge had been rounded smooth.

Maris was having marital problems and wanted to move back to Rochester with two pre-school children. Staying with Mother was the only avenue open to her at the time. She found that Mother was in no state of mind to have young kids underfoot and that she had grown even more irascible. She also found that Connie the mouse, whose superficial demeanor was as apparent to Maris as it was to me, was frequently at the house and had become Mother's almost constant companion.

It didn't take long for Maris' kids to learn what their new grandmother was like. They weren't there more than a week before they became so terrified of Mother's barrages of unwarranted outbursts that they'd literally wet their pants when she walked in the room. They hadn't been raised with the iron hand under which Mother believed all children should cower, so she considered it her duty to discipline them whether they needed it or not.

On one occasion the little girl, all of three years old, was curiously looking through odds and ends in a kitchen table drawer when Mother walked in and slammed the drawer shut on the kid's fingers and screamed at her for touching things that didn't belong to her. The old man had put a golf flag from the fifteenth hole at his club in the back lawn, a memento of his only hole in one, and the flag had remained loosely stuck in the dirt in a far corner of the yard. When Mother caught Maris' young boy playing with it, she asked him what his favorite toy was—his fishing rod—and she took it and hid it on him in retaliation for his having so disrespectfully abused what she called the one keepsake of her husband's memory that she cherished more than anything in the world. No harm had been done to the dumb flag, and I sincerely doubt that she gave a damn about it anyway. The kid had only waved it around and it needed only to be stuck back in the ground again. It was a trumped up reason to get pissed off, and I recognized the behavior only too well.

One day Maris called and said that Mother was threatening to take a belt to the boy because he'd destroyed her flowers. She needed me to come over. When I arrived Mother told me that the little bastard had viciously ripped the bloom off every daffodil in the yard, and she had even saved the decapitations as evidence. The boy, with tears streaming down his face and obviously scared to death, denied having touched the flowers. She had a box full, several dozen of them, and every last one had been neatly cut off with scissors with the same length of stem attached. It couldn't have been more obvious that she'd cut them down herself.

More such episodes followed and Maris finally had to find an apartment she hadn't the means to rent. Her husband subsequently moved back to Rochester and they got back together. Mother went into seclusion. Rudy and I were on her shit list now because we had sided with Maris, while Jim as usual kept his distance to spare himself the meaningless drama for which he had always had so little tolerance.

When I went to the house she wouldn't answer the door, even when she knew I'd seen her though the kitchen window. I had a key, but she obviously didn't care to see me, so I didn't intrude. When I phoned she hung up on me, as I expected, but at least I confirmed she was still breathing. When some of the older grandchildren tried to visit her when they were home from school, we learned she had ignored them as well by pretending she wasn't home. She no longer wanted anything to do with any of us. She had even distanced herself from her longtime friends and was seen almost exclusively in the company of her new, dearest companion, Connie.

Although the old man had not chosen to bequeath his children any cash assets, he did stipulate that we would inherit, after Mother's life use of them, antique furniture, tableware and Oriental carpets that he'd inherited from an uncle back in the sixties, along with a vast collection of books from the same source and those he'd accumulated himself. We'd been led by Mother to believe that much of the furniture, rugs, silver settings, flatware, china, and many books were absolutely priceless, though we would eventually learn otherwise.

Mother had commented to me once that she deserved every penny of the old man's money because of the living hell he'd put her through all their years together. Going by that standard, I figured we kids deserved the same consideration from her with the Hope Diamond and some Saudi Arabian oil fields thrown in, though we were sure she'd leave everything to Save the Sardines before we'd see a penny of it. We began to be concerned for her own sake, however, because we knew that she wasn't wise in the ways of finance and that someone we knew nothing about was apparently managing her holdings.

I sought the advice of an old friend. Salvatore Galli had once been an aspiring artist; but, fearing he'd be confused with the more famous if less-gifted Spanish surrealist, he became an attorney instead. I told him the circumstances and he explained that our mother had every right to do whatever she pleased with her dough, unless we could prove that she was being criminally manipulated, and, of course, we couldn't. Our only other avenue would be to prove her mentally incompetent in order to be given power of attorney and control of her assets—a complex, lengthy, and costly process that would require extensive psychiatric evaluations and expert testimony that might not prove anything. Meanwhile, it was her money and she could invest it in turnip futures if she wanted. He told me our hands were tied but to call him if something came up.

I often felt guilty about leaving my aging mother to fend for herself in that big house, and worried that she may have put too much trust in someone who seemed to have materialized out of nowhere. But my efforts to comfort or counsel her had always been rejected and my motives questioned. She was convinced that we were only after her money, when in fact all we wanted was for her to mellow out a little in her declining years and give up the war. Maris called early one afternoon in late March. Mother was dead.

***

I loved her as much as I hated her. Still do. Always will. I truly believe that's exactly how she wanted it. When I heard the news I felt nothing. I wasn't shocked at all. My contrasting emotions seemed to cancel one another out and leave a vacuum. My heartfelt regret that she had departed on such a sour note was varnished over by my undeniable elation over the burden of anxiety that had been lifted from me. My earnest wish that in her golden years she might have finally come to terms with how adversely she had treated the people who loved her most was overshadowed by my satisfaction that she had finally gotten her due. My sadness over the fact that all the great deeds such an energetic and gregarious lady could have accomplished had been thwarted by the demons within her was upstaged by my jubilation that ding-dong, the wicked witch was dead.

She was found stark naked on her bedroom floor. In light of the totally contradictory manner in which she had lived her life, it was ironically fitting. The woman who had always flaunted her figure so unabashedly was also obsessively modest, and would not have been caught dead without a stitch on.

She had planned a luncheon engagement with the mouse, who had phoned repeatedly with no response, and upon going to the house had gotten no answer to the doorbell. Mother's car was in the garage. Connie had called Jim, though he had no key. The police had been summoned. Officers had broken a small pane in the back door to gain entry. I would learn later that there was no indication of wrongful death. A soiled nightie had been found in the bathroom off her bedroom. She had apparently had an accident in the night and may have been headed to her dresser for fresh sleepwear when she was stricken with what was probably a massive stroke.

The coroner would report that she'd had a peaceful expression on her face, indicative of her having died instantaneously and painlessly with no evidence of trauma or drug overdose, and that she likely never knew what hit her and was probably dead before she slumped to the floor.

When I got to the house my brother and sisters were already there, awaiting the medical examiner. Mother's body was still upstairs, they said, if I wanted to see her. I did not. I had too many conflicting emotions. I would have liked to say goodbye, to see and maybe even kiss on the forehead one last time the woman who had been such a tumultuous influence on my life, who had given me so much joy and pain, so many laughs and sorrows.

I had no desire to see her dead and naked purely out of respect, but my principal reluctance stemmed more from a fear of how I'd react when I saw her. I might be grateful that she'd suffered no pain, or I might have wished that she had. I might have told her how sorry I was for all my transgressions against her, and for hers against me, and that I loved her nonetheless and forgave her.

I might have said that I understood that she had been a sick woman whose reign of terror over her loved ones had been beyond her control, and that she had deserved not our anger but our pity and compassion. Or I might have found myself remembering only the rotten things she'd done to me over the years and bid the crazy bitch good riddance. I honestly wasn't sure I wouldn't spit on her.

24

Fishy

The next afternoon my sisters and I sat in Mother's kitchen, gabbing absently about old times wonderful and awful, hilarious and heartrending, feeling subdued but hardly grief-stricken. The loss of a mother we would have loved to see more of was overwhelmed by the freedom from the one we'd known best, as if the Good Witch of the North would forever have second billing.

All the fun and fantastic times that her dynamic personality had given us paled against the memories of her spitefulness. Often she had estranged herself from us for months on end, during which she would not communicate with one or more of us at all—our punishment, usually, for having stood up to her. So many times over the years, even while we still lived at home, our crime had been only that of defending ourselves against her unjustified wrath. Now that she was gone it seemed like just another rift.

But there was also a ponderous awareness that both our parents were dead, and that an era defined by the triumphs and tribulations of our lives in this big old house had come to an end. Years before, as we had watched our father's health deteriorate, we had accepted his death as inevitable; but we had somehow imagined Mother going on forever, as if, as they say, she was too ornery to die.

She was right next door, another irony. When our childhood neighbors had put that considerable lot with its large imposing house on the market many years before, it had been purchased by an undertaker. The property was zoned for commercial use if maintained in appearance as a residence, but it was Mother who spearheaded a campaign to prevent it. Surmising correctly that the broad side yard in which we had played baseball as kids would be paved for a parking lot, and resenting the very idea of living next to a funeral home, she had canvassed door-to-door for signatures on a petition and had made countless phone calls to muster support, but to no avail. That funeral parlor, having subsequently established itself as a respected component of the community, has since buried just about everyone who had signed that petition, including my parents, who, after several years of an icy relationship with their neighbor, had finally made peace.

We knew that we did not yet have the right to take anything from the house, but that didn't stop us from poking around. Despite being a sloppy housekeeper in general, Mother had always been fastidious about organizing in little containers trifling items that no one else would probably bother keeping—odd bottle tops, empty thread spools, odd fountain pen caps, single cheap cuff links, and the like. In a small wooden box secured with a rubber band in a kitchen drawer, we found what may have symbolized as well as anything my mother's lifelong desperation—a collection of about forty whole wishbones, so dry and colorless that she must have been collecting them for years. Wishes waiting to be wished, dreams tucked away for a rainy day, hopes in safekeeping. The little box spoke volumes to me.

As we discussed what arrangements needed to be made, there

appeared in the driveway Connie the mouse, accompanied by two hardy young men. Not having noticed us through the kitchen window, they came up the walk just as Maris opened the back door to greet them. The mouse was so shocked at the sight of her that she froze and was for some time speechless. Finally she said, "I had no idea anyone was here."

"Apparently not," said Maris. "Would you like to come in?"

"Uh, no, thank you, I don't think so."

"Then what can we do for you?"

Noticeably flustered, the mouse stammered that they'd come to take measurements in order to replace the small pane in the door that the police had broken, though a piece of wood paneling cut to size and securely nailed in place was already sufficient. We wondered why the mouse had acted so frustrated to find us there, and why the chore she ostensibly came to perform required three people, and after dark besides. The mouse withdrew with her cohorts, mumbling something about not wishing to disturb us in our time of sorrow, and departed, leaving us to question her reason for coming. The supposed measurement would have taken a few seconds and they had left without doing it.

Some time later one of us noticed a canvas tote bag hanging on a closet doorknob in the hall. We must have passed it a dozen times. In it we found a four-inch stack of assorted paperwork that included annuity proposals, stock reports, income records, bank statements, life insurance applications, copies of substantial five-figure cashier's checks, investment prospectuses and spreadsheets—all the sort of financial stuff that we had assumed was so far over our mother's head that it might as well have dealt with quantum physics.

Curious. If that satchel contained the details of Mother's financial empire, such as it was, she, like our father, would have kept it more secured than the crown jewels, not hanging on a door knob for anyone to find. We didn't know whether, as executrix of Mother's will, the mouse had authority to enter the house at that point, but it now seemed likely not only that it was the tote bag she'd been after, but that it was important enough to her to break into the house to get it.

She may have asked Mother for the paperwork produced by their financial dealings for some reason and Mother had accumulated it to give her when they met for lunch. Now that Mother was dead, the mouse may have wanted it all the more. We went through it paper by paper. None of us was a financial wizard, but the documents enabled us to conclude that she'd been playing around with close to two million.

There was also a draft of a living irrevocable trust that, upon her death, would authorize all of her assets, including her three-fourths ownership of the cottage, to be turned over to the designated trustee, Connie the mouse. My stomach was turning.

It was my idea, echoed by my sisters, to state in Mother's obituary notice that in lieu of flowers donations could be made in her memory to the National Association for the Prevention of Cruelty to Children. Jim nixed the idea in the name of decency. It would have been, admittedly, a nasty thing to do, however fitting we considered it, and Jim's disinclination prevailed. Since her death he had maintained an air of businesslike respectfulness befitting the loss of our dear departed mom, while the rest of us muddled through by hopscotching among stoicism, amusement, and restraint. Frankly, we were still pissed off at her.

Jim scheduled a memorial service and assumed the role of cruise director. He chose the hymns and prayers and suggested heartwarming anecdotes and appropriate tributes. There were times when my sisters and I had difficulty keeping a straight face, while Jim remained appropriately somber throughout the service. It's entirely likely he was hammered.

We will always find it impossible to explain or justify to others how we could have been so callous toward our own mother even as we saw her off to wherever her spirit was headed. But we were driven by a long and lingering bitterness, and by a consciousness that, like a law of physics, for every commendable deed for which she was recognized as a wife and mother and caregiver, there had been an opposite and equally extraordinary misdeed for which she should have been flogged.

Any psychiatrist could likely explain why I remembered the bad times most, though I must say the tendency came to me quite naturally. I suppose even vicious murderers have kind words said about them over their graves, but while listening to the flowery farewell in church I was reminded of the fruitless attempts I'd made over the years to find my mother an appropriate greeting card that related a heartfelt emotion. No such card existed. On the few occasions that I had searched for one for a birthday or Mother's Day or other observance, my outbursts of laughter in a drug store aisle over the absurdity of sending her such syrupy words of love and admiration could only have been exceeded by her own uproarious laughter upon receiving them. But on those occasions I had also been saddened that she was incapable of believing such sentiments, or even of accepting such a card as an earnest if clumsy endeavor to do and say the right thing. Of course, if I had ever chosen to sidestep the farce by sending a humorous or sarcastic greeting, she'd have rebuked me at length for not having had the civility to send my own mother a decent card. Damned if you do or don't, my mother in a nutshell.

We sent her off in fine fashion, however, with the pastor relating stories of her campaigns through the neighborhood for donations to the Cancer Society, the hundreds of gallons of blood she'd donated to the Red Cross, her many hours of involvement with Rochester General Hospital charities, and even her responsibilities as volunteer driver of a medical transport van, in which she had toted around wheelchair-bound patients who, after one ride with her, had miraculously learned to walk.

***

Two days before the service the mouse summoned us to a meeting in which we children would learn the details of Mother's final wishes. It amounted to an attempt by the mouse and the attorney, a rumple-haired man in his forties who peered at us over half-lens reading glasses perched on the end of his nose, to determine just how acquiescent we'd be in their execution of those wishes.

They began by passing out copies of the will and trust, along with waivers of citation that they hoped we'd all blindly sign so that they could expediently have the will probated. They seemed to stress the expediency factor a little too much for my liking, repeatedly noting that affixing our signatures to the waivers was the easiest and fastest way of settling the matters at hand. I wanted to know a little more about said matters, especially after being struck by the peculiarity of some particulars that suggested that something smelled.

The entirety of the old girl's will was contained on a single page.

Beyond the requisite paragraphs about her being of sound mind and getting her funeral paid for and her debts and taxes remitted, etc., it stated simply that she had directed everything she owned put into a trust she had previously established for her grandchildren, and that the mouse had been designated trustee in addition to her duties as executrix. Period.

That she had left everything in trust for our kids we viewed as both bittersweet and peculiar. She had not been a loving grandmother by any stretch of the imagination, invariably berating many of our kids whenever they visited for what they happened to be wearing, what on earth they'd done with their hair, how they could possibly not adore cauliflower, or why they didn't speak the King's English perfectly. Of course we had not forgotten that two of those grandchildren, Maris's littlest ones, she had treated like dirt.

We were happy that our kids would benefit from her will even if we wouldn't, and that she had at least not donated all her dough to the Hula Hoop Society. At the same time, I don't think we were unreasonable in being a little hurt that out of a kitty of nearly two million dollars our parents had not seen fit to leave their children a dime.

We knew almost immediately that something wasn't right. The mouse announced that as soon as the will was probated she'd begin disposing of the contents of the house in an estate sale. I pointed out that she could do whatever she wanted with Mother's treasured collections of cigarette lighter parts and broken shoelaces, but that the antique furniture, Oriental rugs, silver settings, tableware, books, etc., had been our father's property for Mother's life use only and had been bequeathed to us.

"Where did you get that idea?" asked Matlick from under furled brow.

"From my father's will," said I.

"You did? Well, I can't say that I've actually read your father's will and don't even have a copy of it to tell the truth, but I nevertheless have to question your facts. I can't see how his will has any bearing on the issue. There certainly isn't any stipulation in your mother's will that the antiques and other items you mention were to be dealt with separately."

I said, "Excuse me, I'm a little confused here. You haven't even seen my father's will? Weren't you curious, if not actually obligated as her lawyer, to verify how the hell my mother came to have all these assets?"

The mouse spoke up. "Wait a minute, I think I might just have a copy of Huey's will, in fact … let's see here, oh yes, here it is." She handed it to Matlick, who flipped through the first several pages so fast he couldn't possibly have read a word on any of them, stopping abruptly at the very page containing the appropriate clause.

"Well I'll be darned," he said while speedily scanning the page. "My apologies. You're absolutely right. In fact, it's quite specific. Glad you happened to point that out. I had no idea."

They were testing the waters all right, and my catching the oversight must have come as a blow to the mouse. In addition to her other vocations and amusements, she dealt in antiques. If her mouth had been watering over the prospect of getting her mitts on those furnishings, it must have suddenly gone dry.

I was also intrigued that the documents had been signed by my mother and by the two of them, and that the mouse and lawyer had designated themselves witnesses to each other's signature. I didn't know much about these things, but it seemed to me that a neutral third party of some authority should be involved.

"I'll tell you what," I said. "I have a few questions about these documents and I for one would like more time to examine them before I sign anything."

Matlick's brows were working again. "Well, you're certainly entitled to examine them all you want, but I can assure you that the wording is not going to mysteriously change. The documents are very straightforward and the trust is ironclad in terms of what your mother wished to be done."

"Maybe so," I said, "but I am not obligated to sign this waiver at this time, am I?"

"No, you're not. But unless you intend to contest the will it will only mean delaying the inevitable. You do of course have the right to contest the will, but it is very clear. There really isn't anything in it to contest. I think we can agree that for the benefit of all concerned it would be best to move forward so that these matters don't have to drag on any longer than necessary."

The mouse chimed in again. "The important thing here is to get the trust established as quickly as possible so that it can begin generating profits for the sake of the beneficiaries. The purpose of a trust is to make more money to increase the trust, and the sooner we dispense with these details the sooner we can get the trust up and running and earning revenue."

"Well, I'm sorry," I said. "I don't know about my brother and sisters, and I'm not saying I intend to contest the will. It's just that I'm not really well versed in these matters, and I'm not sure I understand all the particulars. I think that as a lawyer you'll agree that only a damn fool signs a legal document he doesn't understand. I just want some time to look over this stuff." Maris and Rudy said, "So do I," practically in unison. Jim said nothing at all. My sisters and I didn't then know it, but at some point prior to that meeting Jim had already signed the waiver.

I went home and called Salvatore Galli. He expressed his condolences, I thanked him, and we got down to business.

"Strap on your guns," I said. "We're going in." I told him about the pack of papers and that it appeared my mother had been involved with all sorts of investments she probably didn't know much about. I told him we had reason to believe that the executrix had intended to break into the house, and that she and the attorney had tried to pull the wool over our eyes regarding the antiques. I told him about the trust and that there was something strange about the will. Dear friend since high school notwithstanding, he needed to know how I intended to pay for the proposed litigation.

"I have no idea. None of us has diddly squat. I guess I was hoping it could come out of the estate."

"Not if the whole estate is wrapped up in a trust."

"I just don't trust them, Sal. They're hiding something. Something ain't right. Could you at least take a look at this stuff and see what you think?"

"That I can do. If we find something questionable we'll take it from there, but I can't promise anything. If the will is somehow disputable, that's one thing, but it's next to impossible to challenge a trust. Bring the stuff over and I'll take a look."

***

On the steps of the church following Mother's memorial service, Jim turned to us and said, "I have a confession to make. It's something you probably wouldn't ever find out if I didn't say anything, but I think you ought to know because I didn't realize things were going to turn out this way. I'm the one who got Connie involved with Mother. I dealt with her a couple of times through work. She approached me and asked if I'd introduce her to Mother and recommend her as a financial consultant so she could get Mom as a client. I never liked the bitch but I figured Mother probably needed some advice and it wouldn't hurt to introduce her. She offered me five grand to help her get her foot in the door. At any rate, I realize now it was a mistake and I feel kind of shitty about it, the way things are going. I agree that something's funny about this whole thing. If you want to spend the money on lawyers to look into it, you have my blessing. For what it's worth, I got it stuck in my butt anyway. I never saw the money."

25

Gotcha

Three weeks later, seeing the glorious river and getting the cottage up and running again provided a welcome diversion, but it would be the summer of our disbelief. Sal had discovered enough reason to contest the will, and probate remained in limbo. We spent the first weeks of the season grasping at straws while absorbing the provisions of a trust agreement that, while virtually unalterable, were ludicrously ambiguous.

Primarily, it failed to outline how it would benefit the fourteen grandchildren individually. It provided that the principal could be invaded to fund tuition and associated costs at a full-time college or university, but it neglected to determine how much each child was entitled to for that purpose. One or two of the grandchildren could hit up the trust for Harvard Medical School and suck it dry before the other kids got so much as a steno pad out of it.

As it turned out my sibs and I were not left entirely out in the cold, at least theoretically. The trustee could award us from profits generated by the trust annual gifts not to exceed $5,000 each, and in her absolute discretion could refuse requests for the gifts for any reason. That seemed plain enough. The mouse could give each of us up to five grand a year if she felt like it. Given that we had not exactly welcomed her as a loving friend of the family and that the more dough she kept in the trust the greater her commissions would be, we weren't counting on it.

My mother's three-quarters share of the cottage also went into the trust, although as an ultimate benefit to the grandchildren—in that it would be split fourteen ways upon the death of the last of us—it would be all but impossible to administer.

For now, however, in order to utilize the three-quarters interest to generate income for the trust, the mouse as trustee would be duly bound to rent the cottage for most of the season to whomever she pleased, including, it would seem, herself. The very possibility of that prospect felt something like what I'd experienced when the spinal anesthesia wore off after my hemorrhoidectomy back in the eighties.

Meanwhile, Sal and a firm of estate lawyers he had engaged, having pored over the contents of the tote bag, discovered alarming discrepancies between the dollar amounts that Matlick had documented as my Mother's assets and those suggested by the paperwork. Matlick had put my mother's estate at $1.3 million, while our lawyers came up with $1.7 million. Most of that difference, for undetermined reasons, would never be accounted for. Further, my father's estate was estimated to have been more like $1.9 million, and we were unable to establish how my mother had apparently spent some $200,000 over the past few years, since she hadn't made any major purchases we were aware of and had been receiving more than ample income from annuities and her own stocks. Large chunks of assets seemed to have vanished.

As for the cottage, the fantastic turn of events was almost beyond my comprehension. Once upon a time, as many fairy tales begin, my siblings and I had owned half a cottage and the other half had been promised to me by my uncle. Not only had my mother managed to gain majority ownership, in spite of my grandmother's intention that she'd never have any part of it, its destiny was now in the hands of a conniving rodent.

The trustee would now control three-fourths of its occupancy. But if at any time she determined the arrangement too cumbersome for the good of the trust, she had the authority to buy Rudy and me out, assume total ownership for the trust, or sell the cottage altogether. This, Sal explained, was highly possible. The cottage still lacked upgrades necessary to rent it at a high enough rate to be profitable. Since remodeling and maintenance costs would far exceed what could realistically be expected in proceeds from renting it for three-fourths of a limited season, the trustee would likely declare it a liability and take steps to unload it. Sal suggested over the phone that we nevertheless had an option open to us. Rudy and I could offer to buy from the trust its three-fourths interest.

"With what, Sal, pickerel poop? We don't have that kind of money." I said. "This is unbelievable. This cottage was supposed to be ours free and clear, and now we have to *buy* the fucking place?"

"Only three-quarters of it, which, under the appraisal taken when your mom died, would be three-fourths of $92,000."

"It was only worth $64,000 total when we got it four years ago."

"True, but a new bathroom and stairs were put in and some foundation work done and apparently quite a few other improvements."

"Yeah, improvements I made myself. Tell you what, if that's the case, the trust owes me about fifteen grand."

"How so?"

"For the work I've put into it. Half that difference in the appraisal comes from labor I performed. I think twenty bucks an hour for my labor is fair."

"You got paperwork to prove that?"

"I've got receipts for the materials."

"Not good enough. Do you have documents that verify you were contracted to do that work?"

"Of course not. I assumed I was working on my own cottage, or at least the family cottage."

"At the risk of making light of a lousy situation, a lot of lawyers have gotten rich because of what people have assumed. It's a kick in the ass, I'll admit. Unfortunately, it looks as though your mother planned to have the cottage dissolved all along."

"What do you mean?"

"Well, think about it. She bought out your Uncle Tom even though you thought he was going to leave his share to you. Maybe he needed money and really *was* trying to sell his half, difficult as that would be, since who's going to buy half a cottage? In any event your mother stepped in and bought it instead. But if she did that for your sake she'd have turned it over to you and your siblings then and there. Instead she bought Jim and Maris out too. Why would she bother doing that if she wanted you to have the cottage anyway? Because she wanted majority ownership.

"Now, by putting her three-fourths interest in the trust, it would be divided fourteen ways among the grandchildren like everything else when the trust terminated. She had to know how ridiculous it would be to divide three-fourths of the cottage fourteen ways, which is why that living will you came across outlined how the trustee would control the three-fourths, along with the authority to buy you and your sister out. Your mother knew you didn't have the means to turn the tables and buy the three-quarters from the trust, especially after not leaving you any money. In other words, the trustee stood to gain total ownership for the trust and sell the property so that none of the family would end up with it."

"Sal, there's no way my mother would have known enough to plot a scenario like that."

"Unless she was being coached. The more we look at this thing the more it stinks of undue influence, that your mother was being coerced."

"By Connie?"

"Draw your own conclusions."

"But if that twat put the idea in my mother's head, my mother obviously went for it."

"Perhaps."

"But why would the mouse care if we got the cottage or not?"

"Two reasons that I can think of. First, the sale of the cottage and its contents would further enhance the trust, which would be to her benefit. Second, maybe she had an eye on it herself."

"Jesus, Sal. Here I thought my mother wanted control of the cottage so she could rub our noses in it, and all along she was planning to screw us out of it from her grave."

"It sort of looks that way. What, may I ask, did you do to your dear sweet mother to piss her off so much?"

"I got news for you, Sal. She came out of the womb pissed off."

What really poached my pouch about what I was hearing was the vision of my mother watching me do all that work and chuckling under her breath. I was putting time and labor into a property that she knew would be yanked out from under me. I wanted to dig her up and kill her.

The previous year, during the spring and early summer of 1992, the river had reached its highest elevation in more than twenty years. Like many docks and shorefronts, our already deteriorating stone seawall had suffered the consequences. Its hand-laid and mortared stonework had withstood for half a century the battering of summer's thundering wakes and the crunching of winter's shifting ice, and for the last few years stones had wriggled loose and plopped into the river one by one. The high water of the previous season had overflowed the wall and swamped the front yard halfway to the cottage, accelerating the wall's demise. It had protected fifty-six feet of shoreline and included a terrace eight feet wide along its length. The entire affair needed replacing and the cost would be significant.

The cottage roof was also badly in disrepair and may well have been the same one that was on the cottage when I was a kid. The ceilings in the upstairs bedrooms were stained and warped by water damage. Most of the rafters were sagging and cracked and would have to be replaced or reinforced, and the roofing underlayment would need replacing. We hadn't the money to even begin covering these major expenses, let alone come up with or mortgage some $70,000 to buy the trust's three-fourths ownership.

All around me loomed the innumerable tasks of general upkeep and repairs that I now had little inclination to pursue while the future of the cottage remained so dubious. At the same time I felt the need to bolster my optimism by working as usual, as if retiring my tools and taking to a hammock meant admitting defeat. The situation could not have been bleaker. I had waited so long for this chunk of heaven, and for a couple of years, even amidst the turmoil of my mother's domineering and maddening presence, I had enjoyed again and shared with Kay the sounds and sights and smells of my boyhood. Kay had turned a wasteland of yard into a showcase of flourishing gardens. She and Rudy had made a junk pile of a house clean and tidy and comfortable. I had taken up hammer and saw and paintbrush and done a multitude of remodeling jobs on what we thought was our summer home at last. Now it seemed as if it had been dangled before our noses like a carrot that was soon to be snatched away.

The AA Big Book tells of promises that lasting sobriety will fulfill, among them a new freedom and a new happiness, and I had come to believe that the cottage was symbolic of mine. As I had hoped, I had transformed it in my mind from a haven for my drinking to a beacon of my resurrection. When I looked across the river, I knew without question that God was there and watching over me. All my life I had thought that getting the cottage someday was a given. Now I saw it as a gift. I didn't earn it for being sober, but for understanding that it was by the grace of God that I was. Now that the gift might be stripped from me, I couldn't help thinking this must be a test, and a damn cruel one at that.

To a drunk who finally emerges from the miserable hole in which he wasted so much of his life, two years of sobriety seems as unattainable as winning the lottery. Yet, having achieved it, in terms of how fragile and vulnerable his abstemiousness remains against an enemy that waits patiently and eternally to engulf him again, a man with only two years under his belt is still wearing Pampers.

The dire truth hit like a sledgehammer. Losing my cottage would be tragic, but losing my sobriety would be fatal. And so it was that I found myself praying all the more to keep the latter so that I could face losing the former, catching more meetings than usual, listening to the river more often, asking for serenity to accept the things I could not change, and hitching up my diapers.

***

By mid-June—despite mounting allegations that Mother's executrix and lawyer had been naughty and that many discrepancies wanted closer scrutiny—it was decided that the will would nevertheless be admitted to probate so that Connie could proceed with her basic duties as executrix, which included the sale of the household items in order to sell the home.

We'd been bequeathed all the antiques and books, but we didn't know where to put them. We divided the more portable items among ourselves as fairly as possible and according to who really wanted what, but there were a number of oversized and heavy pieces of furniture none of us had room for nor wanted. Only Rudy owned a home, a small house in Canandaigua that she'd bought after her divorce several years before. Jim, also long divorced, lived in a small condo; Kay and I rented a row house; and Maris's small home was a rental as well. The books numbered in the thousands and I took almost all of them. I at least had attic and basement space, and I considered myself the best qualified to determine their value and could devote the time to cataloguing the collection. Much of the furniture ended up in the homes of various friends and our children and some pieces were moved several times.

Meanwhile we had begun to experience the nightmare of the

appraisal game. The items we inherited were evaluated by an appraiser of the mouse's choosing for estate purposes, which by custom were assessed moderately to save on taxes. Therefore, we didn't have a true idea of what they were worth, although we'd eventually discover that most weren't anywhere near as valuable as Mother had thought and that some she'd considered priceless weren't worth much at all.

I quickly learned a little about the world of antiques. No matter how rare or old or sought after an item might be, no matter how many thousands of dollars various people will say it should fetch, it is not worth one penny more than what someone is willing to put in your hand. Unfortunately, the helpful experts from TV's Antiques Road Show aren't likely to drop by, so the only people qualified to accurately appraise your antiques are dealers.

I am not insinuating that all such dealers are shady, but they do make their living in much the same way as used car salesmen. Rare is the dealer, if not a dear friend, who will give you a straightforward idea of what the thing can truthfully fetch on the market. Frankly, he is not in business to make you money. He is in business to make himself money. An appraiser may realize your quaint early American desk is worth $3,000 because he knows of someone in his vast network of fellow dealers and collectors who is willing to cough up that much to acquire it, or because he knows he can sell it for that in his showroom. He won't share that knowledge with you, of course, because, like a car salesman, he certainly can't give you what he hopes to sell it for himself. Instead, his eyes will bug out and he'll gasp and swoon and whistle and whoop over this utterly miraculous find, and tell you excitedly how he might be able to get you as much as $950 for it—which, when he announces sadly that he hadn't previously noticed the half-inch hairline surface scratch in the back corner of the underside of the bottom drawer, will become $650—which, after he discovers that one of the original drawer pulls was replaced, will become $500— which, after he realizes that this particular piece was not actually made in 1778 by the prestigious Horace Hairpie & Co. of Tiddlywinks, Mass., as he had first thought, but is one of thousands of such desks mass-produced in 1782 by the Kindling Bros. Furniture Farm of Dorkington, Delaware, will become $300, from which he'll deduct another $100 because it doesn't have the original dust on it. He will then bless you with a check for $200 and a smile that could melt a musket, as he wraps his new treasure in swaddling clothes and slides it gingerly into his van.

Sal called one day and for once had encouraging news.

"Connie and Matlick have hired lawyers for themselves, and a top-notch firm at that."

"What's that mean?"

"Well, in strictly legal terms, it means we caught them with shit on their shoes and they need attorneys to defend themselves."

"Far out. Then you got them on something?"

"Several things. Stupid things on their part. For starters, they allegedly acted as witnesses for the will while at the same time being beneficiaries of the will. That is to say, as trustee, Connie would receive fees, and Matlick, who was co-executor, would also receive fees, and it is unethical and a breech of their fiduciary duty to be the sole witnesses of a testamentary document from which they will benefit. You were absolutely right. They couldn't just witness each other's signature. They stand to lose their respective licenses for that alone."

"There's more?"

"Yeah, it gets better. Connie is allegedly guilty of gross conflict of interest for being your mother's investment broker, executrix, and trustee all at the same time. That's a definite no-no. Worst of all, the attorney allegedly failed to expose the estate to a skip generation tax, which would clearly be an act of legal malpractice."

"What's that about?"

"When you skip a generation in your will, like your mother did in leaving everything to the grandchildren, there's a generation-skipping tax in addition to or instead of regular estate tax. It was up to Matlick to make provisions for the generation skipping tax and file the proper paperwork and he allegedly ignored it. He could be disbarred for that. We also have reason to suspect undue influence and coercion, but that would be tougher to prove."

"So what happens now?"

"We wait. It's their move. Unfortunately, regardless of what happens to Connie and Matlick, your situation probably won't change, but we'll see."

"Well, maybe we'll at least have the pleasure of watching them burn at the stake."

"Maybe. Maybe not. Sit tight. Go swimming."

26

Miracles

I'm not proud of the way I acted in the aftermath of my mother's death. I should have kept my feelings to myself, but if I appeared to express more remorse over the loss of a property than of a parent, so be it. Unlike her, I was not accustomed to concocting emotions for the sake of appearances, and the truth of it was that I had every right to be pissed. I faced a long-familiar conundrum. How much of her last serving of nastiness was the product of an unmanageable mental instability and how much from a seemingly natural and ingrained malevolence, or were they one and the same? I may not have had any right to feel shortchanged monetarily, but I was crushed to have been calculatingly connived out of my beloved cottage, the one thing I believed I did, in fact, have coming to me.

In time, however, we would learn that the mouse's influence over our mother had been even more far-reaching than we'd realized, and that Mother could not have been an easier mark. Upon weaseling her way into Mother's confidence, she had quickly recognized the perpetual friction in a typical dysfunctional family and had skillfully exploited it, fostering in particular the notion that we kids were selfish and ungrateful moneygrubbers who were circling overhead like vultures.

For his part, Matlick had apparently started out on the right foot. We would later find a letter dated four years before her death, in which he had originally suggested a number of ways Mother might better handle her finances. The letter pointed out that if her estate were settled then, taxes would amount to nearly $500,000, and her executor and attorney together would receive up to $130,000 in combined fees. Each of her children would receive just over $250,000 apiece. However, if she reorganized her estate and mapped out the next few years, she could transfer substantial sums to her children, reduce her estate expenses dramatically by negotiating with her attorney and executor beforehand, reduce and possibly even eliminate federal estate taxes entirely while raising her income considerably, specifically by selling much of her major stock holdings (then paying just 2.4 percent) and reinvesting the proceeds in U.S. long term notes at nearly 9 percent.

By transferring stock and other assets to her children and by making tax-free gifts of $10,000 annually to them, it was possible to arrive eventually at an estate of $600,000, which would be exempt from federal estate taxes. In the case of her summer home, unless she had reason for retaining title, she should gift it to her children immediately and also loan them enough money to fix it up, then forgive the loan the following January.

By making the suggested moves and planning her gifts over the next few years, the letter suggested, she could enjoy an increased and safer income, avoid unnecessary taxes, and maximize the ultimate gift to her children, which could be as high as $400,000 apiece.

The mouse obviously had a better plan: forget the money-hungry children and put the whole shootin' match, cottage and all, in a trust fund from which she as trustee would receive considerable fees for the trust's duration in addition to the ample chunk she'd get as executrix. How the mouse managed to sell this scheme to Matlick as well we have no idea. The greater our estrangement from Mother became, however, the more appealing the mouse's strategy apparently appealed to her.

When Sal's phone call came, his announcement that "they want to settle" meant little to me at first, but from his standpoint it spelled victory. It went beyond nailing the mouse and Matlick for improprieties; it meant a whole new ballgame that included some miracles we had thought impossible.

"What's that mean to us?" I asked.

"It means they're trying to stay out of jail. They're prepared to make concessions."

"Like what?"

"Compensation. The ball's in your court."

"I'm not sure I understand."

"It's a trade-off. You accept a concession and in return agree not to prosecute."

"You mean we can't fry their asses?"

"You could try if you really want to, but it would be foolish under the circumstances. They're willing to settle to avoid going to court. Even appearing in court on the charges could ruin their careers, even if they were cleared. The very fact that they had to answer to the allegations would cook them."

"I want them to cook."

"Yeah, but listen to me. If you choose not to settle and you pursue this all the way to the courtroom, you forfeit any concessions available to you now through the settlement. And if they beat the charges it's you that gets cooked. The legal fees come out of your pocket, and they are mounting as we speak. I don't come cheap, and don't forget that I had to engage another firm to help us with this. They have to be paid too."

"How could we lose? I thought we had them dead to rights."

"Too risky. I'm a damn good litigator, but Connie and Matlick have the best lawyers they could find for this. You never know how it could go. Besides, whether they get indicted or only slapped on the wrist, your circumstances still won't change any. With a settlement at least you've got leverage and bargaining power, and your legal fees will be covered."

"Okay, what about the cottage?"

"What about it?"

"As compensation. Right off the top, ours free and clear. All of it. No strings attached."

"I don't know."

"Look, Sal. We can't say we were screwed out of money, but we can damn sure say we were screwed out of this cottage—quite possibly with undue influence from Connie—after it was supposed to be ours to begin with. Yeah, yeah I know, what we thought and what was supposed to be and what we assumed and what my grandmother intended doesn't mean squat. But if we have compensation coming I'm saying the cottage ought to be it. I think we deserve it."

"Let me look into it. Go fishing."

***

Sal called two days later. "Congratulations. It looks like you own a cottage."

"Say that again."

"Their lawyers went for it, but it's going to take some finagling and we still have to get it by the surrogate court."

"You pulled it off?" My hearted pounded.

"They considered it fair compensation, but like I said there are some complications."

"Like what?"

"Well, it's a little confusing, but when your mother put her three-fourths of the cottage into the trust for the grandchildren, that of course included Jim's and Maris' kids too, even though Jim and Maris previously sold their shares and relinquished their rights to it. So in essence your mother sort of gave their shares back. Jim and Maris still don't have any rights to it, but now their kids do."

"So what happens?"

"Their kids will have to waive the rights to their shares and Jim and Maris will have to be compensated for those shares in their behalf. In fact, all the grandchildren will have to waive their rights to the cottage as beneficiaries of the trust. That shouldn't be a problem. Yours and Rudy's kids will inherit your shares anyway, and each of the other kids only stood to get one fourteenth of three-fourths."

I probably will never fully know about or understand the legal maneuvering that ultimately altered the whole of my mother's estate. Much of the outcome can certainly be attributed to an exceptional attorney who went to bat for us out of genuine empathy, and for me in particular out of the kind of friendship one never forgets. Doors began to open that we had thought impenetrable. Matlick and the mouse may have been even more criminally liable than we'd realized, while the powers that be apparently looked beyond the letter of the law and saw that the trust as it had been structured was a piece of crap.

In any event, since the trust dictated that we children too could invade the principal for educational purposes, it was also decided that as part of the settlement we should presently take advantage of that opportunity in order to acquire working capital with which to make the vital improvements on the cottage. Each of us subsequently received a check for $20,000, and from our front row balcony seats on the wide screened porch, Rudy and I would soon look down upon our hard-earned steel and concrete diploma, bestowed on us by the University of Salvatore Galli College of Seawall Engineering. Jim and Maris benefited in like fashion, for educational purposes as well.

Further good news included a restructuring of the trust that made it infinitely more manageable by dividing it four ways as it should have been to begin with. On another happy note, although the mouse had retained her responsibilities as executrix, we insisted and were consequently satisfied that she be removed as trustee in favor of a bank.

We had hoped to have her ousted as executrix as well, but Sal had insisted that we were obligated to give her something out of the deal as part of the settlement agreement, despite the fact that we suspected she'd already gotten plenty that no one was even aware of. When Connie learned that she was to be replaced as trustee, thereby forfeiting a handsome source of income for many years to come, she commented to me coolly that we were being very foolish because banks were notoriously conservative in their disbursements of annual gifts. I took a great deal of pleasure in replying, "Maybe so, but at least a bank can be trusted."

The unfortunate news was that our mother's original $1.7 million estate—after monumental taxes that could have been avoided altogether, legal expenditures, and six-figure discrepancies never accounted for—now amounted to just over $600,000, which in turn was divided to create four trust funds of about $152,000 each.

This, boys and girls, is precisely what can happen when an unwary widow puts her entire nest egg in a rattlesnake's basket. Sal had graciously kept his fees to a minimum, but the executrix's commission and Matlick's fee were sizeable. Mother had purchased a $200,000 annuity from which she had received an income. There were of course funeral expenses. There were our acquisition of the cottage and subsequent compensations to Jim and Maris, as well as the educational gifts. But there were no outstanding debts to be paid. She'd owed nothing on her house or car and hadn't any credit card balances or loans. Any way we did the math, hundreds of thousands of dollars still could not be accounted for and never would be. It was apparent now that Mother had become so obsessed with keeping us from her dough that she had enabled a con artist to manipulate it for personal gain, and allowed the government to acquire vast sums in taxes instead.

The compromise and settlement agreement ultimately drawn up to amend and restate the original trust was approved and duly signed by a surrogate judge in the fall of 1993, and the matter was finally put to rest.

Kay's younger brother Mickey was married that summer. During the reception at a park overlooking Lake Ontario, the DJ spinning tunes played a song that made me think of my mother. I don't remember what the song was, only that the melody was lovely, and that it reminded me that an appreciation for beautiful music had been something we had always shared. I walked alone to the edge of the cliff and looked across the great lake, instinctively turning to the water for answers as I had so often before, and for the first time since her death a single tear welled up and dropped on my cheek.

If I could have captured that tear and enlarged it into a crystal ball, I would have seen in it not my future but the whole of my past, both glorious and horrendous, both forever forgettable and memorable. And for the first time I realized that amidst all the crippling chaos of the past few years, in spite of the enduring hurt and lingering anger, I missed her.

***

In the fall of 1995, when the new Rochester telephone directories came out, I happened to notice a listing of my mother's name with a post office box and phone number in San Mateo County, CA. Curiosity unfortunately got the best of me and we phoned the number before reporting the discovery to Sal. A woman answered, and when I questioned her she explained that in Rochester many years before she had given birth to a child out of wedlock, had put the child up for adoption, and had left instructions that should the child ever wish to find her, she could be tracked at the address she had just recently listed under that name, which the woman said she had wholly invented, and that it happened to be our mother's full name was merely coincidental.

Upon hearing of this, Sal immediately called and then wrote to the San Mateo district attorney's office. He described the wrongdoings in the settling of Mother's affairs, and expressed his suspicion that annuities sold to Mother may have been outstanding and still unreported to her estate, and that funds from those annuities were being diverted to others holding themselves out in the decedent's identity. He also alerted the San Mateo sheriff's office to report probable criminal activities in that regard, but if an investigation was undertaken, it yielded no results. Through phone calls made two days after alerting the authorities, he learned that the post office box had been abruptly closed and the phone number disconnected. If our suspicions were correct, we'd blown any chance of catching them by alerting them with our original phone call. But if, in fact, annuities were still in effect, someone had been drawing from them for two and a half years. Without an official criminal investigation into a matter of fraud, our only alternative in pursuing it would be the hiring of a private detective whose costly investigation might take months. We let it go.

In the aftermath of the turmoil over the cottage and the settling of the estate, my sisters both commented on how unbelievable it was that I'd survived all the anxiety and anger without drinking. I had to confess that when we had stood on the church steps after Mother's service, the thought crossed my mind that never in my life had I wanted so much to get drunk. It had been a fleeting feeling that mercifully hadn't returned, by the grace no doubt of the same source of comfort and faith that had continued to carry me through the whole ordeal. A single set of footprints in the sand.

It had become my custom upon closing the cottage each fall, when the car had been loaded, the water disconnected, the screens boarded up, to kneel on the seawall and talk to the river. I asked for no favors or special treatment. I asked to be kept sober the rest of that day. To count all my blessings and express my gratitude would have taken hours, and the river knew anyway. All I really asked was for help to guide me so that should I be blessed with another season along this shore, I might return in the spring a better man.

As I knelt by the calm and quiet river late in October, mulling over the extraordinary events of the past couple of years, I felt that perhaps I had finally begun to grow. I had been sober more than five years. It no longer mattered that so much of my mother's money had been unaccounted for. It was long gone. It wasn't important any more what my mother had done to me. She was long dead. No more time should be wasted regretting the worthlessness of my previous life. It had passed. And no longer was this cottage the only thing I ever wanted.

27

Mercy

It seemed inconceivable to me that I could be so blessed. My children and the cottage were part of me again. All those years in which the separation from my kids had continued to widen, I had believed that the cottage was all I wanted or needed or was entitled to. And what would I have done with it? Sit on the porch with my vodka and dope and watch my river and my life flow by, saying to myself in a stoned stupor every day, "man, this is the life," convinced that I was in paradise?

I was about to be blessed yet again. As my daughter Wendy and her fiancé Karl prepared for their spring wedding, they insisted that Kay and I be involved. The news was both fantastic and frightening, for it opened a door I was both eager and terrified to walk through. I had not seen my former wife's parents in twenty-five years, which is how long I figured their bitterness had been festering. There had never been a confrontation. I had merely disappeared, leaving Abby to fend for herself. Now that their granddaughter was getting married, I could only imagine how they felt about my being there to enjoy it.

Abby's father had always been a proud provider who believed that a man cares for his family above anything else. I had been extremely lax in providing monetary support to Abby, partly because I had been either unemployed or unemployable most of the time, but also because I'd had a drug and alcohol habit I supported instead. Had Abby been a harder woman and the laws more stringent at the time, I would surely have been jailed and should have been.

I had argued at length with my counselor in rehab about the guilt I felt over the callousness with which I abandoned my family. Sally had repeatedly blamed my disease, insisting that it was my alcoholism that had left me so open to temptation. My addiction had robbed me of reason and the ability to keep my priorities straight, and had allowed me to think nothing peculiar about spending what money I had on a bag of drugs instead of making sure my kids had shoes. A sober man would not have succumbed to those influences, she said, but her analysis soothed me little. In my mind I hadn't been an innocent victim of alcoholism and addiction who just couldn't help himself. I'd been a garden-variety selfish son of a bitch plain and simple. I hadn't just fallen out of love and parted ways with my wife. I had kicked my family down the stairs and left them there, and no psychological mumble-jumble could explain that reality away.

I didn't even know what Abby had done for money. I'd assumed that her folks or mine had helped her out, but what was inexcusable was that I hadn't even cared, as long as I knew that she and kids weren't actually starving. I would learn much later that before she'd been able to get a full-time job when Jake started school, she'd been on welfare and had barely scraped along.

Abby had filed for divorce early in 1974 and I'd been forced to seek the services of a legal aid attorney. I remember that I'd been furious to discover that the grounds were cruel and inhuman treatment, as though I'd beaten her with a rubber hose. Other than adultery, which was so difficult to prove, they'd been the only grounds available to her in New York State. The divorce decree had dictated that I pay weekly child support of $35—the cost back then of about seven quarts of cheap whiskey or an ounce of decent marijuana, which I must have believed I needed a hell of lot more than a kid needed shoes.

***

I was invited to a small bachelor party for Wendy's fiancé at a suburban restaurant. Karl was a warm and personable young man with a wealth of talent. He had been Wendy's boyfriend for many years and liking him a great deal came easily to me. Jake would be there, along with his stepfather, the wonderful man whom Abby had married, and Abby's father as well. I was surprised even to have been invited, and it would not have shocked me in the least if Abby's father slapped me smartly across the face.

Kay was also apprehensive about going to a bridal shower. She had previously had occasion to meet Abby, but she had never met any of her family. They had no reason to think unkindly toward her, but she was understandably nervous just the same.

I found it almost strange how people in a more stable family look at life and accept life. I had grown up in a household where resentments arose as if instinctively and were destined to smolder indefinitely, where wrongs and mistreatments were swept under the rug but never discarded, endured but rarely repaired, overcome but never forgotten, drowned in booze instead of being dealt with. But in a family like Abby's where family always comes first, where children are cared for no matter what, where problems are faced and fixed, where respect for one another's feelings is paramount, there is little time or inclination even for petty argument, let alone lasting bitterness.

I would not be a member of the wedding party and wouldn't have expected to be, but Wendy insisted that I wear a tux and thus be honored as part of the family. I was, after all, her father. Indeed I was honored, and deeply humbled. Only through my sobriety had I been able to ease slowly and carefully back into my children's lives, and only because of it would I stand proudly with the family as my beautiful daughter walked down the aisle.

When I entered the bachelor party my kids' stepfather embraced me sincerely and kissed my cheek. I had never met the man, and he was treating me like a long lost brother. Karl and Jake both hugged me heartily. And the smile from Abby's father could not have been warmer, or his handshake firmer. Feeling like an outsider when I walked in, I was made to feel like one of the family immediately. At one point Jake's stepfather took me aside and explained apologetically that he would walk Wendy down the aisle and that he hoped I understood. Of course I did. I would not have had it any other way, and told him so. He insisted, now that we had so much to celebrate together, that I have a drink with him. I courteously declined, and could not have been more grateful to be able to.

Kay had been received with equal warmth at the shower, and we were also invited to the rehearsal party in the park, where Abby, bursting with both pride and anxiety over the pending ceremony, welcomed us graciously. Three of her sisters were there, and they could not have been nicer. Even Abby's mother, notoriously reserved and shy and yet the member of the family I feared confronting the most, treated me with the utmost kindness, and that just blew me away. It all seemed so unbelievable.

As Wendy's stepfather escorted her to the altar, Abby stood before the pew in front of us. Wendy looked utterly radiant, and I instinctively took Abby's hand in an attempt to show that I shared her pride regardless of all that had occurred between us. Her hand gripped mine in response, though briefly and almost imperceptibly, and then was withdrawn as her husband and daughter passed, and I understood completely.

A year later, Wendy was awarded her doctorate in special education from Michigan State University, and I was there for the hooding ceremony. Two months after that she gave birth in Rochester to the first of three children. In a former life, if I had still been around at all, I would have heard about them through the grapevine. In this life, I held each of my newborn grandchildren in my arms.

***

I soon had occasion to wear a tux again, when my son and his lovely Laney got married. They shared an apartment on Oxford Street in the city then, directly across the road from the house in which I had rented an apartment many years before. That was where I'd been living with the woman I'd left Abby for, and where my old friend Rob had found me and told me that Abby had gone into labor for the baby whom she would name Jake. Small world.

Abby's father, who had taken Jake under his wing from the beginning and had become his mentor, was said to have cried when Jake asked him to be his best man. He had prepared a speech for the reception, in which he would relate his special love for Jake, and his recollection of recognizing immediately upon meeting Laney that she was the young woman his grandson should marry. He had hoped to get through the speech without succumbing to his emotions. He made it all the way to the second sentence. After his teary address I went to him and hugged him. "Thank you for everything" was all I could think to say. His strong embrace in return was all I needed in response. What I felt in that hug was a mutual understanding that required no words, the sharing of a profound gratitude for Jake and Laney's happiness, and the mending of a wound that had pained me for too many years.

There is still a scar, but it doesn't hurt any more.

28

Jim

For forty-five years my brother and I traveled in different orbits. About the only things we had in common were membership in a screwed-up family, a prodigious fondness for alcohol, and a life-long love for a river. He knocked me around pretty good when we were kids, and when my parents saw the marks or bruises they'd ask me if Jim was responsible, and I'd always say no— not out of fear of his kicking my butt again, but of his getting in trouble. I hated to see my siblings in trouble.

Jim picked on me, ridiculed me, and whacked me every time I turned around, it seemed; but God help any other kid who bothered me the same way. Jim would flatten him. He was three years older than I, which doesn't mean much later on. But when you're nine and your brother is twelve the difference is huge. I was his catcher when he wanted to be a pitcher. He swore the proper distance was forty feet and by the time I finished grade school I'd spent half my life with a sprained thumb. I was his tackler when he wanted to be a running back, his goalie when he took up hockey, and the target he hit balls at when he took up golf, the game that would eventually consume him.

He could have been a stand-up comic. He had a repertoire of antics that turned a routine story into an artistic performance with the facial expressions of Jonathan Winters and the body language of Jackie Gleason. But he possessed as well a darker side in which he harbored a hair-trigger temper and the rage of a wounded beast. Jim withstood Mother's wrath better than the rest of us, I think because, in his own way, he was as nuts as she was.

When we were teenagers, Mother's punishment for our coming home after curfew was to lock us out. That made sense to her for some reason. None of us had a key to the house in those days. We learned to unlock a window somewhere before going out in hopes she wouldn't discover it. When I was still skinny enough to fit a head and shoulder through the milk box opening I could lean inside and unbolt the back door. On the nights I couldn't get in I'd sleep in my father's car, which wasn't too bad in the summer.

Once she locked Jim and me out on a night when we happened to arrive home at the same time. She had her own bedroom, as she'd had for as long as any of us could remember. Jim got a ladder from the garage and propped it against the house under her window. He climbed up and kicked the window out in an explosion of glass, dove into the room with an ear-piercing screech, and landed full length on top of her in bed, collapsing the bed frame with a horrifying crash that shook the whole house. I crawled through the window behind him.

Mother's screaming hit an octave we'd never heard even from her, and when the old man thundered in and demanded to know what the goddam hell was going on, Jim said quietly, "She locked us out again," and we went to bed. Another time he got an ax from the garage and chopped the back door down. The only piece of wood remaining was the three or four inches sticking out from the jamb where the dead bolt was, still securely locked. Jim could be a little unpredictable.

In our twenties he chose a world of country clubs and stylish clothes, snazzy cars and wealthy friends, and I joined my hippie buddies in a world of drugs, patched jeans and long hair. In both our worlds the booze flowed freely, but our paths rarely crossed, except at family gatherings. He didn't think much of my world and I didn't think much of his.

In a way Jim was perhaps more successful than any of us, not that that's saying much. He'd had difficulty learning to read as a child and would always have trouble spelling, so my parents had never expected him to excel academically. He nevertheless made a respectable living in the insurance business, though the bulk of his earnings went toward supporting his big-ticket habits, primarily his membership and requisite spending at Oak Hill Country Club. Oak Hill, host of several PGA major tournaments and the Ryder Cup and long revered as one of the top championship courses in the country, was a more than fitting challenge for his prowess as a golfer; but his greater challenge was keeping up with his fellow members whose wealth better enabled them to belong to such a club.

Had he done a little less drinking and partying and worked harder at controlling his temper and eliminating the erratic nature of his game, he might even have had a shot at becoming a professional golfer, but it was never to be. He was recognized as a streak golfer who often enjoyed intervals of sheer brilliance, but he could never quite master the consistency imperative to competitive golf at the professional level.

In his younger years when he had devoted himself more to pursuing a command of the sport than to the partying lifestyle that tended to come with it, he practiced until his hands bled. Our father was a member of Locust Hill Country Club, and it was there that Jim developed his game. As a young teenager he caddied and worked in the locker room shining shoes for tips, handing out towels, and picking up after the golfers. He hung around the pro shop. He practiced until it was too dark to see. While still in his teens he won the club championship and had a reputation even then as one of the longest hitters around. Eventually he developed the need for a more challenging course, and none could be more so locally than Oak Hill, which Tiger Woods was quoted as calling after the 2003 PGA Championship held there "the hardest, fairest golf course we've ever played." Jim got down to a one handicap in his heyday, which is damn respectable at any club, let alone Oak Hill. He once shot a bogey-free 68 on the championship east course while drinking three six packs in the process, a beer every hole.

When he'd had his cancerous prostate removed in his early fifties, he knew that his lymph nodes had already been invaded as well and that the consequences were inevitable, despite a regimen of radiation and chemo. He had quit drinking and smoking and his health had rallied for a while, but he often complained that since getting off the booze he could no longer break eighty on the links. In his last couple of years he asked to come to the cottage for a weekend here and there, and it was during those visits that we became brothers again. As the cancer spread he struggled to maintain a regular work schedule and played golf sporadically.

I would have loved to play a round with him but he never asked me. I might even have beaten him on an exceptionally good day. I took up golf at the same time I took up sobriety. As a kid I had taken lessons and for a while had tried to play, but my heart wasn't in it. I suppose I was discouraged then by how good my brother was. Ironically, I think now that if I'd stuck with it and continued to play I'd have been just as good or better than Jim had been. Now I find it amusing how much playing golf and staying sober have in common, in terms of the simple attitude of patience each demands, and the one-step-at-a-time procedure each requires to mend one's faults and deficiencies. The sobriety continues to improve.

Jim had been estranged from his four kids for many years. They had spent most of their lives playing second fiddle to a bag of golf clubs and a bottle of booze. He wanted to get back into their lives. Before his prostate operation he had called us and said that he'd like Kay and me to come over to his condo. He had invited my sisters as well, and two of his children who still lived in town, and his girlfriend Rosie. He told us he was tired of his life. He was bored with what he had become and ashamed of the worthlessness of his lifestyle. Everyday he got out of work, went to the club, drank himself stupid, wolfed down a dinner, and went home and passed out in front of the TV, night after night.

He told us he didn't want to drink any longer, and he didn't. He just stopped. He never set foot in an AA meeting, but he never took another drink. I wanted to slap him. I told him it wasn't supposed to be quite that simple. But that was his way. He accomplished things through will power alone. It's doubtful that he had an easy time of it. Quitting drinking is almost the painless part. Totally restructuring your lifestyle in order to live contentedly without drinking is the part that's so hard to do on your own. I'm sure he struggled, but he made it. And the night before his surgery he smoked his last cigarette.

In the aftermath of the operation, knowing that his cancer had not been confined to his prostate, he turned his thoughts even more to family. It meant a great deal to him to make amends to his kids. They rallied around him and it was a joy to see. At the same time he began to gain strength from a source he had probably not acknowledged much before, and with Rosie's encouragement he sought to make peace with his maker as well.

On the last weekend he spent at the cottage we drove to nearby Clayton and walked around the village. He never talked about dying, but he knew it wasn't far off. His former girlfriend of many years had died from cancer after a long and heartbreaking ordeal, and he looked at the inescapable truth of his own future with more fortitude than fear, I think. He probably thought that if she had gone through that, he damn sure could.

We bought ice cream cones and sat on a park bench on the shore, and talked about nothing in particular, watching the river and the boats go by. When we were kids he'd been known around the Point as the Little Admiral because he spent so much time cleaning boats for people, polishing the teakwood and wiping down the seats. That was how he earned rides and got to go fishing, his second love. Over the years he hadn't maintained much interest in our cottage, but he had spent many years fishing with friends several times each summer. One of them owned a large fishing boat and a place on Wolfe Island. One of their favorite fishing spots in the St. Lawrence was where Jim wanted his ashes to go.

As we sat on that park bench, I think he sensed as I did that for the first time in our lives we could talk with one another easily and naturally, even if there was nothing much to say. The towering wall that had stood between us for so many years was no longer there.

What we had done with our lives was no longer important. Our children had let us back into their hearts, and in that we shared an appreciation and a brotherhood like none we'd ever known.

Jim died in 1999 in a hospice at the age of fifty-six with his son at his side. I had been there too for about sixteen hours straight as his consciousness faded in the la la land of morphine. It is thought that while a patient is in such a state of apparent incoherence that he can still hear and understand what people are saying. I don't know if that's true or not. Maybe the nurses just tell you that so that you'll feel free to express yourself to the loved one slipping away. I took his hand and told him that all was well, that he had mended his fences, that he was leaving on a good note, that he had made peace with God, and that he had nothing to be ashamed of any more. And I told him that in spite of all our differences over the years, I had always been proud to be his brother.

I needed to go home for a spell, have dinner with Kay, maybe get a nap. During dinner his son called. His message was brief. "Dad got his tee time."

29

Good Morning

Mid-morning of a late December day in 2006 I signed in at the reception desk of the drug and alcohol detox facility at Main Quest Treatment Center in downtown Rochester. I was directed to a room in which about two-dozen people had gathered. They were in varying degrees of withdrawal, fidgeting in folding chairs arranged along three walls, jerking and yawning, trembling and scratching, playing with their hair, looking about furtively, eyeing me diffidently. They crossed and uncrossed their legs, twitched their feet, pumped their knees up and down like pistons, gripped their hands together. Their gaunt faces exhibited the fear and bewilderment and humiliation that characterized their misery. The scene was so familiar, and the thought came instinctively to mind that there but for the grace of God went I. I took a seat behind a table up front and waited for the group to settle down.

"Good morning. My name is Geoff. I'm an alcoholic."

For a recovering addict, addressing patients in a detox is a vitalizing experience that is at once uplifting and disheartening. How exhilarating it is to share with them my successful journey to sobriety, yet how disquieting to realize that I could so easily be one of them again. I see in their glazed eyes the hopelessness and despair I recall so clearly, and it frightens me to realize that while another failure bides forever within me, another recovery most likely does not.

I can tell them that I know how they feel—physically sick, emotionally spent, socially inept, spiritually bankrupt. I can declare with all the conviction I can muster that if I can get sober so can they, and in theory it is true. But I also know that most of them won't, and therein lies the heartbreak. I can tell them my story and point the way, but I can't shove sobriety down their throats, just as no one could shove it down mine.

This particular detox is where the less advantaged end up. Most of them will likely go back to the sordid lifestyles that helped put them here. Their parents didn't drive shiny convertibles to the country club. They didn't take piano and dancing lessons, nor grow up in Leave It to Beaver neighborhoods. Many of them probably didn't finish high school. It is likely that few if any have health insurance. I doubt that any of them has the wherewithal to advance to an upscale rehab. They can't lay claim, therefore, to any of the advantages that I had known, and that had done me no damn good whatsoever. Addiction doesn't discriminate, and neither does sobriety.

"Thanks for letting me come in and share a few thoughts with you today. I want you to know that you're looking at the last man on earth who thought he'd ever be sitting in front of a roomful of people talking about being sober. Back when I was in a detox just like this one—and I went through three of them because they were such a hoot—I couldn't imagine getting sober at all, let alone being qualified to hand out any advice. And the last thing I figured I needed was for some doofus from Alcoholics Anonymous to come in and talk about how many years he'd

been clean, like that was supposed to inspire me. Well, it didn't inspire me. I figured he was so far out of my league he might as well be some clown who never drank in his life and had no idea what I was going through. It was like being confined to a wheelchair and listening to an Olympic track star. It was beyond my comprehension."

A lanky black man gazes out a window, wearing a look of disgust, almost flaunting his boredom. His mind is already closed. He wants out of here. I see a lost soul in the dark eyes of a Hispanic woman, but I also see curiosity. She wants a way out of her hell.

"You're looking at a guy who couldn't go an hour without a drink, and I drank alcoholically for almost twenty-five years and rarely went a day without drugs. In the end I was drinking almost a half-gallon of vodka a day, morning, noon and night. And while I've been able to string together a number of sober years, it's important for you to understand that I take very little credit for that accomplishment. If you remember only one thing from what I say this morning, it's that I did not get sober by myself. Every time I tried it by myself I failed. I didn't get sober until I stopped thinking that it was me against the world, and finally reached out for help. That same help is available to you. All you have to do is follow the same sort of path to recovery that millions of other addicts have taken, and get your lives back a day at a time. I'll say it again. If I can do it, you can do it."

A pale man in his forties nods at everything I say and looks around for approval. He's been here before, knows the drill. He'll be back again, maybe. There are twenty-six patients in the room, demonstrating twenty-six different ways to slouch in a chair. A guy in his twenties has an elaborate tattoo on his forehead. He's smirking.

"One day at a time isn't a slogan. It's a system. The most terrifying

concept for us is the idea of having to go through life without any kind of buzz. When you've been getting high every day your whole life, that's a scary prospect. That's why we have to think in terms of a day at a time, or an hour at a time if that's what it takes. We overcome today's temptations, deal with today's problems, and somehow get through this day without a drink or a drug. Recovery is a process. You didn't become an addict overnight. You won't get sober overnight.

"I'm not going to try to shock you with all the awful things that happened to me because of my drinking. I've got a few horror stories, but what I went through was probably a walk in the park compared to what some of you have known.

"But this isn't a competition. This isn't a matter of who got the most stitches or totaled the most cars. And it doesn't matter what you're in here for, whether it's booze or coke or meth or heroin. A drug is a drug and an addict is an addict."

There's a girl who looks about twenty-five, yet is probably still a teenager. She is skin and bones and has gnarled hair. I can't imagine what she's been through already. I think she might have been pretty once. She needs sunshine. I wonder how long it's been since she smiled, or had reason to.

"One of the big misconceptions alcoholics have is that if they stay sober for a while, and get their health back, they'll be able to go back out and start using again and it'll take a while to get as bad as they were before. Maybe it took you ten or twenty years of heavy drinking and drugging to get you where you are now, so you think if you get all better and go back out it'll take you another ten years to get this bad again. No it won't. You'll be right back where you were before you know what hit you. Let me repeat that. If you go back out and start

using again, no matter how long you've been clean, you're going to take up your addiction right where you left off. And it will never get better. It will only get worse.

"If you don't do something about your addiction, you're going to die before your time. You're going to fall asleep drunk at the wheel and die in a car crash, fall down stairs and break your neck, overdose, commit suicide, screw some guy out of a bag of dope and get your throat slit, wake up in the wrong bed and get your head blown off, get mugged and murdered staggering home from a bar at three in the morning, have a heart attack or a stroke or die from kidney or liver failure. One way or another your addiction is going to kill you. Count on it. And if you don't care if it does, you might just as well pack up your gear and walk the hell out of here. This treatment center is here for people who want to live.

"We all dream of being able to control our drinking—you know, have one or two and leave it at that, before we get into trouble. But let's be honest with ourselves. That just isn't going to happen. We've never been content with one or two drinks, and there is absolutely no reason to believe we ever will be."

I know I can't possibly reach all these people. Some simply aren't ready to be reached, and perhaps never will be. Yet I know that amidst all the information and suggestions being thrown at them, at some point someone will say something that rings a bell in a few of their heads, that they can personally relate to, that hits close to home. Maybe I can ring a bell or two.

"But the reason for my being here today is to explain how Alcoholics Anonymous fits in. How is AA going to help? The simple concept behind AA is that alcoholics stay sober by helping other

alcoholics stay sober. The only people you're going to see at an AA meeting are people who are going through the same thing you're going through. Look at it this way. If you want to learn to play golf, you don't take piano lessons. You hang around golf courses, take lessons from golf teachers, read golf magazines, talk to other golfers. You want to learn how to stay sober, you learn it from other alcoholics who are staying sober.

"You'll be hearing a lot about having to change the people, places, and things that were part of your alcoholic life, and that's excellent advice. You're on the mend. If you've got a broken leg you don't go skiing. If you've just had open heart surgery you don't play football. If you're fresh out of rehab, you don't go to a New Year's Eve party. But we can't go live in a cave for the rest of our lives either. Your best defense is inner strength, and AA is a good place to find it.

"And that leads us to spirituality, and finding a higher power, which for some people can be a bit of a stumbling block. I'm talking spirituality here, not religion. People in AA don't march around banging drums and carrying signs. But most of us have accepted the existence of a higher power that we believe in. That's all. This doesn't mean we have visions of the Virgin Mary grilling ribs on the back patio. It merely means being open-minded enough to consider the prospect that just maybe we aren't in charge, that there's a power greater than we are and stronger than our addiction is. For most of us that power happens to be God, but it doesn't need to be. Some members of AA who have trouble believing in God have chosen the AA program itself or some other source of inspiration as their higher power. It doesn't matter what or who you chose, as long as you believe and have faith in it.

"*To this day I can't say for sure whether it was my higher power that got me to AA or AA that got me to my higher power. It doesn't matter. But I can tell you this with all honesty because it's absolutely true. The desire to drink has been lifted from me. Let me say that again. I realize it sounds dramatic, but it's the truth. The desire to drink, and, more importantly, the need to drink, has been totally lifted from me, and I don't think that was the work of the tooth fairy, you know what I'm saying?*

"*But please understand this. I've been sober for some time, but I am still an alcoholic. The desire and need to drink are gone, but the lure and compulsion are still there. Alcohol and drugs took me to some special places and showed me many great times, and I know that part of me will always miss those dreamy days when the drugs were working their magic, before they turned nasty and ruined my life. That's why I have to keep my dukes up and stay close to AA.*

"*Let me wrap up with this. The founders of AA never said that they had the only answer, and AA still doesn't claim that today. All they said was that this is what worked for them when everything else they tried had failed. And when other alcoholics tried it the same way they got sober too. It's still working today. There are millions of recovering addicts around the world who will tell you the same thing. This is what worked for us, and it can work for you.*

"*Just don't think of sobriety as being some sort of nightmare. To me, compared to the nightmare that my life had become, it's the greatest show on earth. So I'd like to leave you with a little tip. When I was in detox and rehab and everyone was trying to sell me this concept of sobriety, I had a lot of trouble relating to it, because no matter how I looked at it—one day at a time or however they wanted to package it—it all boiled down to the same thing: that I couldn't drink or drug any more. And that just seemed too inconceivable to me at the time.*

"But if I had been encouraged to think in terms of freedom, it would have made a world of difference. Freedom from throwing up every morning and feeling like crap all the time. Freedom from having to hide, to lie and cheat and steal and hustle to get my next fix. Freedom from the constant guilt. Freedom from having my whole existence controlled by a bottle. Freedom from watching my body wither away because booze was more important to me than food.

"I may not have been sure that I wanted to stop drinking. But there was no question in my mind that I wanted to stop dying. I thank you for your time. I wish you well, and I wish you freedom."

I hope to hell I got to a few of these people. I want them to have what I have. At the very least, I got a booster shot myself. The sight of this detox and the looks on these haggard faces are a wake-up call, a reminder that the crusade surges on. To these struggling patients it is just the beginning. But then, so it is for me, each and every morning.

30

In June

The back door on the cottage never did shut right. It was another of those little jobs one keeps putting off, a project you figure will take an hour at most and ends up taking four. In our first summer after acquiring the cottage a neighbor stopped by as I was prepping a window to paint. I mentioned that I didn't think we'd ever stop fixing up the place, and he said, "You won't. It never ends."

Visitors to the cottage now would not be overly impressed had they not seen how dilapidated and filthy it once was. I cringe now at the memory of having had close friends here when it was in such a sorry state. Much remains to be done, but compared to what we originally walked into, it's almost palatial. Thanks to some knowledgeable neighbors who have been as generous with their help and advice as with their cherished friendship, I have learned a thing or two about repairing and remodeling. The cottage and I have something in common. I'm forever discovering more things that need fixing.

I was re-hanging the screen door when a strange car pulled into the yard. Out stepped two women, one of them Helen Brown, an old family friend whom I hadn't seen in decades. I recognized her immediately. Helen and her late husband Harry had been part of my parents' river gang that vacationed with them at the cottage many years before. There had been four other couples in all and we children had looked upon them as aunts and uncles, so frequently did we see them at parties and picnics and holidays. Helen's husband had been my father's dearest friend, in whom he had often confided about family matters he'd rarely share with others.

Helen and her companion were spending a weekend at a resort in Alex Bay, and Helen had felt the urge, she said, to stop by and see the cottage after all those years. We settled on the porch, and Helen commented on how much the cottage had changed and how much nicer it was, for which I gladly took most of the credit.

I had not seen her since my late teens. That entire river gang, my parents' closest friends, had suddenly virtually vanished. We kids had learned that there had been an affair between one of the men in the group and the wife of another, though at first it had been unclear which of the women it was. How the encounter had even been discovered we couldn't imagine. But when word got out, it had been Mother, not surprisingly, who insisted on circling the wagons to see what exactly should be done about the mortifying situation, while being advised repeatedly by the others to mind her own business.

One simply did not tell my mother to mind her own business, and we later found out that in the heat of the subsequent mayhem someone had commented that at least it was certain the woman in question had not been she, since it was common knowledge what an ice cube she was. Whether by their own choice or Mother's directive we kids never learned, but none of those people had ever set foot in our house again. My father maintained his longtime friendship with them all, but did so without my mother's knowledge.

Helen was pleased to see that the cottage was still in the family, though I felt the need to fill her in on what had come to pass. When she heard how Mother had tried to screw us, she shook her head slowly and chuckled. None of it surprised her in the least. She and her husband had known my parents better than anyone. I told her how difficult it had been to swallow such a bitter pill, to put it all behind me.

"We all had to swallow when it came to your mother," she said, and then related a story about their river-gang vacations that did not surprise me either.

"Your mother wouldn't allow anyone to have a drink until cocktail hour, that was her rule. We'd come in and get cleaned up and gather on the porch for cocktails before dinner. No one was allowed to make a drink until your mother came down and made her grand entrance.

"So all of us would be down here and we could hear your mother upstairs getting ready. And we'd wait and wait and wait. She'd walk around up there for damn near an hour and we knew she was stalling. Nine adults pacing back and forth dying for a drink, and she'd walk around up there forever."

"Just to be a pain."

"Of course."

"And you know, Helen, if you told that story to anyone who didn't know her, they'd never understand why you didn't just tell her to go to hell."

"Well, she was our hostess after all, not that it mattered. She'd be in charge no matter where we were. But we loved her, so we played her game to keep her happy. No one was as much fun as your mother was when she was happy and having a good time. You know that. And sometimes it was like dealing with a baby, giving her what she wanted to keep her quiet. The hardest thing for us was knowing what your father went through, what he put up with all those years. It's just a shame she had to turn so sour in the end against you kids, though. She must have been very bitter. We all knew she was troubled and had a lot of anger inside. But the important thing is that it turned out all right. You managed to keep the cottage, and now your own kids can have it too."

***

In June the river still flows cold. These days it doesn't seem all that warmer in July. I haven't had a drink in seventeen years. It amazes me every day. I gave up pot many years ago as well. I gave up cigarettes too, but not as long ago as I should have. I will pay the price the rest of my days for that. Emphysema has moved in to stay.

I spent too much time hammering the hell out of that twelve-string and now wear hearing aides. I remember so many nights, even in winter, when I'd park in an open lot, pull the Guild from the trunk, and serenade an imaginary audience from the hood of my car. For an acoustic instrument that big-box guitar could make some serious noise. I'd lean the side of my face on top of it, and the higher I was the harder I'd strum, and the harder I strummed the louder I'd sing to hear myself over the din. I frequently got a visit from cops, responding to complaints from neighbors about some God-awful racket at three in the morning.

Five years ago I had major surgery for an abdominal aortic aneurysm as wide as a fire hose. It could have ruptured at any time, and my chances of survival would have been minimal. I left the hospital after eight days with a row of staples down my torso the length of a jacket zipper. About a year ago I started home oxygen therapy for my emphysema. The supplemental oxygen enables me to exercise, to keep on trucking. I'm just now finishing up two months of chemo and radiation treatments for a cancerous tumor on my tongue. God only knows where that tongue has been, but the prognosis is excellent. All three of these medical adventures likely can be traced to my lifelong dedication to consuming only whole grains and fresh fruits and vegetables. Or maybe it was the smoking. At any rate, it seems like they just keep shooting at me, and I'll just keep shooting back. You can't let the bastards take you down.

And despite having tried my damnest to shorten my life, I am still on the right side of the grass—clean, sober, honest and faithful—and amused no end that I spent half my life convinced that I was incapable of being such a man.

Kay has told me that what she notices most in her refurbished if not totally repaired husband are patience and an even disposition. I think back on some of the screaming, cursing tirades I unleashed on undeserving people I was convinced had wronged me, venting an anger that, though triggered by drunkenness, had been rooted in frustration and misery. The memories help me to understand my mother better, and how we can be driven by forces we don't even know are there.

I've mended most of my fences. There were some people whose friendship and trust I abused by using them to accommodate my desires, expecting them to accept the person I was and somehow even love me for it. A couple of them were the best friends a man could ask for, and I just didn't know it at the time. I include them among those to whom words of explanation are unnecessary. One of them is my old drinking partner and longtime friend who lives in the northwest now. I beat him up in my kitchen once, blindsiding him while he was putting his coat on. He was bigger and stronger than I, and I had to make sure he didn't get up. We were very drunk. He hit his head on a counter and would take a few stitches. He forgave me, for that is what friends do, and I later helped him get sober, the best amends I could make.

I look upon the cottage as a reward and as a school. Sometimes, when I forget that it is above all else a gift and a blessing, when I get possessive and obsessive about it, my loved ones have to jack me up a little. It is easy in sobriety to think in terms of having gained some higher level of wisdom. I sometimes slip into thinking that everything would go a hell of a lot smoother if only people did things my way, now that I've rounded up most of my marbles and stumbled across some new ones.

Rudy and I do not always see eye to eye. We have different tastes and tenets. When we clash it is a test of my skills as I face the reality that sobriety entitles me to nothing more than my fair share of life's ups and downs. It doesn't give me the authority to be right all the time, but instead enables me to recognize when I am wrong, and gives me the courage to change. It allows me to see my options and choose wisely among them, and it gives me the inner strength I never had while drinking. I sought inner strength in a bottle of booze, which turned me into even more of a weakling, and found the strength I was searching for when I put the bottle down.

Only in lasting sobriety have I come to understand how unconscious I was to the impact my drinking had on those around me and on my loved ones in particular. How agonizing it is to realize that as powerless as active alcoholics are over their addictions, as long as they remain in the state of oblivion in which they wallow, those who care about them the most are equally as powerless to help them. We who have been shown the way out of our despair wish for them the same salvation. We know they will have to hit their own bottoms, and we pray that they do before the wreckage is irreparable.

I now think of my mother more with amusement and sadness than with bitterness and resentment. For many years I thought in terms strictly of having won in the end, as if, as they say, the best revenge is living well, surviving. But I can't think that way any more. My docket is too full of gratitude. I have a greater understanding now of what I used to think of as my parents' shortcomings. I sometimes feel ashamed of what I put them through. On the other hand, though they gave me countless material things and enabled me to pursue opportunities to which many children are never exposed, brought me up to know right from wrong and taught me proper manners, I could have used a few helpings of self-esteem. Without it you go into battle without much ammunition. If you don't learn self-esteem at home, you look for it somewhere else.

But by far the greatest reward sobriety has given me is something my mother was never able to find. I know how to love, how to show love, and how to *be* loved. There is no finer gift.

***

The river speaks to me most clearly at daybreak, when the water and wind are still. A heron glides in for a landing under six feet of wing and touches down on the lip of the seawall ever so lightly on splayed-toed feet, folding in his great arms. He walks the wall and settles on a spot and stands motionless, his head angled toward the water in readiness to snatch a passing breakfast with his spear-like beak. The river is waking up. The songbirds have been at it since the first hint of light. A fat carp slaps the water after breaching for air. Mother duck leads a train of tiny fuzzy toys along the shore. Chipmunks chatter incessantly. A lone cormorant surfaces after gulping a school of minnows that will never reach basshood. A kayaker swishes by. A dog's bark on Wellesley Island carries across the channel as if he were right next door. The sun peers over the crowns of pines on the horizon and pours gold across the water. The first fishing boat whines by and dawn is done.

Soon the neighborhood kids will commence their yelping and shouting and splashing and giggling. The sounds are especially sweet when they come from the grandchildren who will one day call this cottage theirs. They are playing in and on and by my river and falling in love with it too. The lawn chairs are every which way, wet towels and shirts hanging off them, sandals and sneakers lying around. The sight is beautiful.

The blessings are countless, many of them as simple as the joy of going to bed at night and falling to sleep instead of passing out, of waking with a clear brain that looks forward to the adventures of the day and remembers those of the day before, of feeling the warmth of my sweetie next to me and knowing that my gift of sobriety is hers as well as mine, of having no secrets or anything to lie about.

It is humbling to realize now that while I long regretted not being around to teach my children some lessons for life while they were growing up, it is I who has learned so much from them instead. They have perseverance. They pursue their goals. They work for what they need, with whatever tools they have. They don't waste time thinking about why they can't achieve this or that. They just do it. They have what I never had: motivation, curiosity, plain and simple gumption.

With the exception perhaps of when Wendy was still an infant and couldn't have known, neither of my children nor any of my grandchildren has ever seen me drunk. How I feel about that is indescribable.

While attempting to get an accurate chronology for my story I asked Wendy recently when it was that she and Jake met Kay and me for dinner that first time, when I actually got to meet them. She wasn't quite sure of the exact year either. She said, "How can something so important have gotten so blurred in my mind? I guess it's because what we have now feels like it's always been there." The lady has a way with words.

Not long ago I stopped to see Jake and Laney and their two beautiful children. Jake and I got to talking about one of his cousins who'd been struggling with alcoholism and having a rough time of it. When Jake walked me to my car he said, "I'm not sure if I ever really told you this, but I know how tough it must have been and everything you went through. I just want you to know how proud I am of you."

"You're proud of me?" I asked. "I walked out on you, before you were even born. How can you possibly be proud of me?"

He put his arms around me, held me close, and kissed my cheek. "That wasn't you that walked out," he said. "That was somebody else. *This* is you."

Epilogue

It is hoped that I have not portrayed myself as an authority on getting sober. I am still a student myself. Nor is this account intended as a promotional tool for the fellowship of Alcoholics Anonymous. Indeed, one of AA's twelve traditions specifies that our public relations policy is based on attraction, not promotion. But for me and countless others it was the last house on the street. It must have been the right one. It saved my life.

There are a number of means by which to get sober. AA is one of them. All I know is that for the three years during which I struggled to put the bottle down while eschewing what AA had to offer, I failed again and again; and for the eighteen years since I embraced the fellowship, I haven't drunk a drop. I just can't argue with that. The bottom line is, whatever the hell works.

Many of the expressions, adages, and interpretations used in these pages can be heard in AA rooms everywhere, and I take no credit for their originality. Also, the experiences described in my rehab were only part of what was and is a complex and thoroughly comprehensive program of education and therapy that I couldn't possibly recount in its entirety here. I must emphasize, too, that my numerous failures after rehab were by no means the fault of the program. The rehab didn't fail. I did.

I have omitted recollections of what my sisters endured while growing up. They had their own encounters with our mother and experiences with the men in their lives and relationships with their own children and their own dependencies, and there were surely many incidents I know nothing about. Besides, they're still around and I don't want to have to answer to them. I didn't want to delve into their histories and certainly not into their minds. They'll have to tell their own stories.

I tried to write this book fifteen years ago and several times since, but had to put it aside. I wasn't ready yet. I had growing up to do. My story is not in any way exceptional. Compared to many my life has been a cakewalk. I'm an ordinary Joe, like untold millions of ordinary Joes who could not get through a day without a drink or a drug, and who, by the grace of God, found a way out of the hole. We aren't movie or TV celebrities or sports idols or corporate bigwigs or rock stars or supermodels or politicians or the sons and daughters of multi-millionaires. We may have thought we were that special once, because the stimulants gave us that grandeur. But when the drugs lost their magic and turned on us, we dropped to earth with a thunderous crash and with nothing to show for our foray into greatness but the shattered and scattered debris of our lives.

For most of us the hole has a bottom, and it is only from there that we can see how far we've fallen. I was among the slow learners who had to bounce around down there a while before comprehending that there is nothing further down than the underside of bottom, and nothing below that but nowhere left to hide.

There are drunks and addicts who will never climb out, who will die before their time, and I could well have been one of them. Today I live with the ever-present knowledge that the hole is still out there, around the very next corner, cavernous, concealed attractively by a tempting facade, like a velvety lawn over a pit of quicksand, waiting for me to take a wrong step and blindly stumble in. But I know where the hole is. I keep my distance by keeping the faith, by following a doctrine of *To thine own self be true,* and by never forgetting that I am one drink away from my next drunk. To me, there is no such thing as one drink.

I danced with the demons for twenty-five years. They taught me some fancy footwork. For most of those years I danced gleefully and obliviously, invariably to a different drummer, but always for the sheer joy of the dancing alone, without much thought toward where it would lead me. When the dancing got old, when the demons had finished having their way with me, they left me on the side of the road like a run-over dog.

Having been born again, to be alive at all, I need to give something back. This is my attempt to do that. If it helps even one lost soul crawl out of the hole, the often difficult effort it took to write it will be for me worth every word. If nothing else, the telling alone has been infinitely therapeutic to me personally.

In addition to my wife, who believed that I was worth saving and also worth keeping, I dedicate it to my children, whose unconditional love enabled them to accept me for who I am and not what I was, and who, with their own children, are so much of the reason I'm the luckiest man alive.

Acknowledgements

Several people deserve mention for contributions to this effort either by deed or support. They include, in no particular order, Chris and Robert Koch, for advice, wisdom, and direction; the Hon. Fred. S. Gallina, for enduring friendship and favors huge and small; James P. Flynn, for abiding inspiration and cherished camaraderie; Cindy Haynes, for being my biggest fan and a perfectly good cousin; Robert Marc, for his faith and for his love; Brother Wease, for hawking this book on the airwaves; my river gang friends one and all, for sticking by me in the worst of times; my manuscript readers, for suggestions, opinions, corrections; C.A., for everything; my sister, for loving me anyway, and for supplying many recollections; my wife, for bringing home the bacon while I struggled with this endeavor, and for never once looking over my shoulder; and my brothers and sisters in the rooms of AA, for keeping me upright a day at a time.